Books by Jeremy Hodgson

HISTORICAL ROMANCE

Dance on the Terrace

ADVENTURES IN RESEARCH

Curing Emily

Secret in the Seas

ROMANTIC AFRICAN ADVENTURES

Leap of a Lifetime

LEAP OF A LIFETIME

A ROMANTIC ADVENTURE

JEREMY HODGSON

ISBN: 978-0-6397-9162-3
e-ISBN: 978-0-6397-9163-0

Jeremy William Hodgson
Villa 99, Tamarina Golf Estate
Black River, Mauritius
90922
jwhodgson42@gmail.com

Swahili reading by Priscilla Bancy
Edited by Jane-Anne Hobbs

For my grandchildren Freddy, Manon, Victor and Ella

Swahili Terms

asante-sana—thank you

bibi mkubwa—great grandmother

bibie—madam/wife

bwana—boss

dawa—medicine

duma—cheetah

fisi—hyena

habari za asubuhi—good morning

hakuna matata—no worries

hapana inalala—no, it's sleeping

jambo—hello

jehanamu—hell

kiboko—hippo

kikkoy—pareo/womens' cloth wrapping

kweli kabisa—that is absolutely true

matiti—breasts

mganga, sangoma—witchdoctor or herbal medicine practitioner, male or female

mkubwa—great

mkutano—meeting

mzimu, mizimu—spirit, spirits

nafsi—soul

nimefurahi kukuona—pleased to meet you

njoo—come

nyirakuru—kiha: a grandmother

nidiria—brassiere

simba—lion

tafadhali—please

tembo—elephant

wadudu—insects

waganga—plural of *mganga*

yake fasta—it's fixed

Prologue

Millions of things happened in the twenty-four hours leading up to Marijke's decision. Picking those that might have influenced the course of events is impossible, for the only connection was time, as the night fell or dawn broke around the world.

A company in China that made model electric aeroplanes, and had recently changed ownership, received a request for a quotation from Air Deliveries Inc, an Oman company, to develop an oversized electric model that could carry a payload and would not disturb the neighbours.

A French wine estate owner stood in his cellar sampling the year's production; he used a white wax crayon to print a name on the end of the cask. He had used red or green on others. Then he moved to the next barrel. The name he had written was "Rufisi"; that morning, his investment manager told him he was now the majority shareholder of an association with that name. The white label signalled, "Taste the wine again in three years."

An Indian company that made industrial pulse lasers received an order from the Colombian Police force for a laser that could puncture a car's tyres at three hundred metres. It seemed a reasonable request, for their bank account had received the development cost of the lightweight unit.

On a remote game park in Tanzania, the last rhino with a horn fell with a dart in its backside, only to wake thirty minutes later without the horn. It would take the rhino several days to learn that the horn was no longer there.

Behind a stall, an aged woman searched through a pack of towels in a Nairobi market. She found the one she wanted, then after a pause, picked through a clay bowl of stones to find a blue gemstone that the woman laid on a table; with great care, she stretched a piece of animal hide around the pebble, sewed it closed and attached a leather thong to hang it around her neck. Then she laid down to sleep with a happy smile.

And on a Cape Town street, a snatch-and-grab thief on a scooter ripped the handbag from a young woman pedestrian. She fell, bruised by the hard pavement.

I

———————

It was early; Marijke stopped as she reached for her apartment door handle and thought, *Have I forgotten something?*

With a niggle not to be ignored, she moved slowly through the tiny rooms, hoping to remember what it was. After looking around the kitchen, she moved to the bathroom, examined the shelves and the hook behind the door, and entered the bedroom when nothing triggered a memory. After looking in the cupboard, she turned to look around the room and the bedside table.

As she turned to the door, the memory came. *I put a thousand rand in that drawer.*

Marijke opened the drawer, removed the envelope with the money, and put it into her purse. About to slide the drawer closed, she saw her amulet. She hadn't worn the good luck charm since becoming a boarder at a high school. *It's the only personal thing I have left.*

She removed it, put it in her bag, and left the apartment.

Reaching the street door to her block of apartments, she hesitated in front of the row of letterboxes; *I won't need the keys again*, then pushed them through the slot of her neighbour's box.

Marijke needed to take two buses to reach the Table Mountain cableway. She limped slowly to the bus stop, clutching her bag tightly under her arm.

Behind her, a brief note lay on the table of the vacant apartment.

Dear Mama,

My life has been a total waste: I can't waste any more.

Love to you and Petrus,
Marijke.

The first bus was half empty, and the passengers were mostly those workers like office cleaners who prepared the shops and offices for a day of work by others—mostly women, with one or two men in boots. She could tell by the clothes: flat shoes, overalls, and big bags to carry away anything interesting left lying around. She thought the men would drive or push the complex washing and vacuuming floor polishers around the shopping malls, or empty the waste bins. The streets were similarly half-empty, with a few infrequent cars, two or three queuing at a red traffic light. The leading vehicle inched forward, impatient to continue, the half-asleep driver trying to decide if jumping the mental barrier caused by the red light was worth the risk of a traffic fine.

A few pedestrians were walking their dogs. One woman patiently held the leash while her dog emptied its bladder onto a parked car's wheel. Others were hurrying to work or dawdling half asleep on their way to their first coffee before a day of unattractive drudgery.

No one looks happy; no one is talking.

Arriving at the bus terminus after the first bus, she decided to treat herself to a sugar boost by eating two *Koeksisters* at the café with a cup of coffee. She had always loved the sugary syrup-covered delight.

The woman behind the counter who served her asked, "Miss, are you okay?"

"Why do you ask?"

"You don't look too good, and you limped in. Has someone beat you up?"

"No, a thief on a scooter knocked me down and snatched my handbag last night. I have some big bruises."

"Gee, that's tough; what did you lose?"

"Oh, the usual stuff, lipstick and wipes, but my keys, phone, bank card and ID have gone."

"Miss, I've had lots of mugged customers; I tell them all, put those things in pockets, sew pockets inside your clothes if you can."

"Well, it's too late for me, I blocked the card and phone, but the bank is closed, so I can't replace my card or withdraw money to buy a new phone until Monday."

"Ja, life's not easy. I hope you haven't left any valuables in your apartment; the thief might clean you out while you're gone. You must change the lock."

She's right; it's hell out there. "No, I have the only things of value with me."

The second bus had only three passengers, and she was one of them; it would return with a whole load of workers.

The driver didn't stop at the empty bus shelters; on the other side of the road, the bus shelters held waiting passengers who looked hopefully at the bus going the wrong way, hoping it would collect them on its return.

The bus arrived early, and as Marijke passed the exit door, she saw the driver opening a packet of sandwiches. *He'll sit here and have breakfast until his schedule says to leave. At least he has something to do today.*

The other two passengers leaving the bus at the cableway were employees who entered a side door. Marijke had to wait for the ticket window to open, and for five minutes, she fell into a trance. *When did my life go wrong?*

I was happy as a child, but although I had many friends on the estate, the girls all went their separate ways, and I don't know where any of them are now. Perhaps they weren't real friends; I don't know if they have the same problems. Dad was busy, and Mama doted on Petrus, so they hardly talked to me. Mama never told me about the facts of life; I learned from the other girls whose mothers had told them. I never felt lonely then, but perhaps I was. Maybe I've always been lonely, just hiding it.

When the ticket window shutter rolled up, she bought a ticket and took the first car up the mountain. With no crowd of tourists, and only half a dozen people going up to manage the tourist shops at the top, she could walk around the cabin looking at the view in all directions. The early sun was beginning to light up the city bowl, and as she looked down, she thought, *it looks beautiful in the morning, but that's hell down there.*

The cable car and below were still dark in the mountain's shadow. *The streetlights are still alight.* As the car rose, she saw the furthest rows of lights wink out near the approaching line of sunlight.

It'll be like that if I jump, one moment alive and the next nothing.

Signal Hill to her left was still dark in the early morning. She could see the far edge of the shadow inching towards her as she thought, *I'll never hear the Noon Gun again.*

The cable car entered a dark cave the early light couldn't enter, and with only the night lights on, Marijke almost had to grope her way from the cable car onto the platform after the workers. One of them must have switched on the lights, which came on moments later. With everything closed, it was deathly quiet until the hum of the descending cable car filled the space.

Marijke limped out of the station from the cable car building and slowly along the path in the pale light; as it wandered along, it was sometimes far from the cliff edge and other times closer. She stopped twice.

First to watch a rock hyrax with its young; it depressed her further. *I wanted to be a mother with kids.*

Then she stopped to look at a specimen of fynbos, a plant that struggled to survive on the wind-swept table. She picked four sprays and arranged them in a posy she carried in one hand. *I had a bouquet when I married. When I jump, it would be proper.*

The place she wanted to reach was only three metres from the edge, where a boulder allowed her to sit comfortably and watch the activities in the port area. Marijke had been there several times before when she needed to make a major decision in her life. *And I got them all wrong.*

Marijke found the boulder and sat on it with her bag in her lap, her posy clutched in her hands. *Where did it all go wrong?*

Her mind turned inwards, her eyes staring, unseeing, at the distant horizon. She didn't see the view or the tugboat sweating to move a ship ten times its size in the port, although it was now in sunlight. She thought back to her childhood again; the first thing that stood out was when her dog Ruff died. *I was thirteen, he had been my companion since my first memories, and it hurt.*

As each memory came and left, she felt a dark space growing inside her as the memory took flight, no longer necessary in her life.

She had fallen in love with Hennie, a boy from another estate when they were at school; he was a year ahead. *I gave him my virginity between the grapevines. Was that a mistake?* He was going to Cape Town university to study law. Marijke had decided to follow him to law school. After months in the grapevines, he had left.

Perhaps that was my first mistake; he already had another girlfriend when I got to university. I should have chosen a different career, but what? No one suggested anything else, so it never entered my mind.

While she sat there, her mind registering nothing around her, several people sauntered by on the meandering path; most saw her, and a few looked curiously before continuing.

She remembered changing her course subjects to avoid him, so she graduated with a specialisation in family and criminal law. Later she met an accountant when they both worked on a merger. So she studied for a commercial law diploma at night school, hoping to collaborate with him. Greg proposed after a year, and she accepted. *Was that a mistake? Did Greg start sleeping with other women when I was at night school? Later, I learned that a diploma is not a degree in the legal world.*

A year ago, her father died of a heart attack at sixty. *I remember going to the cellar and emptying every bottle of wine down there.*

Then she remembered the scene where her husband told her he was sterile.

I should have divorced him after the first month, when he stopped trying to please me in bed, just using me and then turning over to sleep; but I was hoping for a child. He said he knew he was sterile and didn't want children. I should have discovered more about him before marrying him; that was my mistake.

Then I learned he'd had a mistress for years.

I'm not even a good lawyer; I lost the last two cases; there's no point in waiting until Monday to visit the bank, back to the life I don't want, and Mama doesn't need my problems; she's grieving for Dad.

As the self-induced review of her life arrived at the present, it seemed her world was a dark and miserable grey; nothing remained, and she was an empty shell. Her despair was total; Marijke had taken the wrong path and achieved nothing. She had no friends. *Dorothy stopped being a friend when the divorce came through. Maybe she has a husband problem.*

Marijke had reached a blank wall. *They say that your life unrolls before you as you die. Mine has been a waste; there's nothing there, and I have nothing to live for.*

A rock on her left, about the size of a football, was near her feet. On it was a giant black ant. Her world had shrunk to nothingness: only the cliff edge, herself, and once she saw it, the ant. *Is it trying to end its life too?*

She watched it run or walk in spurts. *It's lost, like me, trying to find a way out.* Eventually, it reached the side of the rock nearest the cliff edge. *Will it go over?*

After three attempts to climb down, the ant turned back and retraced its steps, following its pheromone trail, until it found a way off the rock and disappeared into the foliage. *It must have a home somewhere. I don't.*

Her eyes were damp in self-pity, so she opened her bag for a tissue and saw the amulet. *Maybe I should have worn that all my life; the* sangoma *did say it would look after me. It's too late now, but perhaps it will help wherever I'm going.*

She took it out, put it over her head, and closed the bag. Her body remembered it as she grasped it with her left hand, and memories flooded in.

The sangoma looked after me from five to sixteen, and I helped her treat hundreds of kids for stings, thorns, scratches and other things. I might have studied to be a doctor if I hadn't had that crush on Hennie, but it's too late now; I've wasted those years. I would be forty if I now tried to become a doctor; too old for children.

Slowly, she took her bag off her lap, placed it carefully beside the rock, and took a deep breath. *This is the end; it will only hurt for a second.*

A week later, fifteen people replied to a police advertisement asking for anyone with knowledge of Marijke's whereabouts to come forward. Three identified the right place. The police inspector found the posy and signs of boot scuff marks on the cliff edge, but the search teams found nothing.

2

Ken Phillips hated cities, big or small. He hated the crowds. When he used to work in Paris, he would visit a psychologist who had asked questions such as, "Do you take buses?"

When Ken admitted that he never took buses except when they were empty in the early morning or late at night, and that his use of the metro system was similar, the psychologist had written on her notepad, *Incipient claustrophobic.*

Then she asked, "How do you travel around?"

"Walk, bicycle, or a small car when it's raining."

"Can you fly?"

"You mean take airline flights?"

"Yes."

"I'm okay in business or first class. I never fly economy; I'm sure I'd have hysterics. I tried it once, and even though I took Valium, I didn't like it."

"What leisure activities do you have?"

"Principally photography. I walk in the country or the mountains and photograph nature. I have superb equipment and take my time; the possibilities are endless, from a landscape or sunset to an insect inside a flower."

"Have you tried the sea?"

"I've dived and done underwater photography, but I prefer to skydive."

She'd drawn a line through *incipient* on the note and added, *Risk-taking tendency.*

"I meant sailing."

"I tried, but I found it boring; I prefer the variety of nature on land."

Observational.

At the end of three sessions, the psychologist had said, "Every animal has a personal space, and when someone or something intrudes into that space, animals run, and people step back. If you imagine the intruder is not there or is a close relative, you can tolerate the presence for the length of a bus ride. Unfortunately, your personal space is much larger than most. There is one trick that might help. Buy earplugs that reduce the level of sounds you hear; this can aid the impression of distance, and it might be easier to tolerate a crowd."

He didn't return. Some weeks later, he found a more drastic solution.

His week in the Cape Town area had been fine; he had spent it visiting estates, tasting and discussing wines. The vineyards and magnificent views made him happy to be there. The wines were superb, and by the end of the week, he had negotiated contracts for several wines that would carry a label over the next five years.

"Selected and bottled exclusively for Rufisi Lodge."

He had only one appointment on Saturday for one of his favourite activities, a skydive at a club north of Cape Town. Still, he had time to spare after an early breakfast, so early that he was alone. He checked out of the hotel, put his rucksack, camera bag and towel in his rental car, and drove away to indulge in his other hobby, photography.

He had never been to Table Mountain, and several people at the vineyards had recommended it as a place of unique fauna and flora. He reached the cableway, parked his rental with his rucksack locked in the boot, and shouldered his camera bag with his towel across it; the mountain could be wet.

He was in the third cabin to ascend that morning, and several passengers looked curiously at him. His casual clothing was unremarkable, but the dark suntan and wide-brimmed bush hat suited a venue far from Cape Town.

"Are you going to jump? If so, please tell me when."

The voice from Marijke's right didn't startle her; it deterred her from standing, as it took several seconds for the words to register. Turning to look at the speaker, she saw, in sequence as she looked up, a pair of scuffed hiking boots, suntanned legs, then khaki shorts and a shirt. A face hidden by shadows cast by the sun behind a wide-brimmed bush hat seemed to have a halo around it. What looked like a large camera bag hung from one shoulder with something like a towel hanging over it. She tried to find an answer but had to refocus. She could only think of one reply.

"Why?"

"Isn't that obvious? I've never seen a suicide jump, and a video of one would go viral on the web. But hang on a moment more. I need to change lenses."

He slung the camera bag before him and began to unzip the cover.

He must be nuts, thought Marijke, but she managed to find an answer. "Why?"

"Well, a lens that zooms between a wide angle and a narrow focus would give a great scene. I'll use a wide angle to show you, the mountain, the scenery and Cape Town. Then I'll zoom in to a full face to capture your expression, exalted or determined, as you decide to jump, then back out to show you running towards the edge, and as you go over the edge and down, I'll zoom in again to keep you in the frame until you go splat. Then I'll go wide angle to show your broken body on the rocks."

Completely, totally, utterly crazy.

"Aren't you going to stop me?"

"Why should I? If you want to go to hell, it's your decision, not mine. Although it would help if you delayed a bit."

He strolled to the cliff's edge and looked down; *I must keep talking.* His boots scuffed the rock.

"Why?"

"It's awfully dark down there, almost night as it's still in shadow; I would have to use a high sensitivity setting, at least a thousand ASA."

"Why?" She looked at and past him. *I never noticed; you can see Cape Town's castle clearly when the sun reaches it.*

"'Cos, it's bad for definition; besides, the whole point of jumping is to see the end coming, and it's too dark for a clear view, so you'll miss the best bit."

Not simply crazy, but a totally deranged psycho.

"Have you left your ID in your bag?"

With her brain still trying to sort itself out, Marijke thought, *Odd question,* as she answered automatically, "Yes, my passport."

Peculiar that she has her passport, not an ID. Was she going somewhere?

"That's excellent. Without a passport, you can't pass through the gates of hell for ages while the ghouls do all the paperwork; even an ID is insufficient. The ghouls love making things difficult, so take their time. Like all civil servants, but hideous ones dripping slime all over the place while asking stupid questions."

He paused, then added, "Oh yes, there are never toilets if you want one."

Crazy is an inadequate description. Insane, demented lunatic might be better.

"I'm not going to hell; I'm going to be dead."

He finished screwing his lenses together and lifted the camera. "Bugger, I forgot the adapter. It'll only take a moment or two more. But you are entirely mistaken on that point."

"What point?" asked Marijke. *Does he really intend to film me committing suicide?*

"Going to be dead. If you believe the authorities, and there are lots of them, they've been positive for over three thousand years that suicides go to hell, to a life of torture and agony for centuries. Dante, the top expert on the subject, wrote that suicides become trees eaten by monsters and grow again from their excrement. Then the monsters eat you again and again. Lots of wailing and groaning without a decent night's sleep. So just a new life like the old one. But it might be better than the alternative."

"What alternative?"

"Not everybody dies after a fall. You might end up in another hell, living bent and twisted in a wheelchair, having your nappy changed twice daily. Come to think of it, probably lots of excrement and few decent nights of sleep as well."

I never thought of that. "Are you an expert on suicide? If not, I must take the chance that you're mistaken."

We're making progress, he thought. *That's an intelligent question.*

"Well, it depends on your point of view. I met somebody once, a nice old guy, who showed me how to commit suicide without it hurting too much, so I tried it. If one experience makes me an expert, then I am."

It gets crazier and crazier. "So, you committed suicide? How can you be here?"

"Well, this old guy, while we were in India, pointed out that there were two ways of considering suicide."

"Mental derangement and drunken stupidity?"

And Ken thought, *Progress—she's thinking.*

"Not at all; he said it was either a stupid desire to punish someone or an excessively extreme method for escaping a failed past. Which are you?"

"Only those two to choose from? Which one were you?"

"The second, but I asked about you."

"I guess I'm also the second."

"Good. The old guy said punishing someone by committing suicide had no guarantee of success; the target might even be pleased, and instead he recommended killing the person you want to punish.

For the other, he said, 'Don't bother drinking; you might do something ridiculous, like climbing a statue to put a hat on its head, then falling off. Just walk away from the past with nothing. When you arrive in hell, you have nothing, not even clothes, so it achieves the same thing.'"

"How did he know that?" *I never thought that lunatics could tell stories, but it seems to make sense.*

"I asked him if he had been there. He said, 'I jumped after a man I knew nothing about shot my wife and child and then shot himself.' The old guy said he was the first type of suicide and damned stupid, thinking he'd have the chance to kill the bastard who shot his wife, but when the old guy reached hell, he realised there was an error in his thinking."

Marijke nodded, "I can understand that. How did he escape?"

"Oh, he said that he noticed no politicians in hell, so he asked why not and learned that they stir up so much trouble talking crap all the time that the devil chucks them out. So, he behaved like a politician, and the devil shifted him to the alternative hell where the politicians can talk forever, but no one listens."

"So far, the story makes sense, but how did he escape?"

She's interested and following the story, thought Ken.

"He said the politicians adore being there because they don't have to stand for re-election. So, there were no guards, and he just strolled out."

"I can imagine that's true. So did you jump?"

"I did. The old guy said I should take a towel and ID with me."

"Why the towel?"

"He didn't say, but it's extremely handy."

"Is that it on your bag?"

"Yes, it keeps the camera cool from the sun. It's useful for all sorts of things. I've had two, the first became very worn and shabby, and I found this one hanging on a washing line. It's much nicer."

So, he stole a towel from a washing line; he's a nutcase who's hardly the most wanted criminal in the world. I'll humour him.

"Why's it nicer?"

"Because it's thicker and softer; quite fluffy, really, but it's the picture that made me choose it."

"What picture?"

He took the towel off the bag, unfolded it and held it up.

"That's an American towel; there's an eagle on it."

"There's a label saying 'Made in China'."

"But the stars under the eagle make it American."

Great, now she's arguing. Useful things, towels.

"I suppose you're right, but I think the eagle likes me."

He's delusional as well. "What was his name?" she asked.

"Who? The eagle?"

"The old guy you're talking about."

"Douglas something."

"And then what?"

"Well, the past is gone. You can start a new life."

"What new life?"

"Who knows? It's up to you to decide what you want the new life to be. In a way, it's the same as jumping off a cliff. You don't know where you'll end up, so you don't know what life you'll have until you arrive."

At least, that makes sense. "So, where did you end up?"

"As expected, in one corner of hell, but I like it there, and I'm improving it."

The craziest story I've ever heard. "You're improving hell?"

"Well, I'm doing my best, not for me but for the others, and only in my little bit of hell. It's fun, although sometimes I think I'm just like Sisyphus."

"Who's he?"

"The guy Hades told to roll a boulder up a hill, and then every time it gets to the top, it rolls down again. I've heard about him but haven't met him yet."

That sounds familiar. "Where, when, and how do I jump?"

Finally, a great question, Ken thought. "Here and now. Come with me."

"With nothing but my passport?" *This is a crazy suggestion, or is it?*

"Exactly, your old life is left behind you."

"To be tortured by a stranger?"

"Well, that's the minimum you can expect in hell, and it will be the least of your agonies if you don't die."

"You said that when you arrive in hell, you have nothing, not even clothes. Can I keep my clothes?"

"Only until you can replace them. Then they go in the bin. If you take them off now, you'll discover a different kind of hell in a police jail cell and then in a mental hospital and probably experience the same torture as in hell. Give me your passport, and then you'll have nothing else left."

She reached into her bag, handed it over, and asked, "Come with you to where?" *At least the first maniac I've met is interesting.*

"Wherever I take you, eventually to hell."

"I don't even know your name."

"Sorry, I didn't realise." *I think we're there.* "Don't you know the name of the doorkeeper to hell?"

"No." She picked up her bag. *It might be more interesting than what I had planned. He's the first person in two years to want to take me somewhere, and he may not be as nuts as he appears to be. I would have been dead, so I have nothing to lose.* She stood up.

So Ken said, "Right, let's go."

She followed him to the cable car. *He's tall, a metre ninety.*

On the rock behind her lay a posy of fynbos.

3

Ken said as they entered the cable car, "Take a good look; it's the last time you'll see this."

That's what I thought when I rode up. I don't belong there anymore. Marijke moved over to the glass wall as if she wanted gaze at the view, although she didn't want to. Instead, Marijke half turned to see him. Without his hat, she had a clear look at his face. *Not bad; he doesn't look like a maniac, and his eyes aren't glittering. I think they're smiling; he has a rugged sort of face. I suppose all maniacs look normal.*

He smiled at her. *Good, she's checking me out, and she's pretty.*

And she thought, *He has a friendly smile too.*

He glanced at her passport. *Marie-Jeanne Coetzee.*

A metre eighty, thick dark hair and huge greenish brown eyes; they'll be lovely if they smile.

He led them to a little white car, and as they drove off, she said, "I thought the transport to hell would be black."

Nice question. We're getting there. "Well, we're not there yet; I'm travelling incognito."

Nuts! "So, where are we going?"

"You wanted to jump, so you need to do one. I'll take you to a jump, but one much higher. It will give you the time to appreciate life and learn something."

Marijke thought it a peculiar reply. *But everything's peculiar this morning, and I did agree to go with him.*

After thirty minutes of silence, while Marijke wondered if she was doing something *really* stupid, Ken drove into a small airfield. She saw a building with a sign above it.

"You're taking me skydiving? I've never done that."

"Well, you'll certainly dive. I'll throw you out over three times higher than Table Mountain."

"Why?"

"So, you can learn something before you die."

He can't intend to kill me, or can he?

She did learn his name was Ken. At least the man running the skydiving show called him that. After introducing her, Ken asked, "Chooky, do you have a suit for her?"

"Sure, Ken. Marie-Jeanne, what size shoes do you wear?"

"Size eight, but everyone calls me Marijke; Marie-Jeanne's only the name for my tombstone."

"Okay."

Ken thought, *She saw me check her passport; her sense of humour is returning!*

Chooky fetched a suit and gave it to her with a pair of soft-soled boots. "Try these; if they don't fit, I have others."

She pulled on the one-piece suit and put on the boots, and Chooky fitted her with a harness, goggles and helmet while Ken kitted up. Then Chooky helped clip a parachute bag on Ken's back and checked everything.

I don't have a parachute; I suppose I'll hang from his harness.

Then Ken said, "Marijke. When you leave the plane's door, spread your arms and legs like this. It's a stable position, gives the longest drop time, and you can see the ground coming up to hit you. That's important."

"Okay." *I guess I'm just as crazy.*

At twelve thousand feet, Ken stood and helped her up. The door rolled up, and she saw the earth far below. She was standing on the edge with Ken behind her, waiting for him to connect to her harness, when she heard his voice. "Remember the position." Then he pushed her out. It took three seconds for her to remember the position and two more to realise she was alone. *He threw me out on my own without a parachute. Oh my God—I'm going to die!*

She couldn't see Ken follow her. After fifteen seconds, he flew down until he was just above her and reached down to clip lines to the loops on her harness; he did so without her noticing because her attention was on the ground. Then he waited another thirty seconds.

First, she seemed to float, the earth still far away. *Skydiving would be fun if I had a parachute.* Then it was approaching fast, for Marijke too fast.

If only an eagle could swoop down and take me to its nest.

Her eyes stopped focusing on the ground as she thought, *Why did I think that?*

Then she saw the ground again, a lot closer and closing—*rapidly.*

She knew death was only seconds away. Her adrenaline levels topped the scale.

I can see people, and they're looking up. They know I'll die.

She could see the colour of their clothes.

But I don't want to die!

At three thousand feet, only seconds later, she felt a massive pull from behind as her fall slowed and then seemed to stop with a jerk. The extreme adrenaline rush brought confusion.

The eagle came and saved me.

Then as the adrenaline subsided, she realised Ken was behind her.

He guided the chute down to a landing, said, "Lift your legs," and landed gently.

He swooped like an eagle.

With the adrenaline falling rapidly, her legs felt like rubber; she couldn't stand. Sagging in her harness, she had to lean against him.

She was grateful when he put his arms around her and held her. When the pickup truck drove up to collect them, she managed to stand on her own. Ken disconnected his harness, removed it, and then removed hers. The truck driver loaded all the gear, and Ken helped her climb into the back for the short drive.

"Ken, is this hell?"

"What do you mean, Marijke?"

"Am I dead?"

"You don't look dead but very much alive."

"But I thought I was going to die. So, you saved me?"

"You were always safe, Marijke; what did you learn?"

"That I don't want to die."

"That's something worth knowing. Are you ready to start your new life now?"

"Doing what?"

"Whatever you want, the past no longer matters. It's gone. Think forward, not back."

"I don't know where to start." *I don't. I really don't. Everything has gone and doesn't matter, as if I did die.*

The truck stopped for them to descend.

Ken remembered his schedule. *I must leave her now; my flight leaves in three hours.*

"You could go home to your parents, talk to them, and work out what you want to do to build a new life."

I can't; I can't go home or to my flat; it's like they're not there. I have nowhere to go. "So, you won't take me to hell?"

Ken thought for a moment. *Marijke has no idea what to do; if I leave her, she might fall into trouble. I like her, and she has her passport. She can't return and jump if I take her away from Cape Town.*

"I said it's up to you to choose. You can come with me to hell; you might learn more."

"Like what torture feels like?"

"That's in the small print."

I'm supposed to be dead anyway, so why not? "Okay."

She has guts. "Then take off your jumpsuit."

Ken took off his suit while Marijke headed to the changerooms, and he called the airline; fortunately, seats were available in business class, so he didn't have to book an alternative flight.

On the drive to the airport, Marijke asked, "Where are we going?"

"Cape Town International."

"Are we flying somewhere?"

"Yes, Nairobi."

"Why there?"

"No flights are going any nearer to hell. We'll spend the night there and take another flight tomorrow. It's a lot quicker than walking."

"Okay." *He'll tell me more when he wants to, not if I ask, and I agreed to go to hell with him. Although not agreed, more like accepted. That's the first time the expression "go to hell" makes sense to me.*

They arrived at the airport just in time to board; Ken had only a small rucksack and his camera bag. With adrenaline ebbing after the jump, Marijke felt tired; however, when the cabin crew served the late lunch, she felt better and cleared the tray.

Ken thought, *Appetite is a good sign*, and then he said, "I never asked, Marijke, why did you have your passport in your bag?"

"A thief on a scooter ripped my bag from my shoulder last night on my way home. I lost my phone, keys, ID, and credit card. The passport and some cash were all I had left in my flat, so I had them with me."

"Big city hell. Were you hurt?"

"Bruised when I fell, and sore at the police station, and it's still tender."

"That's tough; I'm glad nothing broke." *That's not enough to bring on suicide; there must be more, but it could have been the last straw.*

Marijke felt he sounded kind when he replied, "Sleep if you can and forget; the past has gone. We won't be in bed before midnight."

She did, but before sleep came, she had an odd thought, *We must be going to a different hell, one for rich people; business class is more comfortable than a boat on the river Styx. He must be the chief ghoul.*

It was after ten when they cleared immigration and found a hotel limousine waiting for them. It stopped once for Ken to enter a pharmacy and return with a paper packet. Marijke didn't ask what he had bought.

It was another forty minutes before they reached a cottage on the hotel grounds. Marijke hadn't spoken; she'd looked out the window for the whole journey, thinking.

It doesn't look like I imagined hell, but it's certainly different from Cape Town.

"What's this place?"

"The hotel has several cottages; if the main hotel is full, they use them as rooms for the guests."

When they entered the lounge of the cottage, Marijke stopped. "That painting, that's a Botticelli."

"A replica, like all the paintings here, although they were original when the owner decorated the cottage. Do you know it?"

"Yes, it's from an illustrated copy of Dante's poem about hell."

"Then take a good look; you can see where you might have gone. Look for the trees I told you about, the ones the monsters eat."

"I won't; I don't need reminding about the trees. What's the history of this cottage?"

"Like all the others, rich men built them as residences when they came on safari in this region in the 1900s. They decorated them to impress other rich men and women."

"And that picture of a giraffe?"

"That's a Rothschild's giraffe. Baron Rothschild was a keen naturalist and proved that this giraffe differed from the more common subspecies. You can read about it on the web."

"Not right now; I have a more pressing problem. Where's the bathroom?"

"Here." He showed her a bedroom with a massive Victorian double bed and a door to a bathroom.

He handed her a menu when she came out. "What would you like to eat? We have a long day tomorrow, so we should sleep after eating."

"What are you eating?"

"An omelette and fries, with a beer."

"Then I'll have the same, but with a rock shandy."

He ordered, and she wandered around the room, looking at each ornament.

"This is a wonderful collection of African art. It must have taken years to collect; I'm surprised it's still here."

"Like the paintings, they're all replicas. The originals must be in a museum or the Baron's collection. He collected them all over East Africa, from different ethnic groups."

Then she asked, "The skydiving guy called you 'Ken'. Is that your real name, or what do I call you?"

"No, it's not; I earned the nickname in Scotland. You can call me 'Dearest' or '*Bwana*' like everyone in my hell does."

"In Scotland?"

"Yep, the Scots introduced me and said, 'This man is a *sassenach*, d'ye ken?'"

"What is a *sassenach*?"

"An English person. So, people started using 'Ken' as my name."

"Well, I'll stick to *Bwana* until I know you better."

The meal arrived, and after they had eaten, Marijke said, "I have a more practical problem."

"What?"

"I have no clean underwear for tomorrow, so I must wash it, and I have no pyjamas."

"Leave your clothes on the bedroom chair when you shower or bathe. I'll call room service and have them wash your clothes and return them by tomorrow morning; they can also do mine."

"That will leave me naked."

"Me too; don't worry about it."

Now I'll ask the critical question: "Where will you sleep?"

"On the couch."

"Okay." *That's a surprise; I guess I expected something else.*

When she entered the bathroom, Ken placed the paper packet on the bed where she would see it and took her clothes away to a washing basket he had put in the lounge. When she came out, she opened it and was surprised to find two tubes of bruise ointment. Marijke rubbed a liberal smear into the bruises she could reach and climbed into bed. *I've been naked with a man in bed before, but I always wore a nightie or panties at first.*

Ken heard the old Victorian bed squeak, so he entered the bedroom, intending to shower. On her stomach, Marijke said, "*Bwana*, thanks for the ointment; I can't reach high up on my back. Can you rub some in there?"

Ken did, then entered the bathroom, and Marijke thought, *He may be crazy, but he's gentle; he saved my life and bought me the ointment. He should be in the bed and me on the couch.*

Ken showered and left the bathroom naked, his clothes in his hands. Marijke was looking the other way. She wasn't asleep and said, "*Bwana*, the couch is too small for you. You can have half the bed."

"Thanks, Marijke." *I didn't expect that.*

After putting his clothes on the pile in the lounge, he returned and climbed into bed, keeping well to his side. Marijke had her eyes closed, but she peeked. *His body reminds me of a Greek statue, all muscles and suntanned. He lives outdoors.*

I'm in bed naked with a man I met only this morning. That's never happened to me, although I know it has happened to other women.

She opened her eyes. "You said I would lose my clothes when I reached hell, and that's happened. Is this when the torture begins?"

"Oh no, that's too easy; masochists must wait for ages."

"I'm glad to hear that." *He may be nice, but he's completely unhinged.* "So, you think I'm a masochist?"

"Oh yes, high class, top of the tree, none better. An ultimate masochist who wants to suffer a punishment so excruciating that it ends with death."

"I must think about that." *I never thought I was trying to punish myself. If so, why?*

She tried to think, but she was tired. Each time she started a thought, it drifted away. *I have no answer; I must sleep on it.*

4

____

After the first birds began cheeping as dawn broke, Marijke awoke, disoriented for a minute, stood, and entered the bathroom. Ken opened his eyes to see her walking to the door. *Beautiful, naked but for a juju, and she didn't try to hide her nudity.* He smiled. *She's better already. Did she forget me, or is she teasing?*

He feigned sleep as the door opened, and she returned to bed. Once her breathing slowed to a regular rhythm, he rose, collected her washed and ironed clothes from the lounge along with a breakfast menu, and silently put them on the bed.

He dressed and left the cottage to make some calls, then returned. The coffee he'd ordered arrived two minutes later, on a tray, with two cups and a coffee pot.

He heard Marijke go into the bathroom and shower, and she appeared wearing the washed clothes ten minutes later.

"That was quick; women usually take hours."

"So, you have experience with women going to the bathroom in the morning?"

Ken was pleased with the question and smiled. *I think she's fishing. That shows curiosity.* "Of course, starting with my mother, who could drive my father mad while he waited for her to get ready to go out."

He won't admit anything. "Well, I'll try to do better next time. I have no face creams or makeup, so you have me in the raw."

"I like you that way, but you'll fix that this morning. Have a coffee. What do you want for breakfast?"

"I haven't been this hungry in ages. Bacon, sausage, scrambled eggs, toast and marmalade."

Ken nodded. *She probably hasn't eaten well for days.*

"Where did you get that *juju* you wear, Marijke?"

"*Juju?* Do you mean this amulet?"

"Yes, *juju* is the name Africans use for good luck charms in many countries worldwide."

"The *sangoma* who helped to raise me from five to sixteen gave it to me when I left for boarding school; she said it would look after me and bring good luck."

"What's a *sangoma*, and what do you mean helped raise you?"

"A traditional healer. People used to call them witch doctors. My parents were busy during those years, so I played with the other children on the wine estate where I grew up and attended the local school with them. The *sangoma* was a mother to all of us; she fixed our cuts and bruises. I helped her, and she taught me. I learned a lot."

She sighed as she put down her knife and fork, "*Bwana,* that was marvellous. If this is hell, I could stay here. What are we doing today?"

"Oh, hell is just down the road. First, you will take a taxi; the driver speaks English, tell him what you want, and he'll take you to the shops. Remember to buy sunscreen, enough for at least two months. You have until twelve-thirty to return. Then we have lunch and take a taxi to the airport for a flight to Dar es Salaam. That's the next stop on the way to hell."

"I don't have any money." She had a slight feeling of achievement. *He slipped up; he expects me to be in his hell for at least two months.*

Ken handed her a wad of Kenyan notes. "Here, this should cover it."

Marijke sat beside the driver. *I'll ask him for some Swahili words.*

Marijke opened the window on her side, for she wanted to hear and smell. *It's quite different from Cape Town.* The air that blew into the car was pleasantly cool; she knew Nairobi's altitude was higher than Johannesburg's. *There are also far more people on the streets than in Cape Town, and they aren't rushing around. But there's something else.*

It took Marijke ten minutes to realise what it was. *The people are talking to each other, smiling and laughing.*

As they pulled up in front of a large shop with Western ladies' clothing in the window, she realised, *Those clothes don't seem right. I died; this is somewhere else where I must start a new life. I must begin by wearing the clothes the women wear here.* She told the driver, who, once he understood what he considered a crazy request, took her to an open-air market, parked the taxi, and led her down alleyways between packed stalls to the clothing section.

When Mama Keita learned she had a client ready to buy six dresses, shoes, night dresses and underwear, she had her two daughters come to help from nearby stalls. The panties were no problem, but the bra was.

When Marijke removed her dress, Mama said, "My *sidiria* won't do; you have high *Matiti*." It took fifteen minutes to find a dozen flat boxes of bras from other stalls and for Marijke to try them on. She bought six. The night dresses surprised Marijke. "Mama, these are short and almost see-through."

"It's too hot to wear anything to bed; we wrap a *kikkoy* around us and undo the knot. The young women buy these for *special* occasions."

"Then I'll take this red one and some *kikkoys*." *Maybe I'll have a special occasion.*

After selecting six *kikkoys*, Marijke thought, *I don't have a towel. Ken said I must have one.*

"Mama, I need a small towel."

"I'll call the *mganga* who sells them."

What's a mganga?

When the woman arrived, visibly far older than the young woman beside her who carried a bundle of towels, Marijke knew immediately. She would have recognised a South African *sangoma* without the amulets hanging around her neck. The one on her father's estate who administered medicines to all the kids, including her, looked the same.

She has lovely eyes.

A flood of memories returned, and Marijke couldn't help herself; as she had done on the estate, she did a little girl's respectful bob. The woman's eyes widened in surprise, and then she examined Marijke closely. Marijke didn't move, and when the woman looked into her eyes, she met her gaze directly.

They can see right into me. I hope what they see is good.

After a moment, the *mganga* smiled and spoke to the young girl beside her. Then the girl searched through the towels and handed one to Marijke.

Marijke caressed the towel. "This is beautiful, the cheetah is lovely, and it likes me."

Mama Keita translated, and the *mganga* replied. Then Mama said, "She asks if she can see your *juju*."

Marijke lifted off her amulet and handed it to the *mganga*—who held it with both hands to her forehead, then closed her eyes for over a minute. When she opened them again and spoke, her eyes were warm and smiling. Mama translated: "A *mganga* gave this to you as a mark of her respect to a young *mganga*. She was your mother and your teacher."

Marijke, amazed, said nothing, then nodded.

The *mganga* handed it back, then took an amulet from her neck and reached up to hang it around Marijke's neck; the gesture was unmistakable, so Marijke bowed her head for her to do so. Then the *mganga* spoke again.

Marijke could hear the respect in Mama's voice as she translated, "She waited today for you; the towel is a gift to your spirit, your *mzimu*, and the *juju* is a gift from one *mganga* to another."

She waited for me? How could she know I was coming?

"Please tell her that I and my *mzimu* thank her, but I have come with nothing but money to buy the clothes; I cannot give her what I wish to give."

"She says that she knows, and you will return here to buy your wedding dress, so you may make your gift when you return after your voyage."

So, I've been a mganga *since I was sixteen and never knew it? And how does she know I'm not married? Or that I shall return?*

The *mganga* left, and then Mama Keita smiled conspiratorially. "She also said I must not make the wedding dress too tight."

Marijke thought, *Does that mean what I think it means?*

When Marijke had dressed in her new underwear and one of the multicoloured loose dresses, she said, "Mama, I don't need my old clothes now; please give them to someone."

"Then I shall give you something." Mama fitted a beaded headdress to Marijke's head. "There, you look just like a Kenyan woman. No one will speak English to you."

"I shall learn Swahili."

"I know, *Bibie*, already you are speaking some Swahili."

I am! I know all the words for these clothes. Why does it seem effortless?

It took the final hour for her to visit a beauty shop; the driver had to carry a box of sunscreens, perfumes, creams, shampoos, two hairbrushes, and a lady's razor to the taxi.

Ken was waiting when she stepped from the taxi; he gaped when he saw how she had dressed and heard her say *"Asante-Sana"* to the driver. *Incredible! What a surprise. She has jumped into a new life.*

Marijke grinned at him; he was so obviously amazed. "Do you approve, *Bwana?*"

"Marijke, you're beautiful and a delightful surprise. *I'm staggered; she's like a different woman, and what a smile!* Where did you buy the *juju?*"

"A *mganga* in the market gave it to me."

This puzzled Ken, and it showed. *That's even more of a surprise; I've never heard of it happening before.*

There must be something about Marijke that I haven't noticed; choosing to wear Kenyan clothes is special. "Does that make you a *mganga*?"

"The *mganga* in the market said the *sangoma* of my childhood gave me the *juju* I came with as a young *mganga*, so maybe I've been one for years but never knew it. But I'm only a learner."

"Well, that's surprising; I never thought of a white *mganga*."

"*Bwana*, in South Africa, there are several hundred white *sangomas*, and in Europe and worldwide, many thousands. Just think of the witches and wizards throughout history."

"Do you want to be a Kenyan in your new life?"

"No, *Bwana*, you have the wrong tense. I *am* one."

"I don't follow you, Marijke."

"I ran barefoot for my first sixteen years with children from the Cape farm community, and I belong in African culture. I never saw myself as a white girl.

"Then I tried to become a city girl, and I failed; you gave me a second chance, and today I found the culture to which I belong. I feel gloriously free and happy. I must learn how an African adult behaves because I was a child. I'll learn Swahili so I can speak to other adults who speak it."

"Well, you seem to be doing okay so far, and I have much to learn. You can teach me. We'll have lunch after we put those things in the suitcase I bought."

"Okay, *Bwana*." *Funny, I feel like a different person already.*

"Marijke, why did you buy a towel?"

"Someone I met recommended it to me; he said it was important to have one when travelling. The *mganga* chose it for me; I love the cheetah picture. I didn't steal it off a washing line."

Ken remembered: *Neither did I, but I won't tell her that. She's much better, and now she's taking the Mickey.*

Marijke thought, *I'll not tell him the* mganga *gave it to me; he won't believe it.*

Ken said as they walked to the restaurant for lunch, "You're going to be a sensation, Marijke. Are you ready for it?"

"Why a sensation, *Bwana*? Except when I was young and with other girls, no one noticed me. There will be other Kenyan women dressed like me. Nobody ever looks at people in a restaurant. All they see is a dress or a suit with a head on top. Lawyers are not flamboyant like artists."

Ken thought, *She's like a rose that's spent a lifetime in the shade when it needed sunshine. The dress is her sunshine.*

"You'll see, Marijke. You're not a lawyer now but the most spectacular woman in the hotel. People will look at you today and every day."

"And you, *Bwana*, will they look at you?"

"If they do, it will only be to think, 'He's a lucky guy'." *I know how she must have felt. They never saw me when I worked at a bank; I was only one cog among thousands.*

Ken was right, and it was a completely new experience for Marijke. She had never been a sensation in a restaurant. A soberly dressed woman is unnoticeable unless alone, but a tall white woman in exotic clothes with a Kenyan headdress is not. Marijke knew the men and women diners were examining her openly and revelled in it.

Ken watched, amused—and pleased. He didn't ask himself why the staff gave her far more attention than other diners.

Then an American woman came to the table and asked, "My dear, I must ask, where did you buy that beautiful dress? I really must get one for myself."

"Ask a taxi driver to take you to see Mama Keita in the market. She and her daughters can fit you out with everything."

"Thank you, I shall go this afternoon."

Ken asked, "Marijke, do you enjoy being a sensation?"

"*Bwana*, it's a new experience for me; already, my life has changed. *Asante-Sana*, it's a lot better than being dead."

"Because you are making it better. Continue, and you will find out what you want from life." *Kweli kabisa—that is absolutely true.*

It's metamorphosis; I thought I had found a caterpillar, and now a beautiful butterfly has appeared. I must wait until it learns to fly.

5

———————

By the time they had checked in at the Blue Sapphire Hotel in Dar es Salaam near the airport, Ken was beginning to wonder. He had never before experienced the exceptional service they'd received at the airports and the hotel reception.

Marijke changed before dinner. Ken was relaxing in an armchair by the window when she came out of the bathroom. It was the first time he had seen her made-up with her hair arranged for the evening. *She's stunning, even without the headpiece.* He reacted as any man would and stood immediately.

"*Bwana,* please answer a question that's bothering me. Why did you bring me here?"

"I told you, it's just a stop on the way to hell. I know this hotel must remind you of Cape Town, but it's close to the airport and to the road we must take, and Lucas has family nearby; like me, he doesn't like the big city."

"Who's Lucas?" *I'll remember they don't like cities.*

"You'll meet him tomorrow; where I go, he goes; having a buddy with you is necessary for survival in hell. He's also the number two at the lodge. When I'm away, he's the manager. He's collecting our monthly shopping; Dar is a much older city than Nairobi; it existed along with Zanzibar for centuries as an Arab port. The European

33

colonials didn't have the impact they did in Nairobi, which the British set up from scratch, so the type of cottage we stayed in doesn't exist here."

"I didn't mean that at all; I meant, why did you take me with you from Cape Town?" *I've almost forgotten why I was there!* "As a start, you could tell me why you talked to me on the mountain."

"That's easy; you looked so miserable that my soft heart said to cheer you up." *It wasn't just that she looked miserable; I felt unhappy when I saw her and terrified that she would jump.*

"That's not true; you couldn't see my face."

"No, I couldn't." *True, but I walked along the path two metres behind her, and she didn't notice me, so I turned to look closer.* "But I was there to take photos in the early light; I thought you might make a good subject, so I came over. You looked desperately miserable and alone from the slumped way you were sitting."

"So, you spun a yarn about hell and jumping off high places to divert me?"

"You can say so, but every bit of it is true; at least, to me it is."

"So why did you push me out of that plane?"

"I had arranged the jump as the last thing to do before leaving Cape Town, and I thought you had to learn that you don't want to die."

"You almost gave me a heart attack. I could have died in mid-air."

"I thought you looked healthy, so I didn't think that would happen. It did work, though, didn't it?"

"Yes, and then you were going to leave me. That's what I'm asking; why did you bring me?"

She's far better but still lacking confidence.

"I can't answer that, Marijke; I don't know. I did offer to take you to hell, although I expected you to leave me in a hurry after the jump. When you said you didn't know where to start, I thought, what difference does it make to you where you begin a new life? So, I offered again. I was amazed when you said yes, but now I'm glad." *Kweli kabisa.*

"Why?"

"Put that beaded headdress on, Marijke; then I'll show you."

She fetched it from her suitcase and returned wearing the headdress.

There must be a better word than stunning—she's glowing. "Now, come to the big mirror by the door and stand before it."

Ken stood beside her.

"Look carefully, Marijke. Have you ever seen a more beautiful woman?"

"It's the dress and the makeup."

"No, they make beautiful into magnificent; what's inside them must be right, and it shows."

Ken says I'm beautiful; no one has ever said that to me. "Looking lovely" *is the most they said.*

"Now, let's go for dinner; you'll be a sensation again."

Marijke felt the same pride when the diners remarked on her presence, and the staff vied to serve her. *Ken's enjoying the attention; is it because he's pleased for me?*

Ken wondered, *The servers have never given me the attention Marijke's getting. Is it the* jujus *or her beauty?*

"Marijke, can you tell me why you came with me after the skydive?"

"I don't know, it was just a feeling that I belonged with you after you saved me."

She must have been confused after the jump.

Marijke mused when she slipped into bed, wearing a *kikkoy. Funny, I could have worn my underwear, but the elastic's uncomfortable, and I like being in bed with Ken like this. Will he try to make love to me tonight? That's odd; I wouldn't have thought "to make love" yesterday.*

At breakfast, Ken told her, "If there's any shopping you need to do, now's the time to say so. We're driving to hell today, and there are no towns to buy anything except basic foodstuffs."

"*Bwana*, I don't know what I'll need in hell; I have everything I can imagine. What do you do if you need things?"

"Make a list, email it to a shop, and send someone with a truck on a two-day drive to fetch it, usually once a month."

"Is there no faster way?"

"There's a lodge not far away with an airstrip, so someone can fly in with a small plane in an emergency. Also, the plane's pilot doesn't mind bringing a small packet when they fly tourists to that lodge if they don't have too much baggage."

"Okay, then I'm ready." *Is this where the new life begins? Or has it begun already, during the skydive or in the Nairobi market?*

The double cab four-by-four pickup already had a small mountain of things in the back; it was fortunate that she and Ken had little baggage. On the door, there was a logo of a cheetah and a hippopotamus beside a river, with *Rufisi, Nyerere National Park* written below.

Ken introduced the two men with it, "Marijke, this is Lucas; he looks after the lodge and me. Lucas, this is my *Bibie*."

"*Nimefurahi kukuona*, nice to meet you, Lucas." *Ken said Bibie—that means wife.* She shook hands with Lucas. *He's Ken's age and handsome, with the same confident look of authority as our winery manager, and Lucas wears a* juju.

"You are very welcome, *Bibie*; we have all worried about who *Bwana* might bring to the lodge."

"Wait until you know more about me, Lucas. You might change your mind."

Then she asked Ken, "*Bwana*, are we going to a lodge in the Nyerere game reserve?"

"We are. That's where you'll live with me until you decide to leave."

I'm beginning to feel I want her to stay; I didn't expect that.

Marijke thought, *A lawyer would interpret that as a marriage proposal—an invitation to stay forever.*

"But that's not hell, *Bwana*."

"It is. You'll learn that people suffer from a lack of medical treatment; there are no vets for the animals; poachers kill indiscriminately; and the predators eat anything, including people, alive.

"The mosquitos are as big as a jet; snakes, scorpions, and huge spiders scuttle around, and the flies never cease to annoy you. It's worse than hell; in hell, you at least know what to expect."

"Are there ghouls with whips?"

Now she's pulling my leg again. I'll tell her about the Glooper. "I haven't seen any with whips; there are lots who keep hell clean, so they must have brooms and stuff. I call the boss ghoul the 'Glooper'; his breath stinks horribly. We stay away from him because he can swallow a motor car or person whole."

"Where is the 'Glooper?'" *Is this another piece of his imagination? He probably means the scavengers.*

"Ask a ranger for the entrance to *jehanamu*—hell—and they might show you."

"I can do without going near that, but what will I do?"

"I've no idea; it's up to you. The staff and I will do our best to make sure nothing eats you, but you aren't a paying guest at the lodge, so if you don't like it, tell me. I'll ask a ranger to drive you back here, and you can fly back to South Africa."

Marijke thought, *I might not stay; he might not want me to. But I won't go back to Cape Town; I would go somewhere else. I'll have to be desperate to return.*

"If you find something interesting to do, ask Lucas or me for help."

I'll never be a lawyer again. I must learn what I can do. Once I know the lay of the land, I'll find something.

Ken introduced the driver. "Marijke, please meet Amali; he's an apprentice ranger and our driver. Like Lucas, he attended a mission school and learned to speak excellent English."

She shook hands. "*Nimefurahi kukuona*, Amali." *Very young, twenty-plus, with friendly eyes.*

"What do apprentice rangers have to learn, Amali?"

"*Bibie*, number one is not to be rude to obnoxious guests—that's difficult. Then I must learn all the roads in the park and all about the animals and the birds. *Bwana* says it takes three years, but I'll do it in two!"

Ken added, "I think he will, but it gets harder to learn about the rarer animals, so we'll see. I must assign someone to show you around and keep you out of trouble for a month or two; I think Amali might do an excellent job." He turned to Amali and asked, "Would you like that?"

"With pleasure, *Bwana*."

Marijke agreed, "I appreciate that, on condition Amali speaks Swahili with me as much as we can."

She asked Ken, "Do your paying guests do this drive?"

"I try to avoid the tick-off tourists; I want the serious ones who come for a week or more, but if the drive would be too hard on them, I'll arrange a charter flight to that nearby lodge and pick them up from there."

"What's a tick-off tourist?"

"One that flies in and wants to see the big five in two days—ticks them off the list of things to see—and then flies off to see the flamingos at Lake Manyara. I visited one of the exclusive lodges in Kruger Park, and that's the kind they want. That lodge even gives them fancy certificates."

"And you don't?"

"We can if they want one, but finding leopard and rhino is difficult, so we don't advertise. Marijke, there are cushions and pillows in the rear seat; arrange them so you are comfortable and they protect you. It's a long drive, and there are smooth parts, but the truck will chuck you around on the bad road. I'll be in the rear with you."

Marijke looked out the open window as they drove out of Dar. She thought the air was much hotter and more humid than Nairobi, but the two cities were alike in many ways. As they left the city for the open country, she found a resemblance to the Karoo: dry, short bushveld with savannah patches. It was only then that she thought, *Dar smells fishy. Out here, that's gone.*

Six hours later, twenty kilometres after passing through the park gates, they arrived at the Rufiji River; the lodge was a further ten kilometres along the bank. Marijke had seen the wild game in South Africa, but the scenery here was utterly different: a vast open plain of short grass, a kaleidoscope of greens under the angled sunlight. She had never seen some of the antelopes, especially the dainty Thomson's gazelles.

"*Bwana*, it looks like someone mows the lawn."

"The someone is hippos; I agree they make it look like that."

Marijke marvelled at the variety and density of wildlife. After a picnic lunch, she had dozed, woken often when the vehicle had to negotiate a piece of road washed out by the rains and rocked violently from side to side. Lucas or Ken had to descend and lock the front axle three times to traverse deep mud sections.

"*Bwana*, is it always like this?"

"No, we are in the wet season, usually six months starting in November; then there's the dry season. That's a more comfortable hell, with a much shorter route from Dar with a heavily loaded truck. The wet season has compensations; we don't have as many visitors, they usually fly in, and we have few commercial poachers. It's the time when we can build and improve."

He added, "Our hell is always hot because we are close to the equator."

The second time they stopped to lock the axles, Lucas said, "*Bwana—duma*."

Ken looked up, "Where?"

Lucas pointed. Thirty metres away, two cheetahs lay before a clump of brush.

Marijke exclaimed, "They're beautiful."

Ken said, "The *duma* is not as beautiful as the leopard, but far less dangerous to man."

"Well, I think they're beautiful; I love them."

"Wait until you see the leopards."

With its mass of hippos, the Rufiji River amazed her. "*Bwana*, there are more hippos in this river than in the whole of South Africa!"

"No, but you won't find a concentration like this one. The hippos feed at night and are very territorial. The sides of the river are a perfect feeding area for them. There also used to be rhinos, but we've only three; they hide, and we cut off their horns to discourage poachers. The lodge doesn't have a waterhole; it's close to the river, and guests can sit on the veranda and view the game coming to drink, so walking in front of it at night is a substantial risk. At dusk and dawn, we see them all: the herds, the elephants, and the predators."

"Okay, I've been to game lodges. Do you eat with the guests at night?"

"Yes, I do; I think you should come as well. The staff will expect it."

"So do I."

Ken thought, *Now how am I supposed to interpret that? Does she want to be part of the lodge and my life? That's unexpected but pleasing.*

Amali stopped at a long bungalow with a thatched reed roof and a veranda along the entire length. Four men came to unload everything, and Ken led her up to the porch.

"Welcome to my bungalow, Marijke. There's only one bedroom, but the bed is as big as the one in Nairobi. The house is spacious and comfortable; I hope you like it here. We'll go for dinner after a shower and clean up, then have an early night. I have breakfast on the veranda at six; then, I'm busy all day. If I'm at the lodge, I have lunch with the rangers in the dining room. You can come any time, whether I'm there or not, and then we have dinner with the guests between eight and nine in the boma.

"Amali will show you around until you know the layout. I said you could do whatever you want, but please remember always: there are no fences around the lodge and no electric wires. I won't have them as we are in the animals' territory. They stay away most of the time, but you could meet anything in the lodge area—elephants, lions, cheetahs or hyenas—so we must be careful at night. You can go on a game drive as often as you wish if there's a spare seat; you'll learn a small bit of the area that way. Ask the rangers once you know them."

"Why only a small bit?"

"This park is three times the size of Kruger; a small bit is a lot."

"Where do the staff come from, and where do they live?"

"The rangers have accommodation behind the garage and the workshop. Lucas does too. The others come from half a dozen villages. The nearest is less than a kilometre away, it was there before the Selous Park declaration in 1896, but it's a bigger village now there's work for them."

"Okay, *Bwana*, I'll go for a shower."

6

———————

By the end of the following day, Marijke had been everywhere except the workshop and the villages. The lodge area was on a flat plain. In front was lush grass; *hippo food*, she thought; then reeds before the river. Behind the lodge was thick thorny bush, then further from the river, acacia trees dotted thinned-out bushveld until a mixture of different trees created a dense forest. However, nothing was more than four or five metres tall except those within the lodge area. *The builders must have chosen this site because of the trees; they supply shade and character.* No rocky hills were within sight, but she could see hills to the north when she looked at a map on the wall in the lodge's lounge.

After carefully looking, she decided the bungalow was the first building on the site and had initially been the lodge lounge, dining room, and probably a toilet block. The new lodge's main building was thirty metres closer to the river, later extended to include the outdoor boma dining area and the two offices.

What seemed unusual were the materials used in the construction, until she realised that the building blocks were only balls of sand from the river mixed with cement and probably formed and cured in hessian sacks before assembly into walls. *I haven't seen rocks anywhere.* The shape and the pattern of sacking on the outside of many blocks supplied the clue. The roof and veranda were made from tree trunks and branches trimmed by hand, with a covering of reeds from the river. There wasn't a straight line anywhere. All the floors were coloured cement, now highly polished. She thought building the lodge with only manual labour and without wheelbarrows had been possible with imported cement.

She found the lodge kitchen huge. The two wood-fired cast-iron cooking ranges were enormous; a separate room had a battery of modern fridges and chest freezers, and another was the pantry with a stock of food. The pantry's door fascinated her for five minutes; very thick and tapered inwards, it closed hermetically. The bottom swung in a shallow arc-shaped pool of something oily with a stepping stone in the centre. She decided to ask Ken about it later.

She followed the concreted path leading to the cottage rooms, each a different shape and size, and all with thatched reed roofs, and she could see the odd corner of a solar panel on one or two. She visited one where two women were cleaning.

"*Jambo*. May I look?" Two fingers to her eyes and then pointing inside made it clear; smiles and nods were the answer.

The materials were the same, but an animal horn instead of a metal door handle, handmade cupboards, and a washbasin of solid concrete showed economy with an effort at decoration; the only out-of-place item was the white toilet pan. The beds and chairs and low table were all hand carved. Marijke thought them beautiful as the woodcarver had followed the twisting grain of the timber, so each piece was a work of art; nothing was straight, like the main building.

Walking around the back of the cottage, Marijke found a wood-fired boiler for hot water.

The trees around the lodge were full of birds; she thought the birdlife was far more interesting than it was in South Africa.

Marijke had lunch with the rangers, but Ken didn't come. When she asked where he was, one of the rangers said, "He's gone to the other side of the park; we heard a lion has killed a man."

"But why did *Bwana* go?"

"It's bad for the park when that happens; if the villagers complain to the authorities, they might come to shoot the lion and shoot several. *Bwana* will find out what happened. It might be an accident, but if younger males eject an old male from the pride, the old lion might hunt people as easy prey, and *Bwana* must shoot it."

"Is that part of a lodge manager's job?"

"No, but *Bwana* is different; he worries about everyone in the park."

So, he's the self-appointed guardian of the people here; he must look after everyone in his hell. It's what he said on Table Mountain; it was true. I'm beginning to understand him better.

"Is it dangerous?"

"It can be, but he has our tracker and Lucas with him, and *Bwana* is careful. He knows how much damage a lion can do to a man."

Odd. I hardly know Ken, but I'll worry until he returns.

She found the rangers interesting, and they vied to tell her stories about the lodge and the game. Then she asked, "The lodge builders used handmade blocks, but I can see only mud everywhere when the blocks have sand. Where does that come from?"

One replied, "When we build an extra cottage for guests, we must fetch it from a pit about five kilometres away. There's a higher area where the rains have washed off the clay. The tractor has a bucket to dig the sand out, and we use an old truck to bring it here. The truck's in the workshop for repair; I think it may be hopeless. We managed to transport enough for the last cottage we built before it broke down. We finished that cottage last week."

"There's lots of sand?"

"Tons and tons, the top layer is too fine, the middle layer is what we want, and the bottom layer is bigger gravel."

Another ranger added, "If you dig away the mud right here, I guess you'll find the same deep down, but it will be far down. The river deposits the silt yearly when it floods, and that's been happening for centuries."

"Thanks, guys; I'm finding out all about the lodge. I won't ask what you think of the *Bwana*; you'd never tell me anything bad about him."

"Nothing like that to tell, *Bibie*; he's the best lodge manager I've known."

The murmur of agreement told her a lot.

After lunch, she found a copy of a Helm field guide to the birds of East Africa in the lodge lounge, and as the afternoon breeze cooled the air, she sat down at a table on the veranda overlooking the river. She paged through the book, looking for a picture of the bird she had seen earlier, and then Ken came to find her.

"Hello, Marijke; how was your day?"

"How is the lion?" *Strange, I feel relieved he's back safely.*

"I had to shoot it. It was thin, probably ejected by a younger male a couple of weeks ago, and his first meal was the man he killed in desperation. Two or three weeks more, and the hyenas would have killed him, but he might have killed another man first."

"That's a shame." *Ken did say it was hell here.*

"Amali said he showed you everything today."

"He did, except for the garage and the workshop. Rufisi's bigger than I thought. And I've learned the rules, like not drinking the bath water, and having a bath or shower at night when the water's hot. Amali did offer to have a fire lit under the water boiler in the morning, but I told him the water was hot enough. He also showed me the solar farm; I didn't think it would be that big."

"It's only for the kitchen deep freezers and fridges, the water purification plant, and the air conditioning when needed. The roof panels power the lighting and the fans. We add at least one cottage for guests yearly, but we must stop soon because the dining areas will be too small."

"Can you explain the design of the pantry door?"

"We fill that pool by the door with water containing a strong dose of insecticide, so the door bottom is a death trap for insects. That's also why there are no windows, and the ceiling is a steel sheet. The insects are part of the hell I described. The cockroaches ate their way through the plaster ceiling we had before. Once insects lay eggs in the pantry, it's only a week before we must throw away the food and sterilise the room. During the wet season, the river sometimes floods; the plain becomes a mud bath for at least half of what you can see, and the insects come in clouds because the water covers the grass."

"But why is there so much food in the pantry?"

"Everything comes from Dar. We could halve the amount if we made a bi-monthly trip, but monthly is cheaper if we manage to keep the *wadudu*, the insects, out."

"Can you grow vegetables like lettuce here?"

"Oh yes, everything grows well with the soil near the river; it holds ten thousand years of animal dung. And we pump the water; sunshine is free."

"So why don't you grow lettuce?"

"Birds eat it if they can reach it, as do mice, rats, moles and other little beasties. Then warthogs and bushpigs have a go, and finally, the elephants and hippos can take a fancy to it and destroy any defences we build. In the wet season, the *wadudu* can do untold damage as the caterpillars eat their way through the foliage."

"No monkeys or baboons?"

"The baboons will probably come once they smell the plants, but this bush is unsuitable for monkeys. Too short and too thick. But their relative, the galago, is common."

"Well, perhaps I'll try to prove you wrong about growing greens once I've looked at everything."

Ken thought, *That's unexpected; I hope she doesn't become depressed when it doesn't work. I must help so that doesn't happen.*

"You're welcome to try. Ask if you need help. What are you doing with that book?"

"Trying to find a picture of a bird I saw today."

"Are you keen on birds?"

"Not excessively, although I have favourites; there are so many here that learning about the birds should be much easier."

That's great. She loves cheetahs and birds; I think she'll like it here. "Which ones are your favourites?"

"The malachite kingfisher and the lilac-breasted roller, although I think the honeyguide is the most fascinating."

"Is that why you chose the colourful dresses?"

"I didn't think so then; perhaps that's the inner me expressing itself."

"And doing so marvellously. Do you know how to find birds in one of these bird books?"

"No, is there a special way?"

"Yes, all the birdwatchers know. Start at the beginning. The first chapters tell you what to note about a bird, whether it hops or walks, what kind of beak it has, the colour of its legs, and things like that. They note those things when they see a bird they don't know.

"Once you can do that, finding the section that includes the bird is easy, and looking at the pictures to identify it is possible. If you know the name, it's easy; you look in the index."

She looked it up and said, "Yes, this is the one I know."

"Did it come and show you some honey?"

"Yes, *Bwana*, I was about seven when I followed one across the estate I lived on; it took me several minutes to understand that this excited little bird wanted me to follow it. It showed me a hive in a dead tree. I could see the honeycombs in a split of the tree trunk."

"Did the bees sting you?"

"No, I knew about bees; I had watched the *sangoma* removing stings from other kids, but the bird was so excited I had to help, so I fetched a long stick, poked the combs, and then ran away as fast as I could."

Ken laughed, then thought, *How could she possibly have become a lawyer? I mustn't ask, it'll remind her of her past, and it's better if the memories grey out. Although I'm not any better, I studied accounting and economics and worked in a bank, so I know what it's like to be in the wrong world.*

"*Bwana*, tell me about the predators; what are they like? What should I know about them?"

"They are all different; each has a different hunting method, but they have highly developed hunting computers."

"That's a funny way to describe them."

"It's the only description I could think of when one of our visitors asked. I told her to think of a tennis player; when the ball comes streaking at him, his action is the same as a predator. He attacks it. He doesn't think, 'Oh look, here's a ball; what should I do with it?' He doesn't think; he reaches out, hits it, and hopefully, it goes where he wants.

"I call that the attack or hunting computer, and predators are all programmed differently. I'll describe what I think their hunting programmes must be like.

"Cheetahs are not dangerous to people unless cornered. They're glorious to watch. They watch and plan, choose the prey they think is most vulnerable, look carefully at the terrain, and calculate the probability of success. Once it's good enough, they burst into a sprint."

"I'll ask the rangers to find one for me," said Marijke.

"Lions are different; like most predators, they will take advantage of a gift, but they do much the same as a cheetah, watch and calculate. They can charge over a short distance, so they must calculate the distance right and include how far the prey will go and in what direction. I believe they don't actively hunt people; they ignore us because, without experience, they don't have data to feed their hunting computers."

"So, I must avoid being a gift. That should be easy."

"No, Marijke, it's not; a lion can be still and silent, invisible in the long grass until you are too close. We must watch for other signs, like a swarm of flies. Don't go walking alone outside the lodge area without a ranger."

"Okay."

"Leopards and the other cats are pouncers; they will stalk their prey silently, or sit hidden in a tree or on a high rock and wait for something to come in range. When the calculation shows they can pounce, they do, and they are magnificent in a leap, up or down."

I hope to see one someday, but I must watch for one hiding.

"The *fisi*, or hyena, are different again; they don't have the big cats' claws or fangs. All they have is a massive, powerful jaw, so they must seize a leg in their jaws, and they can suffer a kick in the face. We call them cowardly, but I believe their computers are far more sophisticated; they calculate the probability not of reaching their prey but of success overall. There's a saying that if you're taller than a hyena, it won't attack. I don't think that's true, but it's a factor included in the attack calculation. All predators have patience, but the hyena marries this with the ability to travel long distances. If they think the chance of success is low, they'll go elsewhere."

"That's nice to know. And wild dogs?"

"They're like wolves; once they're hungry, they'll chase something to exhaustion as a pack and then attack."

"Okay, I'll avoid them like the plague."

"You don't have to; they don't hunt people. If you ignore them, they will come close and look at you. But don't shoo one away. Think of them as a pack. A gesture at one is a gesture to all, so if they are close, sit, don't move, and say nothing."

Marijke put the bird book on the table. "*Bwana*, I'll read about birds tomorrow. Right now, I want to shower and talk to the guests when they come for tea and the game drive. Amali has only four guests, so I have a seat; he says he'll find some lions. I'll see you after the game drive."

7

———————

There were only seven guests in two vehicles for the drive that afternoon. The wet season wasn't popular. Two couples were Americans; the youngest Marijke thought were honeymooners, and the older couple were retirees doing everything on their bucket list. They had brought their daughter, who looked about thirty-five and was rather severely dressed. The last couple were English, apparently veteran safari-goers.

When she greeted the young couple, she found her guess right; Jennifer and Sean were from New York and had come to East Africa because Jennifer said she had a family tie to East Africa but didn't know where.

"Don't you have any clues?"

"Only one: my great-grandmother married a man named Meir, a German name, so we chose Rufisi because Tanganyika was a German colony, as were Rwanda and Burundi. We're visiting Rwanda to see the mountain gorillas before returning to New York. It may be our only trip to Africa, at least for many years."

Marijke couldn't miss her body language; a caress of her tummy was enough for Marijke to know Jennifer was pregnant.

The older couple and their daughter came from Milwaukee. It was their first visit to Africa, and they said they loved it and the animals;

50

however, Marijke suspected that their daughter didn't feel the same. She remembered the wife of one of the law firm's partners and thought the daughter belonged in a group of similar women; her comment about Rufisi when Marijke asked was, "I'll be glad to return home. The sunrises over the lake are as superb as here, and the smells nowhere near as bad."

Marijke thought, *I would have felt the same a few days ago; once used to a smell, it becomes unnoticeable, and I don't miss the metallic taste of pollution.*

The English couple, in contrast, were sympathetic; Marijke liked them and asked many questions. Anne and John Trevelyan, sixty-five, had come from the Luangwa Valley park in Zambia and had taken the *Liemba* steamer north to Kigali on Lake Tanganyika and then the train to Dar. They travelled with only a rucksack each and would visit Zanzibar after a week at the lodge.

They were enthusiastic about Rufisi. Marijke decided it was a pleasure to welcome guests like them. Jennifer, Sean, and the Trevelyans were with her, Amali and an experienced ranger in the safari wagon.

Ken was waiting on the steps when Amali drove his guests and Marijke back up to the lodge.

"Hello, Marijke; how was the drive?"

"Wonderful, we saw a pride of seven lions; the male reminded me of a guy I met at university."

"That's an unlikely comparison; why?"

"Well, my crowd of girls called him Adonis behind his back. He seemed never to be without at least two girls trailing behind him. One day I saw him lying on the grass in the park, and six girls were lounging around him, and like the male lion, he was on his back!"

Ken laughed. "Tell Amali we'll call him Adonis. You've named your first Rufisi animal!"

"Ken, I want a rock shandy. Would you like a beer while you tell me why you live here?"

"Did I say I would tell you?"

"No, but I'm asking."

Maybe it will help her.

Marijke waved, and when the bartender came, she surprised Ken when she asked for their drinks in Swahili. *"Bia moja na Duma tafadhali."*

"Marijke, how can he know a cheetah is a rock shandy?"

"I wanted one this morning, so I taught him, and he said he would call it a *Duma;* you need a cocktail menu with animal and bird names. I'll look up cocktail mixes on the web and make a list. They'll be popular, and Omari will enjoy mixing them. He knows a lot about cocktails already. Do you know he worked at a Dar hotel before coming here?"

"Yes, I did, but I never thought of a cocktail menu." *Things will change with her here.*

"Okay, now you can finally tell me how you ended up here."

"I worked in finance, in a bank, but one day decided to jump. Not like you, just out of finance."

"Woman problem?"

"Sort of, but not with a girlfriend. I had several, and then one for three years, but I wasn't in love; I don't think she loved me either, and after the first year, it was just convenience. We never lived together."

Ken paused, "I was never close to my father; he was away a lot when I was young; my mother was both parents in one. When she died suddenly, the world seemed empty, and I didn't like the women or the men in big city life; I don't like cities at all, so I decided to resign and go around the world."

Marijke absorbed this. *So, it wasn't a girlfriend; it was his mother, but he was like me, in a life he didn't want to live, in a hell where he didn't want to be. He must have had problems like me to end up as a banker.*

"I was a twenty-four-year-old backpacker," he continued. "Most people took me for a hippy or a madman; I met the man in India on my travels, then after two years, I ended up here while hitching from Dar to Kigoma. A lion mauled the manager of the lodge about three days later. It was a tiny lodge then, like an oversized campsite, so I stayed as the manager until he returned, which he never did. If he had, I would have stayed anyway. I love this place, it may be hell, but it's a hell one man can do something to improve, while a big city is a hell that no one can change."

He did say he was improving hell. "Who owns it?"

"I don't know the details; when I arrived, I learned there were twenty shares and fifteen owners; four had two shares. I bought the last share when I decided to stay. It's their holiday place, and they still pay the annual maintenance fee. The owners did come initially, but we haven't had an owner's visit for a year because the lodge is doing well, always full and growing, although it never pays dividends."

"Who manages the owner's association?"

"Why do you want to know?"

"I was a lawyer and studied commercial law, so it's natural to ask." *I shouldn't ask—that's my past.*

"There's a notary in Dar; he sends me a paper every year to sign, approving a resolution to continue as before with an adjustment, if necessary, in the annual levy."

"No annual meeting?"

"No, I suppose they have a quorum without me, and it's a long trip, especially in the wet season."

Marijke couldn't avoid thinking, *That's an odd way of running an association. I must forget about the legal stuff, but I can't forget those last two cases I lost; they were the final straw in a career I hated.*

Ken thought, *Maybe I should ask the next time I visit Dar; I've no idea who the other shareholders are now.*

"You've done a lot since you came here. Did you build the new lodge?"

"Yes, we replaced the tents; there were just four then because only the owners came; we built the cottages in the same place, then we built the new lodge and started adding cottages."

"*Bwana*, what are your plans? What do you build next?"

"Two more cottages. Any more and the lodge will need more

management, and it will be too commercial. That's about it, except to make it the best lodge in the park. I'm not sure how I'll do that."

"*Bwana*, please look at me."

Ken turned to her. "Why?"

"I want to look into your eyes." She did for over a minute.

"What do you see, Marijke?" *She has lovely eyes; I think she's trying to see into my mind.*

"*Bwana*, do you have a dream of the future?" *He has thought of something that he's not telling me.*

"Yes, Marijke, a distant dream that I think is impossible to attain." Ken looked away. *How could she see that in my eyes?*

"Tell me, *please*."

I suppose I can. "I'd like to see rhinos, with their horns, grazing on the plain in front of the lodge."

"Why's that an impossible dream?"

"I could buy white rhinos from the Hluhluwe-Umfolozi reserve in KwaZulu-Natal. It would be expensive to transport them here, but they'd be dead within three months, hunted by the rhino horn poachers."

"Is that your only dream?"

"The other is even more impossible. Do you know about the great tuskers?"

"Elephants with huge tusks?"

"Yes, I used to think they were just old to grow those tusks, but the scientists have found that the DNA of the great tuskers is a little different from the others. The last DNA pool is in the Tembe Elephant Park in KwaZulu-Natal. Getting one of the males here is unthinkable, but perhaps the sperm of one could inseminate elephant cows here."

He has dreams, and they are good ones. Like I once had.

"Marijke, why did you want to look in my eyes?"

"*Bwana*, I'm only a *mganga* beginner, but I've realised the *mganga* have something in common. Their eyes can see into a person; I'm practising."

"So, you are a *mganga?*"

"A beginner. The old *mganga* in the market said I was."

"Can you see what I'm thinking?"

"No, but what you're thinking about shows something in your eyes. I could feel you hadn't told me a dream."

"Have you always been able to do this?" *Incredible. Lying to a mganga must be impossible.*

"I suppose so, although I didn't know it. The *sangoma* at home told me several times that I had beautiful eyes; I now think she meant *sangoma's* eyes."

"They are herbalists, Marijke. Do you know about herbs?"

"Plant medicines, *Bwana*, it's about much more than herbs and some animal bits. I learned all the plants the *sangoma* used; I can recognise them and know what they do, but I've no idea if they grow here, and if they do, perhaps they don't have the same effect. There may also be others I don't know; I must learn."

Ken felt this was beyond him, "Okay, let's go for dinner; we can talk some more afterwards." *If Marijke had stayed on that wine estate, she would have learned.*

8

———

After the boma dinner and the entertainment for the guests, Marijke said, "*Bwana*, I'll wait for you on our veranda while you say goodnight to everyone."

"Stay with me, Marijke; I'm sure the guests want to know more about you, and then we'll go to the bungalow together."

Fifteen minutes later, after saying good night, she had fielded several questions about how she liked being at Rufisi. One was from a rather voluble woman who said, "It's a wonderful place to visit, but it must be boring living here with only animals to watch every day; I couldn't live without the excitement of the city."

Marijke replied, "You should try a wine estate holiday, ma'am; the only excitement comes from watching the grapes grow. I find Rufisi far more exciting."

Ken thought her reply delightful, and as they left for the bungalow, he couldn't help grinning as he said, "Maybe Adonis thinks Rufisi is like a wine estate."

"More like a personal paradise," she replied as they sat on the veranda.

Then she asked, "Do you like living cut off from the outside world?"

"I would love it, but our clients wouldn't. Hasn't Amali told you?"

"What?"

"The office has internet; it's slow but can manage voice calls with one person. Emails and messages are okay. I use it late at night to search the web for information. A tower behind the workshop has a dish on the top. Since the lion mauled the first manager, I keep one satphone in the office strictly for emergencies.

"Our website tells clients that if they want comms, they must bring their satphones; it makes it exciting to think they're going on safari in darkest Africa."

"So, I can check on the web if I'm stuck identifying birds?"

"Yes, but the Wi-Fi only works in the lounge. You must go there."

"Okay, I can do that."

"Remember to tell one of the night watchmen; you could easily meet a leopard on your way to the bungalow."

"Oh, I can scare any wild animals. I'll carry my *bobbejaan sakkie.*"

"What's that?"

He doesn't know, and he's curious; yippee! "I'll tell you one day."

It amazed Ken that she wasn't terrified of meeting a leopard at night.

After breakfast, Marijke washed her cheetah towel and hung it over the veranda rail. *I could put it in the lodge laundry, but this is special and needs a cool wash.*

Amali had come to show her the workshop. Marijke was reading about bird characterisation when three barefoot children trotted past the bungalow. The littlest, she thought, was about five, the two others in front a year or two older.

"Amali, where did those children come from?"

He replied in Swahili, and she thought she understood what he said: "They are the cooks' children, and their mothers have gone to a market far away, so the cooks must look after them."

"Why have the mothers gone?" *Far away probably means the next village.*

"To buy vegetables."

"Can't they grow them at the village?"

"Keeping the animals from eating what grows is difficult, so a bigger village has to grow them as they have children to scare the animals and the birds."

That's something to remember if I try to grow lettuce, Marijke thought. "But nobody seems to be watching the children."

"We all do, *Bibie*; it's the same in a village. They know they must stay in the lodge grounds."

"Okay, Amali, I want to finish reading this before going to the workshop."

"I'll wait, *Bibie*; I have a book to read. I'm studying the galago."

"The bushbaby?"

"Yes, there are many in the park; on an evening drive, we often see them. I must know all about them so I can tell the tourists."

About an hour later, Marijke heard a child crying, looked up, and saw the youngest limping towards the kitchens. As he passed before her, she stood up, descended the steps to meet him, and took him by the hand. About to ask his problem, she noticed blood on his bare foot and saw a grazed knee with blood dripping from it.

"*Njoo, njoo*, little one." She led him, still crying, to the veranda, picked him up and carried him up the steps; Amali heard her voice and came onto the porch.

"What's his name, Amali?"

"Andwele."

"Have we any medicines here?"

"A box in the lodge office, *Bibie*."

"Then please fetch it and bring a bowl with water to wash his leg."

She found antiseptic in the box, washed the scrape, and then around the knee. Andwele stopped crying and sat fascinated as she used a pair of tweezers from the box to remove some tiny stones from the deepest scrape. Then, after drying the area, she painted everything with a double layer of mercurochrome.

Amali had watched her doing it and, when Andwele trotted away, said, "It looks like he's proud of his injury now."

"Amali, has the government vaccinated the children?"

"Some, *Bibie*, they come and do some. Most of the people here don't believe the government officers. They say that the government wants to make everyone sterile."

"That's nonsense but not new. So, Andwele has not had a tetanus vaccination?"

"I do not think so, *Bibie*."

"Well, I must watch him. Tell his parents to bring him to me if he gets a fever. Please fetch the pad of paper in the lounge, and the pen, then help me put everything in this box on the table. I want to make an inventory."

She found four items beyond their expiry date; the plaster bandages were within a few days of expiry, the aspirin and paracetamol phials were near empty, and only three sleeping pills remained. She wrote down everything that was there.

"Amali, is there no other medicine at the lodge?"

"Not that I know of, *Bibie*, except one of the rangers takes something for his heart; he brings it with him after his leave."

"What about a snakebite kit?"

"I think there's one in the office, *Bibie*; I have seen a tin box there."

"Please, can you fetch that too?"

Amali arrived with a white tin box, and Marijke opened it. After a check of the contents, she said, "Amali, this is useless and dangerous; put it up high on the cupboard in the lounge where no one can find it until I know how to dispose of it, *tafadhali*.

"I must make a shopping list; we need much more than this, and I must find out about snake bites. You've been waiting long enough; let's visit the workshop."

It was like a workshop anywhere, although it seemed untidy to Marijke's untrained eye. Most of the area seemed to be dirt soaked with old oil to keep the dust down, although the work areas were concrete.

As she and Amali left after meeting the staff, Marijke spotted something interesting.

"Amali, what's that over there by the bush?"

"It's the elephant pen, *Bibie.* We haven't used it since I've been here."

Amazed, she asked, "Have they kept elephants in there?"

"Yes, *Bibie*, the rangers told me. Sometimes a female dies before weaning her baby, and there's no other female to feed it. They need milk for up to two years, or the baby will die. If this happens, we must capture it if we can. Often it's feeble when the elephants leave it, so it's not difficult. Then it stays here until we can send it to a zoo."

"That's a shame, but letting it die is worse. Can't you give it back to the herd?"

"I don't know, *Bibie*. The rangers said the baby grows at the lodge; it can wander freely and doesn't leave because it knows the milk is here. They don't know how to make it return to the herd. A zoo soon takes it."

Marijke added this to her private list of things to uncover.

Lunch with the rangers was enjoyable; they talked about their jobs and the animals, building a picture of the lodge and its activities for Marijke. As a visitor to game lodges in South Africa, she had learned about the game, taken game drives and experienced short educational walks, but she had never seen what happened in the background.

Associations with her memories built until the mental picture formed. *It's like a wine farm; the lodge is like the great house with the staff. The workshop is the same, but the workers check on the animals instead of the grapes. But here there are no worker families and no farm.*

I must think about this; the lodge is not a place to raise children. It would be a much happier place if there were families. I played with the children daily when they did their chores at the farm.

When Ken came to shower for dinner, he saw the array of medicines on the table. "Marijke, what's all this?"

"The total medicine stock, *Bwana*, including the expired items. But not including the useless, outdated and dangerous snake-bite kit."

"Why are they here?"

"Andwele grazed his knee; he was in tears. I cleaned it with antiseptic, removed a few rocks, and gave it a good coat of mercurochrome. Then I looked at what was in the medicine box. I'm going to make a list of what's needed."

"Have you had medical training?"

"Not at all, except for about eleven years when I often helped our local *sangoma* fixing injuries, grazes, minor cuts, stings and thorns. You don't have anywhere near enough medical stuff, but I can make a list with some help from the web."

"Did your *sangoma* use Western medicines?"

"*Bwana*, I can see you have much to learn. A *sangoma* treats anything that people ask them to treat. Sometimes they send someone to a hospital or treat them with herbal medicines, but they are like all doctors; they have the urge to cure, and when a *sangoma* learns of medications that can help, they will use them. But as most of them don't ask for money, except in cities, they can't buy them. Our *sangoma* could have whatever she needed because my father bought it, so I learned about them."

"Why don't they charge?"

"Partly tradition, but money is useless if there's nowhere to spend it. It's far better to receive a gift from a grateful patient, something to eat or use."

For five days, when she dined with Ken and the clients, she put a plain folded paper bag, her *bobbejaan sakkie*, in a pocket of her dress; after dinner, she sat in the lounge with Ken's tablet to search the web, pencil and paper beside her. She thought, *Ridiculous, modern and stone-age technology together, but it's easier than copying and pasting with a finger on a tablet.*

Ken didn't tell her, but he asked for an extra security guard to keep watch until she returned to the bungalow.

Five days later, she had a composite list from various sources; one was a circumnavigating yacht skipper, another a doctor from Doctors

Without Borders, and one from the Australian Royal Flying Doctor Service – RFDS. The list kept by a hospital outpatient department was laughable, as the department had access to immediate and much bigger supplies.

Marijke decided, *I might not know how to use all these medicines, but I can learn and call in an emergency. I've found something to do, and it will help everyone, especially the children.*

The RFDS list was the most extensive, and they recommended storing the medicines by injury class in five storage cases.

When she climbed into bed that evening, Ken was already there.

"*Bwana*, I have the list, and I need five wooden boxes; each must be identifiable, painted in distinct colours or something else. I also need a small fridge."

"The truck goes in two and a half weeks; give your list to the office and ask Lucas to find a woodcarver for your boxes. For the fridge, see if you can arrange something with the kitchen, and have a look at the cooler boxes they have."

"No, *Bwana*, I want a lockable fridge, and I'll have the key. Some of the medicines are poisonous if taken incorrectly."

"Okay, find what you want, and I'll buy it for you, even if we import it."

"I want to order the medicines myself; then I can discuss what's available."

"The office has the pharmacy email. We have an account."

"Thanks, *Bwana*." *He's not objecting; as he said, I can try anything.*

Ken thought: *Well, she's undoubtedly determined. She's found something to do. That's a good sign.*

9

———————

"Lucas, do you know a woodcarver who can make medicine boxes smaller than this one, so they're easy to carry?" Marijke asked.

"Yes, *Bibie*, there's one in the village to the east. He's excellent and uses tambotie wood."

"Then tell Amali which village or take me to see him, *tafadhali*."

Lucas took her. Before leaving, she put her folded paper bag in her pocket. It became a habit; she never left the lodge without it.

The reception in the village made the sensation in the Nairobi hotel seem lukewarm in comparison. The *mganga*, who Marijke thought impressive, greeted her and Lucas. He was tall and thin, with white hair and a lined face, and his eyes were alive, switching from serious to amused in seconds. When Marijke looked at his face, she remembered a man on her father's estate. Her Swahili allowed her to say, "*Nimefurahi kukuona, Baba.*"

His eyes told her. *He knows I called him* Baba *out of respect.*

Lucas introduced a second *mganga*: "This is *Bibi Mkubwa*, the *mganga* of my village."

Marijke greeted her the same way, thinking, *I can tell a* mganga, *it's not the* jujus; *it's in the eyes, they see inside you. I wonder why she's here. Mkubwa* must mean great, like mkhulu *in Zulu.*

The village's *mganga* asked her to sit on his right at the reception with village elders, a position of status visible to all. The villagers knew all about her, her ordering medicines and treating Andwele's knee.

The meeting began with a cross-examination, with Lucas as the translator.

"*Bibie*, the *mganga* wants to know where you got the *jujus* you wear and if he can look at them."

She lifted the *juju* from South Africa over her head and handed it to him. He took it with both hands as a precious item.

"Lucas, please tell him it was a gift from the *mganga* near my home. She gave it to me when I left home for high school when I was sixteen. She was a second mother and my teacher for eleven years."

After carefully examining it and discussing it with *Bibi Mkubwa*, he said, "It is many years old; it will need repair when the stitches break. Please bring it to us when that happens."

After Lucas translated, the *mganga* returned it. Marijke received it in both hands and replaced it around her neck, then carefully lifted the juju given to her in Nairobi over her head and handed it to him.

He again held out both hands to receive it, as Marijke said, "Lucas, please tell him it was a gift from a *mganga* in a Nairobi market, a *Bibi Mkubwa*. She said I would return to buy another dress, but the *juju* would protect me until I learn more."

After an animated discussion between the two *waganga*, he handed it back, so she used both hands to receive it and then put it back around her neck as the *mganga* turned to Lucas and spoke.

"*Bibie*, he says they know of the *mganga*," Lucas translated, "who they know as The Great Elephant, who carries many elephant *mizimu*. For her to have given a *juju* to you confirms his beliefs. What is it that the village can do for you?"

After explaining what she wanted in broken Swahili, enhanced by Lucas, they called the woodcarver, and within an hour, a crude reed model of a storage case, the right size, lay in front of Marijke. Then a problem arose. Lucas had difficulty translating the woodcarver's question into English.

"*Bibie*, the man is a woodcarver; he must carve a picture on the box. His *nafsi*, the thing that makes him a woodcarver, will insist. The picture is of your *mzimu*, for you will use the box. He wants to know what your *mzimu* is."

Marijke already understood what a *mzimu* was; Mama Keita had translated it as spirit, but she didn't know what stood for her *mzimu*. She thought, "Nafsi" *must mean "soul" or "talent"*.

It seemed to Marijke that everyone in the circle was holding their breath as she thought of an answer. She didn't close her eyes; she tilted her head back and looked at the sky, her hands folded in her lap, seeing nothing; then she reached up with one hand and grasped her latest *juju*. She reflected: *What makes me happy when I see other creatures? Which ones do I love? Dolphins? Birds? Yes, the malachite kingfisher.*

Then the image of the cheetahs, when she had arrived at the lodge, came to the fore. *Cheetahs, yes, they are beautiful, and I love looking at them—and that's why the* mganga *chose a cheetah towel. It's my* mzimu, *or at least one of them.*

Her eyes focused, and she looked at Lucas with a smile. "Lucas, I have three *mizimu*, and I need the help of the *mganga* to decide which one the woodcarver should carve on the boxes. One is a *mzimu* of the air. He shows himself as a little bird when I need him. I shall show him to you if I see him. His name in the book is the malachite kingfisher. You can tell me his Swahili name when we're back at Rufisi. The second swims in the oceans; he's free and happily dances on the water with others. That *mzimu* will not be happy on a box. The third is of this land, the *duma mzimu*."

In the ensuing argument, Marijke understood little. Only that one faction wanted the bird, for it could see great distances into the future, and the other wanted the cheetah, for it was the fleetest runner, and the *mzimu* would help her and any patient to flee an evil *mzimu*.

The cheetah won.

And Marijke thought, *The* waganga *have become experts on people with three* mizimu.

Marijke thanked them all but then had another problem. The *mganga* said something to Lucas, and he translated it.

"*Bibie*, the *mganga* says the *mzimu* of *Bwana* must be strong to live with a cheetah *mzimu*. He knows this is true but wants to know what that *mzimu* is; I think he doesn't dare ask *Bwana*."

Hell, how do I answer that? "Lucas, I don't know; I haven't asked, but I shall ask my *mzimu* to help. Perhaps I'll not get an answer at once."

After Lucas translated, she did as she had done the first time, gazing unseeingly at the sky, and asked herself, *If Ken has an* mzimu, *what is it? He's a free spirit and has wandered the world for years. Something that fits in Rufisi, not a reptile, not something that crawls; lion or leopard doesn't feel right.*

Then her memory brought back the skydive and a recollection of her thought. *If only an eagle would pluck me from the sky and take me to its nest. Ken did just that! And Rufisi is his nest where he keeps his towel!*

She lowered her head and looked at the *mganga* with a lovely smile. Had he been a Christian, he would have crossed himself; instead, from his sitting position, he bowed deeply forward.

"Not long ago, my *mzimu* was weak," Marijke said, "for we lived in a city. We fell from a great height, and my *mzimu* called for help. The eagle *mzimu* saved us and brought me here."

That was when the old Marijke died, and when the parachute opened, the new me was born. Thank you, eagle spirit.

Ken heard the whole story from Lucas and was impressed. *Marijke's a woman who belongs in this Africa, entirely out of place in a big city; no wonder she was about to jump off a mountain. I hope she stays once she learns what she wants to do.*

Later, he asked Marijke: "I learned from Lucas you are now a woman with three spirits. Did you choose them?"

"No, *Bwana*, they chose me. Did Lucas tell you about your *mzimu*?"

"No. So I have a *mzimu* too?"

"Yes, an eagle. You've had it for ages; it probably made you jump."

"How do you know?"

"The eagle is a free creature that travels great distances and sees many things, and when you pushed me from the plane, I asked for an eagle to save me and take me to its nest. You did, and I know now: it's why I said yes when you said I could come with you."

Ken had nothing to say.

Later that night, Ken said, "Marijke, you seem to be learning Swahili faster than I did. I struggled for a long time, but you seem relaxed and learning it rapidly."

"*Bwana*, it took me a few days to realise why. It's an African language, and many words are the same as in the Bantu languages. Although pronounced differently, the structure is the same. Throughout Southern Africa, people can understand the language of others because the languages are similar. On the farms, the bosses and the workers all speak the local dialect, and I'm no different. I was the only white girl on the estate, so from babyhood, my nurse taught me her language. Until high school, my friends and playmates were girls of every skin shade, and we spoke either Afrikaans or the local dialect. *Bwana*, all I need to do is learn the words that fit into what I already speak. It's like adding another synonym to my vocabulary."

"Then I shall speak Swahili with you and improve my Swahili too."

In six months, she will have integrated here. She will never leave unless there's a problem. And that makes me happy. I must ensure there are no problems.

Once Marijke had ordered the medicines, her thoughts turned to something else. *I thought since the first day, it would be much happier here if there was a farm and families. I don't know if I'll stay here, but if I can do it, it'll help Ken.*

She looked for Amali. *He's always around; Ken did tell him to look after me; I'm glad he does because I would be a drag if Amali weren't here.*

When she found him, she said, "Amali, is there a village that grows vegetables? Not just a small amount but a vegetable farm with enough to sell."

"I shall ask Lucas, then come to tell you."

Lucas returned with Amali and said, "There is the one that the women from my village visit, but they don't sell to other villages. The biggest vegetable farm is in the mountains."

"Then I'll ask *Bwana* if we can visit it."

Ken joined Marijke and the rangers for lunch, and she thought, *I'm sure he's coming to lunch more often.* She said, "*Bwana*, I want to visit a mountain village."

"Why?"

"Because Lucas says that they grow vegetables."

"It's not the same there, Marijke. I don't know if the elephants go there, but the village will be much higher than here, and the insect population will be far smaller. Lucas can take you. How far is the one he told you about?"

"He said a two-to-three-hour drive; if we leave early, we can return before nightfall."

"When?"

"I must receive an invitation first."

That's a surprise; I wonder how she'll do that. "Well, let me know; Amali can also go with you. Lucas will need help if there's a muddy patch."

"Lucas can drive, *Bwana*; I'll ask two of the villagers to come with us."

"Okay, it's your expedition." Then Ken thought, *I suppose it's easy when you have three spirits. Marijke's already a different woman; she has no lack of confidence, and she's enjoying herself.*

"*Bwana*, why is what we eat here with the rangers so different from the dinners?"

"Well, the kitchen has a menu for breakfast and lunch that never changes; the clients choose from the buffet.

"The ranger's lunch is different because we are here permanently; we have some variety as the kitchen decides what to feed us. The dinner menu repeats every two weeks, so we know what to buy with little waste. Why do you ask?"

"Because some of the things I've eaten here are delicious but they don't appear at dinners."

"You mean the local dishes?"

"Yes, that colossal banana fried with onions, tomato, chillies and garlic. I'm sure the clients would like to try them."

Ken thought, *It's her idea; I'll encourage her to do it.*

"Marijke, organise it with the kitchen, but be careful; the clients aren't used to what we eat at lunch."

"Okay, just one dish each night."

Two days later, the bush telegraph relayed a message that she would be a welcome guest, and Marijke left at six the following morning with Lucas and two stalwart young men from his village. They arrived two and a half hours later, after struggling through only two patches not far from the lodge, where the mud required particular care.

The welcome included everyone in the village and began with a plate of mixed vegetables and salad; Marijke complimented the *mganga* on the quality and freshness and asked to see where they grew them. The crowd trooped off to a nearby collection of mesh-covered frames protected from elephants by a deep rock-lined trench, and then the *mganga* explained how they had built them with stones from the hillside as a base with the surrounding low walls leaning outwards. The *mganga* insisted the height was critical to protect against warthogs and the cemented floor inside against burrowing animals.

Marijke asked about insects and learned they had no problem in the daytime, and two girls showed how they picked caterpillars off leaves and washed the plants with soapy water for aphids. The soap looked homemade. Then the *mganga* pointed out flat boxes high up. "These are our night friends. They eat the insects. We have small boxes here with four or five bats in each and others around the village with large families. We swap the ones inside the nets with others outside every two weeks to be sure the bats have enough to eat."

"How can I get some?"

"We will give you three boxes with bats. Fix them to trees where it's warm, and make more boxes. We'll give you an empty one to use as a model. The bats will find and use the empty ones, so you will soon have many bats."

As they strolled back to the village, the *mganga* pointed out the bat boxes; Marijke estimated there were thirty around the settlement and probably more, further away.

When they returned, it was late; they arrived at the same time as the game drive vehicles. Ken had already showered; she could see that from the state of the bathroom, so Marijke hurried to shower and then to the boma for dinner.

In bed that night, Ken asked, "Did you enjoy your visit to the village?"

"Yes, I learned how they manage to grow vegetables. It's huge; they must have expanded the business for years."

"How do they stop the warthogs and rodents?"

Marijke explained.

"And how about the insects?"

"They say the day ones aren't a problem." She explained what they did with caterpillars and aphids.

"And the night ones?"

"There're bats."

"They're bats? So, they're crazy? I did say it was ridiculous to grow vegetables here."

"No, you're not listening." Marijke sat upright; the sheet and *kikkoy* dropped to her waist, and she spread her arms and flapped them. "Not batty, but the small black—"

Realising he was not looking at her or listening but concentrating on her jiggling boobs, she blushed, laid back and pulled up the sheet.

"You're not listening to me."

"I was."

"No, you weren't; you were looking at my boobs."

"I've been looking at them when you come to bed most days. So, what's new."

"They were jiggling."

"I know, and they looked lovely. Now you've ruined my pleasure. Go on."

I'll teach him. Marijke sat up again, and the sheet fell. "Well, listen to me, don't look at my boobs. The little furry beasts are bats." She flapped her arms. "They have lots and gave me some that I shall nail to trees."

They are *lovely.*

"Nail the bats to the trees?" Ken asked.

"That proves you're not concentrating. The boxes, silly."

"I'm not interested in bats right now. Marijke, will you marry me?"

Shocked, Marijke had to think. *He can't be serious; he doesn't know me at all. It's because he's bemused by jiggling boobs.*

She laid back and pulled up the sheet. "No, it contravenes the latest rule in my list."

"What rule?"

"Never agree to marry a man just after you've shown him your boobs."

"Why?"

"Because it's not a serious proposal."

"Oh, how long does 'just after' last?"

"At least a week or two, probably months."

"Okay, I'll wait; let's sleep."

It took Marijke an hour to fall asleep; her thoughts raced. *He asked me to marry him. Do I want to? Do I know enough about him? Am I ready to marry again? What if it goes wrong? I'll have to wait until I'm sure I won't mess up my new life.*

10

The village had given Marijke three boxes with bats and one old empty one. She had the workshop crew nail the occupied ones to the trees, then asked them to make forty more from boxwood, and the workshop fixed them in places Marijke chose. She liked sitting on the bungalow veranda at sunset and watching the bats flit around, catching insects while her thoughts wandered. *It'll take some time for them to multiply; what shall I do now?*

After dinner in the boma, the staff usually performed traditional African songs and dances for the guests. Marijke had sat with Ken for the first few days, then Ken asked, "Marijke, you can, I'm sure, answer the guests' questions; if you could sit at another table, I can give one of the rangers a night off." *It should help her to feel she belongs, and she might get some ideas from the guests.*

"Okay, I'd like that." *Ken promoted me. From a non-paying guest to unpaid lodge staff. At least, that's a step forward.* "Listening to men discussing the merits of safari vehicles is boring."

Ken cringed. *Oww!*

Marijke found she made a difference. *The women all talk a lot more.*

The guests thought Marijke, dressed as she was, could tell them about the traditional songs.

I should learn these songs and dances. That's what I'll do, Marijke thought.

Marijke visited two women who cleaned rooms while the guests were on game drives.

Her Swahili was improving daily, not the city Swahili, but the everyday countryside version, so Marijke hatched a plan with the two women. They would meet every evening when the women stopped working, behind the workshop, where they would dance and sing. Translating the songs was a problem, even with Amali's help, but as the days passed, she began to sense the songs' real meaning and the women's feelings when they sang, sometimes joyful and sometimes sad. She enjoyed it immensely; it was liberating, and she relaxed and felt like she was one with them.

They sing marvellously and harmonise naturally; I wonder if I can find a song known to the visitors that will suit their voices. I must listen to some.

She only had to say once that no one was to tell *Bwana*. If the cheetah *mzimu* wanted it, none would, but several others came and joined their classes, including Lucas.

It allowed her to talk to Lucas alone, so one night after the practice, she asked, "Lucas, why do you wear your *juju?*"

"*Bibie*, the *mganga* gave it to me after the lion mauled the last lodge manager. She told me to wear it to protect me from the lions."

"Do you know what your *mzimu* is?"

"Yes, *Bibie*, the honey badger."

"I have heard stories about honey badgers; that's a powerful *mzimu*; I expect lions will stay away from them."

"I hope so, *Bibie*."

Marijke had an idea at dinner one night, and once Ken had come to bed, she asked, "*Bwana*, you said you were improving your hell. It's also mine. Can I do some improving too?"

"You are already improving the medical treatment and filling the lodge with bats."

"But this is sort of different."

What is she going to suggest now? Ken wondered.

"The dinners need to give the guests more of a real African experience," Marijke said.

"We have them in the boma," Ken replied, "with a fire in the middle, and the staff dance and sing in traditional costumes. Isn't that enough?"

"It's good but lacks a beginning and something spiritual, something with feeling. The lodge does what all the lodges in South Africa do; to me, it feels commercial."

"What do you mean?"

"Sort of, 'Dear guest, here's your entertainment; now sleep and rise early for the next game drive.'"

"What do you suggest?"

"Let me try something. I'll organise it with the kitchen staff."

"Okay." *I'm not sure if Marijke's trying to help me or wants to have fun.*

"*Bwana*, Lucas told me his *mzimu* is the honey badger, and the *mganga* gave him his *juju* after a lion mauled the last lodge manager. Can you tell me what happened?"

Ken told her the story. "I had been here only three days, Marijke; the lodge didn't employ me; I was passing through, so I was a guest. It happened shortly before lunch; I had returned from a game drive and was in the lounge when Lucas arrived in one of the jeeps at top speed. There was a lot of shouting, so I went out and saw Lucas covered in blood. I couldn't understand a word of Swahili, but when one of the rangers grabbed the medicine box and sprinted out to join him, I took my camera off the table and rushed out too.

"We drove about three kilometres to where Johan, the manager, was lying in a pool of blood under a lion, I didn't know whose blood it was, and we arrived just in time to scare off two hyenas. We lifted the dead lion off Johan and found he was still alive but badly mauled on his chest, back and shoulders, with terrible claw cuts on his legs. Lucas and I did our best with antiseptic and bandages to close the wounds and stop the bleeding, loaded him in the safari wagon, and brought him back to the lodge. Lucas told me about the satphone, so I called Lodge Air. The plane came from Dar, and we took him straight to the airstrip; it took off just before nightfall. I learned that the hospital sent him to South Africa after a few days.

"Then the next day, Lucas showed me an envelope in the office labelled 'EMERGENCY INSTRUCTIONS'. I called the Dar notary and told him what had happened. He called back two days later and asked if I would stay as the manager until Johan's return.

"When Johan gave notice a month later, I was asked to take the job."

"But what about the blood all over Lucas?"

"Marijke, it seems unbelievable, but when the lion knocked Johan down, Lucas couldn't shoot for fear of hitting Johan, so he darted in, put the muzzle of his rifle to the side of the lion's head, and fired. The explosion blew brains and blood back that covered him. He did the right thing. He came back to the lodge for help as quickly as he could.

"I took only a few photographs, but they proved what had happened when the police and park officials enquired about it."

"But why were Lucas and Johan there?"

"They were following the trail of poachers from a hippo kill near the river, and as I warned you, lions are invisible in the bush if they don't move, so Johan didn't know it was there, and he was walking too far ahead of the jeep. A tracker might have smelled its presence."

"So, the *mganga* gave Lucas a *juju*?"

"Yes, she said only a honey badger would have courageously dashed up to a lion and bitten it."

The following night Marijke stood and tapped her glass for attention once the guests had arrived. It surprised Ken.

She smiled, "We have a surprise for you tonight. We're out of potatoes to roast, so we are serving an East African dish in their place: Chef Faraji has prepared *Matoke*, a giant banana fried with onions, tomato, chillies and garlic. He does have a few roast potatoes left, so if the garlic might affect marital relations, he'll be happy to serve you. Please enjoy."

Amidst laughter, the guests all tried the *Matoke*. Ken watched, listened and heard them saying: "Superb, delicious, great idea; I never knew they ate such delicious food in the country."

Several thanked the chef.

Later, Ken said, "Marijke, you've changed Rufisi. Will you organise different dishes for each night?"

"No, *Bwana*, the chef and the office will print menus and attach the recipes, and the guests will find them in their cottages on arrival."

And probably reduce our food bill as well, Ken thought.

Three nights later, the meat dish was impala. Ken noticed Marijke was not at her table and sensed an anticipation among the staff and the rangers. *What is she up to?*

When the last guests had taken their seats, three kitchen staff arrived, followed by Marijke; one carried the impala steaks in a flat steel serving pan, holding it high. The two others carried flaming torches on long poles. The leader reverently placed the impala platter on the serving table and stood back as Marijke stood between the flaring torches, wearing her beaded headdress.

Ken's heart was thumping. *My God, she's beautiful, and what a grand entrance!*

There was a stir of comments between the diners until Marijke raised her arms, and a deafening silence fell, disturbed only by the crackle and crunch of burning wood. It seemed even the crickets stopped chirruping.

"We welcome our guests who have come from far away, and tonight we have impala, a buck that gave up its life to feed us only a day ago. Our traditions date from the Stone Age, when our ancestors sat by a fire and thanked the animal's spirits for feeding them."

She raised her head to look at the black, star-filled night, and most diners did the same.

First in Swahili and then in English, she said, "*Kwa niaba ya wote hapa, nashukuru roho ya impala kwa kutupatia chakula kula usiku wa leo.* On behalf of all here, I thank the spirit of the impala for giving us food to eat tonight."

Then she lowered her arms and sat at her table as the ranger at another table stood and said to his guests, "Come, we'll serve ourselves."

The Englishwoman beside Ken said, "I didn't know that; it's fascinating and appropriate."

"Didn't know what, ma'am?"

"That people said grace in the Stone Age; now I know it, it seems natural that they would do so."

"The San of the Kalahari thank the spirit of the animal they kill as it dies; in one way or another, it's a practice that has never died."

Marijke told me that. We shall thank the spirits at dinner every night; I'm sure the staff all think it's a good thing to do, and it certainly impresses the guests.

It makes us feel better. Marijke has improved our corner of hell and improved me too.

"Marijke, thank you, you did it just right."

"What, *Bwana?*"

"Saying grace at dinner. From where did the idea come?"

"One of my *mizimu* must have suggested it; it just came to me."

"Then let them suggest other things."

"They've already suggested something, *Bwana.*"

"What?" *I should have expected that.*

"Name the cottages. It makes it more friendly than numbers. Names like 'Warthog' and 'Jackal', and then make up a story for each one for when a guest asks why the cottage name is 'Warthog'. A tale like, 'A warthog had its home in a hole beside it.'"

"Why's it more friendly?"

"*Bwana*, have you ever heard someone say in a home, 'I sleep in Bedroom One?' It's always something like 'the Blue Bedroom'.

"Let the staff choose the names and the rangers the stories; then they will feel the lodge belongs to them.

"*Bwana*, I have another idea. Name the path going east, 'Leopard Walk,' and the one going west, 'Cheetah Run.' It makes the lodge different and brings home that we are in Africa, not a Caribbean holiday resort."

"We'll do that, Marijke." *I never thought of it, but she's right.* "But can I ask you how many rules, like the jiggling boobs rule, you have in your rule book?"

"I haven't written them down; I remember them." *I should have expected that question.* "About fifteen, I guess. I was fifteen when I learned the first, and then one or two each year since then."

"What was the first?"

I can remember that clearly. "I swam with the kids at a waterfall with a pool; for years, we always swam there naked until one day when I was thirteen. I wasn't conscious that I had boobs and curves, and one of the older boys looked at me and then disappeared into the bushes. I asked an older girl where he had gone. She said, 'Marijke, he saw your naked body and has gone to masturbate. He can't help it; boys have wet dreams.' Then I learned why she was wearing a swimming costume.

"Of course, I wanted to know what masturbation and wet dreams were, so she told me then added, 'Be kind to the boys and wear a swimsuit.'

"So, my first rule was: 'Don't show your naked body to men.'"

"But you showed me yours after we met. I expected you would use a towel or bathrobe in the Nairobi hotel bedroom."

"Oh, that rule I made in my past world, I thought it didn't apply in hell; you did say I would lose my clothes. But I wouldn't be here if I had known all the rules before I was seventeen."

"So, you've scrapped those old rules?"

"Yes, I've only *some* new ones, although some old ones might still apply. I must think about it."

Marijke asked herself: *Does Ken have rules too? He may be different from what I know of him. And if so, what are they? I must find out.*

"*Bwana*, I want to know something. Why didn't you book two bedrooms at the Nairobi hotel? Then in Dar, and then here?"

"Take them one at a time, Marijke; I didn't know you very well that first night, and I felt I should keep you close. I intended to sleep on the couch until you invited me to sleep in the bed. Maybe I was afraid you would have a nightmare or disappear if you had a separate room.

"Then you did your magic trick and changed into a Kenyan woman, which was wonderful, and in Dar, it had gone so well in Nairobi that I didn't think of changing because I was enjoying your company."

"And here?"

"Let's just say I wanted you beside me day and night by then."

"But you haven't even tried to kiss me."

"Marijke, I told you I'll never leave here. I don't go away except when I must make a short trip for business. And you are trying to find what you want to do with your life and where. I'm afraid of a relationship that might end. I'll kiss you the day you say you'll never leave Rufisi."

Marijke thought about what he had said. *His bond to Rufisi must be something irresistible. He proposed, and it must be agony sleeping with me. So what's stopping him from just kissing me? I suppose it's his way of allowing me the freedom to decide. I'll have to find out.*

Later, Ken thought about his letter to the German Embassy, four months before his trip to South Africa. He had asked if it was possible for a student doctor, in their final year, to come to Rufisi to provide medical treatment to the people.

He had not yet had a reply, for the letter had gone from desk to desk in the cavern of government as each recipient tried to find somewhere to send it. A system that should, eventually, find someone who would deal with it.

We don't need a student doctor now; we have someone far better.

—————

11

Their latest guests, Sakkie and Ina De Wet, arrived while Marijke danced with the staff women behind the workshop. After Ken greeted them and they listened to the welcome song by eight of the staff, he took them to their cottage.

"Please, if you'd like an evening game drive, I have a ranger and safari vehicle waiting to take you. Dinner will be after your return."

They accepted, so Marijke didn't meet them until they arrived in the boma, when Ken introduced her as his companion and said, "Everyone calls her *Bibie*, just as I'm called *Bwana*."

Marijke didn't miss it. *So, he's promoted me to companion!*

Sakkie looked keenly at her, then asked, "*Bibie*, do you have an older sister in Cape Town?"

Ken wondered, *How will she answer that?*

"I might have, sir; I have no idea where my father went or what he did before I was born. Why do you ask?"

Ken smiled. *Brilliant.*

Ina tittered. Sakkie laughed and said, "You remind me of a woman I met at a meeting. She was much older and married, though, and she never spoke."

"Dressed like me in Cape Town?"

He laughed again at the thought. "Not at all, plain Cape Town business. I think it's your face and eyes that brought the memory."

"Well, I must ask my mother if she knows something! As you are new arrivals, Ken is your host tonight and can answer all your questions about Rufisi and Nyerere Park."

Ken showed them to his table, thinking, *Masterful. What a woman.*

In bed that night, Marijke asked, "*Bwana*, did I look older when you saw me on the mountain?"

"Yes, Marijke, but that's not surprising; how you felt made you look older."

"How old?"

"I thought you were late-thirties to forty. I was shocked when I saw your birth date in your passport and discovered you were twenty-seven."

Marijke thought about this in silence for two minutes, then asked, "You asked a forty-year-old woman to visit hell with you. Why?"

"Thirty-five, but it didn't matter; I was beginning to like you."

"And now, how old do I look?"

Dad warned me about answering this question. Let me answer in the way he suggested. "What answer do you want, the truth about what I see or what I feel?"

"Both."

"I see a young woman under twenty-eight, say twenty-six, but if I felt you, I'm sure you would be twenty-three or four."

"Silly, not that kind of feel."

Ken laughed. "No, every day when I talk to you, I feel I'm with a young woman learning and experiencing the first joys of adult life, a woman that age. But now it's your turn; what do you see and feel about me?"

"*Bwana*, I can only say that you seem older than you are at times, and at other times younger, much younger, but it's reassuring to know what you will be like when you are older. I think we are both learning together."

She's right on that one. "Marijke, do you remember Sakkie De Wet from your time in Cape Town?"

"No; in the beginning, I was only at those meetings to increase the billable hours, although the boss said listen and learn."

Ken felt cold as he remembered the meetings he had attended at the bank. *My God, what a life, but I can remember much the same.*

Then she asked, "And when I come to bed, how old am I?"

Diversion is the only tactic; I'll tell the truth, Ken thought. "I see a beautiful young woman of twenty-four; you make me feel I'm the same age, and I feel a terrible urge to tickle you and hear you laugh."

"Let's sleep. You can delay tickling to the future." *He's still nuts; I hope he stays like that when he's older.*

The following day a Frenchman and his wife came to stay; he was a keen birder and needed special facilities. When Ken met them and welcomed them to the lodge, he found his guests had very rudimentary English, so he switched to his mother tongue, "*Monsieur,* it will please me if you speak *Français* so that I can practice."

His guests were delighted, and they chattered away while he told them about the lodge and the arrangements he had made for their birdwatching. They needed a vehicle that would provide a solid platform for powerful telephoto lenses. He had a safari wagon with hydraulic stilts for that purpose. He didn't see Marijke enter the lounge and listen for a while before she strolled over and said in French, "*Monsieur et Madame du Pont,* may I introduce myself? I'm Marie-Jeanne and must look after the tasks that *mon mari* forgets."

Ken looked flabbergasted as she turned to him and said charmingly, "Is it not so, *mon cheri?*"

Madame du Pont chuckled. "All men are the same; they would forget to don underwear if we didn't tell them to."

After their guests left for their room, Ken turned to Marijke and asked, "Why didn't you tell me you speak French?"

"Well, why didn't you tell *me?*"

I suspected yesterday that he was different. He's French; he speaks it as well as my mother. "Simply because we never thought of it," she replied. "Now we know we have a secret language we can use when we don't want the staff to understand what we say. However, you must be forgiving; you speak it perfectly, while I haven't spoken it often since childhood. My mother is French."

"Why not since childhood? Is she still alive?"

"Yes. Mother doted on my brother and often ignored me. I didn't mind, I adored my father, but he died a little under a year ago. She lives with my brother."

"And how did Marie-Jeanne become Marijke?" *I'm beginning to understand why she was on the mountain. She lost her father and was not close to her mother, so she had no family support. She was in a job she hated.*

"It's my name, but ask six-year-old South African kids in the Cape to say Marie-Jeanne, and they say 'Mari-je'; anything small gets 'kie' added to the name, so I became 'Marijekie'. Later I dolled up the spelling. I didn't want to be French like Mama, but Afrikaans like Dad."

It sounds like she lived in hell for a long time. "Well, I'm glad to learn I'm your husband now. Is that only when we speak French?"

"We're both confused, *Bwana*; I'm sometimes 'my *Bibie*', or 'companion', and you are '*Bwana*' or 'my husband'. Let's not read too much into it; you can be '*mon mari*', and I can be '*ma femme*' if we speak French."

"Okay."

Marijke decided the opportunity to speak French and learn about birds was a godsend. She spent as much time as possible with the du Ponts on their birdwatching trips. Then hours every evening in the lounge. Before they left, she spoke much better French and asked Mr du Pont about her project: "One of the problems with growing vegetables here is the insects. I can put a huge birdcage around the vegetable beds, but how do I keep the insects under control?"

"I've seen several insect-eating bird species that would do the job, but I'm afraid you won't eliminate all the insects," he replied.

"Why not?"

"No matter how well the birds catch flying insects, there's a problem when the insects land. There is a species that will eat the caterpillars or the insects off the plants, but only one of the species I've seen is likely to go under the plants and eat the insects that creep in there. Then the insects lay eggs, and you have caterpillars eating the plants from below."

"Is there no solution?"

"I can't think of one, only pesticides. For that reason, vegetables grow in closed plastic sheeted sheds in Spain."

"*Cheri*, how about toads?" asked Madame du Pont.

"*Oui*, if there are toads here. With a basin of water with reeds at each end of the vegetable bed, or all around it, and fifty toads, they would devour the insects before they laid eggs."

Ken had just come into the lounge. Marijke said, "*Bwana*, please come over here."

He did, and after he greeted the du Ponts, Marijke asked, "Are there toads in the river, *Bwana?*"

"Of course, Marijke, snakes love them."

"Then I must collect toads as well as bats. And keep them away from the guests because of the croaking, and protect them from snakes." *That may not be easy. I must get a mongoose family—perhaps mongoose and jackals. My idea is more complicated than I thought; I need an entire ecosystem.*

After the du Ponts left, Marijke put the bird book back in the lounge bookcase; leaving it lying around was untidy, and the book might suffer damage. She found its place, then glanced along the row of books before leaving. One of them, published in 1942, had a French title. *Les Animaux de Selous* by Lionel La Salle. She took it out and opened it; the flyleaf had a dedication in French, dated two years ago.

To: d'Yquem, Phillipe / Ken Phillips / *Bwana*.

I leave with precious memories of the paradise you have created; this history of our heaven must remain here, in its proper place.

Avec tout notre gratitude, Louis et Soraya de La Vallee Poussin.

So, Bwana is Phillipe d'Yquem, and "Ken" is an English pronunciation—"de ye Ken". But Bwana suits me fine. I'll stay with that, and I'll bet that Louis is one of the owners who hasn't been back; he called it "our heaven".

The next morning as Marijke finished breakfast, Andwele arrived clutching a young Thomson's gazelle to his chest. From what he said, she understood that it had an injury, and Andwele wanted her to fix it as she had fixed him.

Amali came onto the veranda. So she asked, "Amali, Andwele says the gazelle is hurt, but I don't understand how it is hurt."

Amali asked Andwele, then replied, "It has a broken foreleg, *Bibie*. An accident often happens when they put a leg into a hole. He thinks you can fix it like you fixed his knee."

"What's the normal procedure, Amali?"

"Someone would cut its throat, and it would go in the pot. A three-legged antelope is prey predators can easily catch and eat."

"That would make Andwele unhappy; I can have a look. *Njoo hapa*, Andwele." She patted the floor beside her to show him where to sit. The first problem was how to keep the gazelle calm. It was calm when held tightly in Andwele's arms but struggled to flee once he slackened his grip.

"Amali, can you fetch the medicine box, *tafadhali*."

She broke one sleeping pill in two, then into quarters. *I wonder if that's too much.*

She crushed a quarter tablet into powder using two teaspoons, mixed in several drops of water, and with Andwele still holding the gazelle, she dribbled a little of the mixture into its mouth. *I'll wait a bit and see if it takes effect.*

Five minutes later, she gave it more; a bit later, it seemed less agitated. *I think that will do the trick.*

Another five minutes and the gazelle slept. Andwele asked, "Is it dying?"

Amali replied, "*Hapana inalala.* No, it's sleeping."

Marijke then examined the leg. She could feel the break in the thin bone and tried to pull the bone on each side away to align it; after some careful twisting and pulling, it seemed to fit together, and when she released it, it stayed that way.

"*Yake fasta,*" announced Andwele.

Marijke thought, *He's only five and thinks I've fixed it. I must explain.* "Amali, can you explain to Andwele that I have no *dawa*, medicine, like the red one I put on his knee, but I'll protect the leg while the gazelle makes *dawa* for itself?"

Amali did; Marijke thought his explanation excellent, and the way he invoked the help of the gazelle's *mzimu* was genius: "Andwele, *Bibie* has no *dawa* for the Tommy, so she can't fix it like she did your knee. She will call on the gazelle's *mzimu* to make *dawa* for it and protect the leg from evil *mzimu* while it gets better."

Seeing Andwele's big eyes, Marijke was sure he understood. "Amali, can you find two thin straight sticks for splints on the leg?"

Amali brought half a dozen dry sticks, and Marijke chose and taped two carefully to the leg, then used a plaster of Paris bandage to wrap the leg. She wanted to laugh; the little gazelle looked so odd.

"Andwele, stay here with the youngster until he wakes up. Amali, we need a wire-fenced space with a box for it to sleep in. Can you organise it?"

"At once, *Bibie.*"

Ken came to fetch Marijke for lunch.

He didn't fetch me for the first week. I feel he likes talking to me.

"Marijke, what's this about a Tommy? Amali asked permission to have the men build a pen and a box."

Ken hadn't noticed Andwele in the corner of the veranda, so

Marijke pointed, and he burst out laughing. "I've never seen a Tommy with a plaster cast. Will it recover?"

"I hope so; Andwele is attached to it already."

"Why's it sleeping?"

"I think I overdosed it with a sleeping pill."

Ken thought this hilarious. "You have a gift, Marijke, of making things happen. And I'm sure it's going to surprise me." *Will Marijke be our vet?* "I can hardly wait to see what you do next."

The baby gazelle was a sensation; all the kids came to see it during the three weeks it staggered around the cage with the leg in plaster. It healed perfectly but liked to stay in its cage unless it could walk beside Andwele. The children brought other injured animals and birds, and within a week, she had a baby warthog in the gazelle's cage.

Marijke thought they liked each other.

12

The medicines arrived, Marijke began unpacking them, and three young men and the woodcarver arrived with the medicine boxes. *I should have expected them; the village must know the truck with the medicines came from the city.*

"They are beautiful!" Smoothly polished, with the distinctive hardwood grain visible, the tops were a work of art. Each box had a carving of a cheetah in a different position: walking, jumping, stalking, looking back, and on the last, the cheetah lay on the top with its tail hanging over the edge. Marijke looked carefully; the artist had burned the cheetah's spots into the wood with a hot nail.

"Amali, please tell the artist that the medicines I'll keep in these boxes will gain a great force from the cheetah *mzimu*, for she will be happy with the beauty of these carvings."

Amali did; Marijke could see how pleased the artist was. "Can you ask him about payment? And then take him to *Bwana*, who will pay him."

"The boxes are a gift from the village, *Bibie*. The *mganga* has ordered it."

My God, they would be worth thousands in Cape Town, and they're giving them to me. What can I do? She thought for a moment. *Bwana can give him another order and pay for it, and the lodge can sell his carvings.*

"Amali, I thank the village for their gift; the medicines they hold will do much to help everyone. This man is a talented artist; it's a shame his work is unknown to others.

"Please take him to see *Bwana*. Tell *Bwana* I want a table in the lounge with many animals and a cheetah in the centre. Perhaps a glass top may need to cover it to protect the carvings. *Bwana* must pay for it; it's the eagle's gift to my cheetah *mzimu*.

"The artist must also make many more small carvings that the tourists can buy, whatever his *nafsi* wants him to carve, whole animals, or pictures like the tops of these boxes. When a tourist buys a carving, the office will give him the money, but a part of that money must be for things the village needs." *I hope that sounded as firm and positive as I wanted.*

Marijke would learn that a *mganga* with three *mizimu* had enormous power to do good. Over the years, the village's carvings would appear in collections worldwide.

Ken came to take her for lunch; when he arrived, Marijke had nearly finished packing the medicines into the boxes.

"Marijke, what the devil have you got me into now?"

He doesn't sound angry. "I won't tell you until you look at these boxes."

Ken looked, and Marijke watched him and thought, *He loves them. I can sense it from how he caresses the pictures; I feel the cheetahs purring. If he stroked me like that, I would purr too.*

"They're magnificent; I can feel the tail of that cheetah twitching the way they wave their tails," Ken said.

"They are a gift from the village."

This shocked Ken, until he realised, *She found a way to pay for them without hurting their pride. Brilliant!*

"The artist will bring carvings for sale, *Bwana*; you fix the selling price and give him all the money."

"I understand. I'll tell the office we will arrange shipment if a visitor buys something too big to carry away."

After two weeks of song practice, as she and Ken left the bungalow for the boma dinner, Ken noticed she was wearing the beaded headdress. *She seems glowing.* "Marijke, you look beautiful every night, but tonight you are radiant."

"Thank you, *Bwana*. I'm glad you like my dress."

Ken knew. *It's not her dress; it's her and much more than like.*

When the performance was about to begin, she excused herself from her table and joined the others outside the boma. The procession of singing and foot-stamping men came in, followed by the women dancing and clapping to their song. It took Ken over a minute to recognise Marijke. It was one of the women guests who asked, "Isn't that your wife? She's marvellous."

He could only say, "Yes, ma'am." *I couldn't say it better.*

That night Ken asked, "You must have practised that dance; why haven't I heard about it?"

"Because I asked them not to tell you."

"Marijke, all the staff obey you without question, even though women in Tanzania don't usually hold a managerial role." *She's born with natural authority, she has only to ask, and people do what she wants. Is that new, or was she like that before?*

He asked, "What did you do before I met you?"

"You're wrong about the women here, *Bwana*; the *waganga* are primarily women, and although seen as medical people, they have much to do with managing daily life.

"As you know, I was a lawyer, not a particularly good one; I lost the last two cases just before I met you. Now I can do what I want for the first time, not what others dictate. Only the partners wield any authority in an association; the others must toe the line.

"Why the staff accept my orders, I don't know; it may be because I'm your *Bibie*."

"I don't think so, Marijke; they like doing what you ask."

"As they follow you. Maybe I'm copying you."

"Why did you learn the songs?"

"The guests asked questions about what the songs meant, and I couldn't answer them, so I decided to learn them. The translations don't tell you much; the songs are more feelings than words. I sensed this, sang with them, and then the songs took over. The songs express joy, sadness, happiness and misery, not the words, but the sounds and the way they sing. I learned no one arranges the harmonies; they come from individuals expressing different feelings naturally and change with their moods. It's made me a better person and taught me much about understanding the people here. And if the guests can understand, I can tell them.

"You asked why they accept my orders: partly because they know I can understand them and are happy to do what I want.

"If this lodge becomes a happy place to live and work, the people will sing all the time, spontaneously."

The following day when Marijke finished breakfast, she saw three young boys sitting in the shade of a tree next to the bungalow. "Amali, please explain; what are those boys doing?"

"They are waiting for you to hang your towel on the railing, *Bibie*."

"Why, Amali?"

"I asked them; they said it's the sign that you will give them medicine. When Andwele came, both times, your towel was on the railing. Now that is the sign. It's like those I have seen on office doors in Dar that say 'Open' or 'Closed'. But few of our older people can read. The *waganga* all have a sign."

"What does the *mganga* in your village use?"

"She uses a broom leaning against the side of the door. The broom is straw, without a handle, like those the cleaners use to sweep. She refuses people if the brush is down; it says she's busy. They can see her with their problems if the brush is up."

They probably invented the idea a thousand years before the so-called civilised people thought of an "Open" and "Closed" sign.

"Okay, Amali, I'll hang out the towel and see what's wrong with them."

Is there a link with the expression "Throw in the towel"? Ken was right; towels are useful for all sorts of things.

Only one of the boys was ill; the other two had come to ensure he reached the bungalow.

"Amali, I understand this boy has pain in his stomach. Do you know anything about it?"

"Yes, *Bibie*, it's common. *Bwana* says it comes from the water, and the people must boil the water they drink. We call it *kiboko* belly. That's the Swahili name for hippo."

"But why?"

"The hippo sprays a liquid excrement with great force, *Bibie*."

Hippo guts—Gippo guts. My God.

"Bring the jumping cheetah box, Amali." *The boy will need water with salt and sugar.*

"And send someone to the kitchen for three one-litre bottles of our drinking water and put a teaspoon of salt and four teaspoons of sugar in each."

Now, is it diarrhoea or dysentery? I have Imodium for diarrhoea.

Amali returned, so she asked him, "How long has he had it, Amali, and has he seen blood in his excrement? Lastly, does he get it often?"

"He says two days, no blood, but sometimes many people simultaneously suffer from the same evil. The *mganga* treats them with plants."

"I think I know which plants. Does anyone die?"

"Not often, *Bibie*."

But they sometimes do.

Marijke took the Imodium from the box. "Amali, I'm not sure which bacteria bring this sickness. I shall ask *Bwana* if he knows. I'll give the boy some medicine now. He's to finish the three water bottles, but only drink a mouthful each time, until tomorrow morning, and then he must come here again."

She gave the boy the Imodium, made sure he swallowed the tablets and left to find Ken. She found him in the workshop.

"*Bwana*, do you know about diarrhoea and dysentery in the villages?"

"Yes, Marijke, and cholera. What do you want to know?"

"What I can do about it."

"It's the same all over Africa, polluted drinking water.

"Look around; a million animals and humans crap in or around the river. And sometimes, the e-coli count is high; other times, there are all sorts of bugs. The people choose not to go for vaccinations, although they are free at government clinics.

"You saw our water-treatment plant; the staff at the lodge rarely have a problem. Look carefully at the staff living in villages when they go home. They take bottles of our water. The other villagers only have river water, and despite telling them to boil all drinking water, they don't."

"Can't the villages install filters?"

"Money and electrical power, Marijke. A bacterial filter needs pressure, which means pumps and electricity. The *waganga* do an excellent job with treatment, so I have relied on them."

"Well, I'll think about it."

It started slowly, with a child or teenager coming to her after breakfast when she sat on the veranda and hung her towel on the rail.

She had to treat cuts, broken toes, festering blowfly sores, scorpion stings and spider bites—not only people but also dogs mauled in a fight with other dogs, baboons or a marauding genet.

Marijke didn't ask for compensation, but gifts began to arrive, often on two or four legs. The hen house, closed in a heavy mesh around and on top, expanded. The original Tommy's shed grew to be the same heavy mesh and housed the warthog and five goats; four needed daily milking—and then a villager gave her a baby pig.

The strangest gift was a two-foot-long python. She draped it around her neck and looked for Ken.

"Marijke, is that a real snake around your neck?"

"Yes, *Bwana*, a present. I came to ask if I can keep it."

"You will terrify every staff member at the lodge, but if you can be sure it can't escape, you can. Do you like snakes?"

"Not really. I had a brown house snake when I was thirteen, after my dog Ruff died, and I didn't want another dog. I found it in the garden and kept it for three years, then let it go because I was growing up."

"Then why do you want to keep this python?"

"I'll keep it in a box with a glass lid on the veranda, and then I'll show it to all the kids with all the information I can read about pythons and their habitat, so they know something about pythons and won't kill them if they come across one."

"Why?"

"If you try to kill a snake, it'll strike, and venomous snakes will kill. It's far better that they learn to avoid them all."

"That's a great idea, Marijke; I wouldn't have thought of that."

Sometimes she would take the python out and let the children touch it.

And sometimes she asked herself, *Am I doing something that will lead to trouble?*

She would ask herself the same question multiple times.

13

Marijke finished bandaging her last patient. The twelve-year-old boy had arrived limping, and she found a vicious thorn that pierced his foot before breaking off under the skin. She injected lignocaine around the thorn, waited for it to take effect, then made a deep cut before she could reach and draw it out with a pair of pliers that Amali had fetched from the workshop and sterilised in boiling water. She decided she needed pliers for her medicine box. She used a syringe to inject an antiseptic into the hole, irrigating the full depth.

A feeling of hunger and then a niggle of worry made her ask Amali. "The *Bwana* hasn't come for lunch; where is he?"

"He went to look at the hippo carcass by the river, *Bibie*, to check if poachers shot it for its teeth."

"Who's with him?" The worry grew.

"I'll ask one of the rangers."

"Quickly, Amali, I feel there's something wrong."

Amali was back in four minutes in a safari wagon. He stopped and told Marijke, "He was alone, *Bibie*."

She snatched the towel from the veranda railing and threw herself in.

"Damned fool. Drive, Amali, fast. Do you know where the hippo lies?"

"Yes, *Bibie.* The rangers will come once they have fetched a car."

Ken had driven to the carcass, a kilometre upriver from the lodge and only fifty metres from the water. After scrutinising it, as he found both massive lower canine teeth in place, with no sign of a bullet wound, he concluded it had died from natural causes. Preoccupied with his examination, Ken hadn't noticed two hyenas that approached silently. He saw them when he turned from the carcass to walk to the Land Rover. Ken had his rifle, so he felt no fear, but kept his eyes on them as he backed towards the vehicle, twenty metres away. Five steps later, his left foot stepped into a rabbit hole, and Ken fell backwards, twisting his ankle. The rifle flew behind him when he flung his hands out to break his fall.

He didn't see the hyenas leap back ten metres when they saw the sudden movement, but Ken reacted quickly.

Lifting his injured foot from the hole and crawling rapidly to recover the rifle, he used it as a crutch to stand, balanced on one leg, for the ankle was agonising. He knew hyenas feared attacking something taller than them.

Then it was a standoff. Ken could hobble using the rifle but couldn't shoot or stand on one leg with the rifle ready. He knew they would retreat a short distance if he fired the rifle in the air, but they would return ever closer when he didn't hit one. Ken was sure the recoil would knock him back if he fired from the shoulder while standing on one leg. Still using the rifle as a crutch, Ken stepped back; with each step he took towards the vehicle, the hyenas came closer until they were eight metres away. He was sure the attack was coming, so he lifted the rifle to shoot; he wouldn't miss at eight metres and hoped the other hyena would flee far enough for him to reach the wagon.

"Amali, there's his wagon. I can't see him."

"I can see it, *Bibie,* and I see *fisi;* he must be on the other side of the wagon."

"Faster, Amali, faster."

"Any faster, and I'll break the vehicle."

"Stop between him and the *fisi*."

The hyenas heard the roaring vehicle before Ken, who was concentrating on the moment they would attack. This new element in the hyena attack computer caused the programme to recalculate with a check on all inputs. Ken waited.

When the Land Rover roared between him and the hyena and screeched to a stop, he let himself fall as he heard Marijke, who had leapt out on the other side, waving the towel in the air as she charged the hyenas. "Bugger off, you carrion-eating ghouls from hell, or I'll send you back there."

Amali was only a second after her, rifle at the ready.

The hyenas rebooted their attack computer.

After a rapid calculation using advanced calculus, the Fibonacci series, and stochastic logic that included a factor for a multi-coloured monster with a furiously waving long neck and a terrifying scream, they decided the probabilities were not in their favour, so they turned and loped away to begin a new life.

Marijke turned to Amali and asked, "Where's my idiot husband?"

"Back here, *Bibie*; he has a broken ankle."

Four more rangers in another safari wagon arrived as she reached him.

"Then lay him on the seat of a wagon, *tafadhali*. Amali, you can drive as fast as you like; I hope it hurts him, so he'll learn a lesson."

She sat next to Ken as Amali drove tenderly at a crawl back to the bungalow. "*Bwana*, is it broken?"

"I don't think so, just a bad sprain."

"What happened?"

"The *fisi* came, and I was backing up to my truck when I put a foot in a hole, lost my balance and tumbled backwards."

"You told me when you brought me here that a man needs a buddy to survive; why in the hell did you go alone?"

"Everyone was busy, and it's not far."

"If a leopard can eat you between the lounge and the bungalow, anywhere is too far."

Amali eased to a halt.

"Carry him onto the veranda and bring the sleeping cheetah box."

"Ken, rest. I'll give you a pillow; your boot can stay on until the painkiller and the muscle relaxant I'll give you take effect."

Marijke gave him a pillow and then the pills. *I'll give him three, not two.* "Amali, please bring us a bucket of crushed ice and two small towels in twenty minutes."

The pain diminished; Marijke cut off the boot with the help of Amali, felt the ankle and found no break. After an hour with the foot in a compress of ice wrapped in towels that she replaced twice, she bound his foot and ankle tightly with an elastic bandage.

"Okay, guys, now put him on the bed. Amali, he'll need a crutch. Can you ask the carpenter to make one?"

After undressing him, Marijke said, "*Bwana*, you must lie here for five days; Amali will bring you a crutch to reach the bathroom. You'd better think about what you want me to do while you're incapacitated."

"Marijke, did I hear you ask Amali, 'Where's my idiot husband?'"

Marijke thought, then grinned at him, "I might have said it, a slip of the tongue."

He smiled back. "Or a Freudian slip? Revealing how you think of me?"

"An idiot? Yes."

"I meant the husband bit."

"Well, I'm still one up on you if it was."

"What do you mean? I haven't made any slips."

"Two, *Bwana*; remember when you introduced Lucas to me."

He did and recalled saying, *"Lucas, this is my Bibie."—Okay, I must give her that one.*

"Okay, Marijke, I'll plead guilty; I did say, 'my wife'. But that makes us even."

"Don't you remember the other?"

Ken tried to remember. *Maybe the painkiller had too much effect.* "No, I can't."

"I asked if we were coming to this lodge."

Then he remembered his words. "*We are; that's where you'll live with me until you decide to leave.*"

"What's wrong with that?"

"That's a marriage proposal."

"No, it's not; no judge would agree."

"It depends on the lawyer, *Bwana*; I was one, and I could make it stick."

"I thought you said you were a bad one."

"I never said that. Every lawyer loses cases; I said that I hated the profession."

Ken had to struggle with the thought and conclusion. *I like the idea that I've proposed.*

"Okay, Marijke, I'll give you that one too; I've proposed twice; I'll wait until you say yes."

"More than that, Bwana; I've stopped counting. Sleep now; I'll have your dinner served in bed." She smiled; he thought it was a tender one.

Ken thought, *I didn't imagine that's how it would end, but I'm thrilled.*

Marijke came at least twice a day to tell Ken what was happening. She found time to sit and talk. Most of their discussions were about everyday things that had happened, the guests, and minor problems with the staff that made Ken think, *She knows more about the personal issues of the team than I ever learned, and I suppose that's normal.*

He asked, "Marijke, have you had any more ideas to improve things, like saying grace?"

Marijke answered, "A few, *Bwana*; I must sort them out between the possible and impossible. There's one that I think we should do immediately and another that may take years. The first is easy."

"Tell me." *She said "we" again. And she's thinking in years!*

"The lodge needs a shop; it can be tiny to begin with, just a cupboard with a glass front next to the office."

"And what do we sell?"

"The first thing is a stock of sun creams and lotions of different strengths; the guests sometimes forget or run out. Then toiletries: toothpaste, toothbrushes, and razors and creams. I've had to give some of mine to the women. If there's a factory packaging creams under licence, we might order packaging with a Rufisi label."

"What else?"

"Caps, teeshirts and shirts for both sexes with 'Rufisi Lodge' written on them. Free advertising. The woodcarvings can move into the shop. Then I'll look around the villages and see if there are handicrafts that we can sell, like grass bags or placemats."

"We'll soon have no cupboard space."

"I know, but if we do the guests' necessities, you will have the time to build a shop next to the office or the boma. Put that on our to-do list."

"And what's the second one, my ... Marijke."

Marijke caught it with a smile. *He almost said "my dear" or "my darling"!*

"Several guests have asked me where the giraffes are. I asked Lucas the first time, and he said there were only a few and far from here. Can't we buy some?"

"That's a double problem; the bush around here is too short for giraffes; they need a place where the trees are taller. There's a suitable valley about ten kilometres from here, but it's fifteen kilometres long and has dense vegetation at the far end. There are few giraffes, as hunters are keen on them, so they prefer the denser bush areas. It's a three-hour drive with little chance of seeing them.

"Then, if we did bring giraffes from Manyara or the Serengeti, the hunters would return."

"If I can think of a solution, I'll tell you," said Marijke.

"I've tried to find a solution, but the poachers override everything."

The morning Ken was due to start walking again, Marijke said before she left the bed, "Stay there; I'll do the morning check and return for breakfast. I'll help you up, and we can eat together on the veranda."

Ken watched her as she entered the bathroom. *She gets more beautiful every day.*

Marijke returned half an hour later. "Ken, there's something new. Lucas says two poacher pickups were hunting east of us; one has gone to *jehanamu* or hell, and the other is up to its axles close to the entrance. What is that about, and what do I do?"

"That's one of the gloopers. Send the tracker to learn the story, then send the tractor to collect the pickup."

"Okay, I'll be back in five minutes, and you can tell me what a glooper is."

She was back in three.

"Marijke, the plain in front of us appears to be mud, but that's only the top half a metre, deep enough to halt a vehicle. Under that, it's the same clay, but it's so dense that water only seeps down very slowly and below it, probably fifty metres down, are the sand and gravel layers like our sand pit. So, the mud is like nearly dry clay and hard. But there are two places where I'm sure there is an underground spring bringing water up, and for a forty-metre circle, the mud is soft and sloppy down to the gravel. It's like quicksand; anything that falls in there disappears. Most animals know and avoid those two spots, but an animal disappears when it forgets in a panic, chased by a predator. When the carcass is deep down and rots without air, bubbles of stinking gas rise slowly, expand and burst on the surface with a noise like 'Glooop'."

"So, if you fall in, you're dead?"

"No, don't panic; lie flat, and swim; you can reach the side slowly. Animals and people who don't know struggle and sink."

"And nothing comes out?"

"It's over fifty metres to the gravel bottom; we will never know what's down there."

"Okay, the tracker will tell us what happened later. Let's have breakfast."

While they ate, Ken asked, "Will it hurt to tell me why you hated practising law?"

"No, it won't; that's history." Marijke told him about her lost cases: messy divorce matters, domestic violence and abuse, and unfair judgments.

When she had finished, Ken thought, *I can imagine that brought on depression.* Then he asked, "It's nearly two months since you arrived; how do you feel about being here?"

"I feel I belong, but I still can't imagine what life I want to lead, which worries me."

She does belong. More than anyone I know. "Hakuna matata, continue; I'm sure you will discover what you want to do." *And I hope it's here with me, but I promised no pressure.*

Then Marijke thought, Hakuna Matata. *That's the song I need, with much harmonising. I wonder if there's a Swahili translation. I'll show the children the* Lion King *film and teach them the English version, and Amali can tell them what it means and let them use Swahili words.*

"Marijke, I must ask the Dar office to apply for a work permit; your visitor's stamp expires in a month. It can be a fixed-term permit or apply for a permanent one. I'll say I need you as an assistant manager. What would you like me to do?"

Marijke thought about it: *Is a permanent permit a commitment?*

"*Bwana*, I said a moment ago that I've no idea what life I want to lead; it may be years before I know. Apply for a permanent one; staying for life is not an obligation."

"Can you request a copy of your degree certificate from Cape Town?"

"Of course, I'll ask the university to send one by email."

When she gave the document to Ken three days later, she noticed he had a slight limp. "*Bwana*, you're limping. Does your ankle still hurt?"

"Not really. It's tender; I guess I don't put my full weight on it. It will wear off."

"Then come to the bungalow; let me see if there's any swelling, and you can have an elastic bandage for a few days."

Ken submitted willingly: *I like Marijke looking after me.*

"*Bwana*, I don't think it's your ankle; you have something in your heel, like a thorn or a piece of glass. I must take it out."

Ken feigned alarm, "Oh no, are you going to cut me open?"

"Don't be a ninny, only a small cut."

"I'll faint."

Marijke grinned at him. "Okay, I'll use lignocaine."

"You'll stick needles into my foot?"

"Only if you insist, *Bwana*. I could ask Lucas and Amali to hold you down."

"I'll grit my teeth and shut my eyes. Go ahead, slice me up."

Ken screwed his eyes up but watched.

Marijke said two minutes later, "I don't know where you found it, but it's the tip of a porcupine quill. I'll clean the hole and put a plaster over it."

14

A week later, an out-of-breath teenage boy jogged up to the veranda. Amali had to translate again because the boy spoke no Swahili, only Ndengereko: "The *mganga* in his village has a young man with a broken leg in her hut. The boy has asked you to fix it like you did the baby gazelle."

I'm not a doctor, but I can look and decide how to take him to a doctor.

"Amali, load all the boxes in a safari wagon and drive us there, *tafadhali.*"

The boy in the hut was visibly in pain. *His leg is beginning to swell; it's probably not much different to the gazelle, but a sleeping pill won't work, and I can't risk an overdose.*

"Amali, can you explain to the *mganga* that this boy is much bigger than the gazelle; I don't have *dawa* that will make him sleep so he cannot feel pain when I try to fix it. He will move or struggle and defeat my efforts to straighten it. We must take him to a hospital or doctor where that *dawa* exists."

Amali explained, and it seemed an argument followed. Finally, Amali said, "The *mganga* says she has *dawa*, and she can do it."

Marijke hesitated. *That sounds unlikely, but I've learned nothing is impossible; I'll let her try.*

She spoke to the *mganga*: "Please do it, and I'll judge if the boy is deep enough in sleep."

Marijke watched while the *mganga* ground up several dried herbs to a fine powder, then added drops of water until she had a thin paste that she fed to the boy in sips from a wooden spoon. Then she began crooning, a rhythmic chant that sounded like a lullaby to Marijke. At the same time, she waved her hands in intricate patterns in front of the boy's eyes.

Marijke asked herself, *Is this drug-assisted hypnosis?*

Five minutes later, the boy was asleep. Marijke could touch his leg without reaction, so she began to probe, feeling for the bones and the break. *It won't be easy to align them, as the ends are lying side by side, but it's possible.*

"Amali, I need to pull the leg down. Point your finger at me." He did, and she placed her finger overlapping his by a centimetre. "Your finger is the top of the bone; the bottom lies beside it like my finger; I must pull it down like this until the ends meet. With the baby gazelle, I could do it with a hand on each side; here, I can pull only one side. You and the *mganga* must hold the boy and the top of his leg so it doesn't move."

Amali explained it to the *mganga*, and then they positioned themselves on either side of the boy, facing his feet, while Marijke faced the opposite way, her hands just above his knee.

"Right, I'll pull."

She pulled steadily, and as the strain built, she felt the bone rubbing against the other. She had almost reached the limit of her strength when she felt a click as it moved slightly across the other, so summoning a reserve of power, Marijke pulled harder until she felt the bone had finally aligned itself. When she relaxed, sweat pouring off her brow, she leaned forward, probed, and felt good bone alignment.

She sighed in relief, and the *mganga* said something to Amali and fetched a wet cloth that Marijke accepted with thanks.

"Okay, Amali, thank you for holding him. Bring me the box with the jumping cheetah and fetch a gourd of water big enough to put my hand in."

Amali had seen what she did with the gazelle, and ten minutes later, with Amali holding the leg up and the *mganga* on one side with Marijke on the other to wrap the bandage around the leg, the plaster cast was complete.

"He mustn't walk for three weeks. Then, I'll come and take it off."

As they left, Marijke asked Amali, "What did the *mganga* say when I aligned the bone?"

"The *mzimu* of the cheetah came to help with your last pull."

Ken, of course, learned what she had done. He said nothing but was surprised when Marijke spent several days visiting the *mganga* with Amali as her translator.

She asked the *mganga* to show her the plants the *mganga* used and talked about those she recognised and those she didn't. By the end of the third day, the *mganga* had learned that Marijke was no amateur, for she knew most of the common plant treatments.

Marijke soon sensed the *mganga* was sharing her knowledge freely, as one sister to another. It gave her a feeling of belonging that she had never experienced as a lawyer.

Her Swahili improved as she spent her days in the village and talked to the men and the women.

On the fourth day, she sensed a feeling of anticipation when she arrived in the village. *They expect something special to happen today,* she thought.

When she saw the *mganga*, another village's *mganga* was with her, and many villagers were watching. After the traditional greetings and an introduction to the other *mganga* from an upriver settlement, the village's *mganga* said, "*Bibie,* the *waganga* have met. We want to give *Bwana* an eagle *juju*. The *mganga* of a mountain village has sent us a *juju* for him."

She unrolled an animal hide packet, showed her a *juju*, and then rolled it up again. "Can *Bwana* come here so we can give it to him?"

"I'll bring him tomorrow."

"You told Amali about your bird *mzimu*, the bird that tells the future. Upriver, there are many of these birds, where the water is clear of mud. The *mganga* of a village there has brought a *juju* for you." The other *mganga* unrolled a packet and lifted a small *juju*. She lifted it above her head and implored, "I call on the *mzimu* of the weather bird to help you see the future when you need it." Then she placed it around Marijke's neck. Marijke reached up and held it.

"I thank you and your villagers; I feel its happiness. Why do you call it the weather bird?"

"The bird can see the future; it tells us when floods are coming. It builds its nest much higher in the riverbank, and the people who live near tell everyone that floods are coming."

When Ken came to bed, Marijke said, "*Bwana*, tomorrow you must come with me to the village. They want to present you with an eagle *juju*."

"So, I'm to wear one too? Why?"

"Two reasons, *Bwana*. When you have a problem and hold the *juju*, sometimes the *mzimu* helps to find a solution. Mine helps me often. I want you to wear it."

Ken thought, *If she wants me to wear it, she cares, and that's a good enough reason for me.*

"Then it shows the villagers have profound respect for you. They want the *juju* to help you and that you will stay. It's their sign that you belong with them."

And Ken had another thought: *That's new. Is it because the people want her to stay too?*

Ken duly received his *juju* in a simple ceremony where everyone applauded, and a choir sang a praise song.

When they returned to the lodge, Marijke had a stock of herbs and two herb mixes—the ones used to hypnotise the boy, and another that the *mganga* told her had magical properties to fight infection.

She tried it on the animals and then the human cuts and abrasions and found it better than anything she had in the medicine boxes.

That night when Ken came to bed, Marijke asked, "*Bwana*, before we left Dar, you said that both you and Lucas disliked cities. I can understand Lucas not liking them, as he was born here in the open country, but you said you were born in Paris. Why don't you like cities?"

"I don't honestly know; when I was a kid, I don't think I disliked cities, but it began at university and then worsened as the years passed. It's not that I don't *like* them; it's just that I feel uncomfortable in crowds and have the urge to escape from a crowd."

"Was it bad enough to see a psychologist?" *Is this the cause of his bond with Rufisi?*

"I did once. The shrink asked many questions, but after three sessions, I stopped."

"Why?"

"She said I was a claustrophobic risk-taker and recommended earplugs."

Marijke laughed. *He would look like Frankenstein with plugs coming out of his ears.* When she stopped laughing, she asked, "Why a risk-taker?"

"Because of my skydiving."

"I don't see a link; when you threw me out of the plane, for the first few seconds, I was exhilarated by the feeling until I remembered I had no parachute."

"Me neither. I told the shrink I scuba-dived to photograph the fish and didn't feel claustrophobic."

"How bad is the feeling you have in a city?"

"It's worn away a lot since I left the job in the city. I told you I never lived with a girlfriend; I didn't want to because having someone so close to me was always uncomfortable." *It was hard to find a girlfriend,* Ken thought.

"I had two single beds in my Paris flat. If Andrea stayed the night, she slept in one of them. Nairobi was the first time I've ever slept all night in a bed with a woman."

"But you don't mind me being with you or sleeping in the same bed? It must be terrible to have such a strong feeling."

"I can't explain it, Marijke; I haven't had that feeling since I met you. In Nairobi, my first thought was to sleep on the couch, but for the first time ever, I wanted to sleep beside a woman, and then you invited me to, and since then, I like having you beside me."

"That's reassuring. You pushed me from a plane, but now I know you won't push me out of bed. Let's sleep."

"I'll never do that."

She didn't need to visit to remove the plaster from the boy who broke his leg. The villagers brought him to her to do it. They gave her a billy goat, and she mused, *I need that food supply. I'll now have baby goats as well.*

Marijke received a permanent Tanzanian residence document and a stamp in her passport and thought, *It's not a commitment to stay, but it's nice to know that if I start something, I can finish it.*

Taking the plaster off the boy's leg raised a worry to the surface of her mind. The following night she told Ken: "I need to visit a hospital, but I don't know which one."

"What for?"

"I'm worried I haven't had a severe wound to treat. The worst I've had are cuts I've managed with tape, but one of these days, it will be a wound needing stitches and a general anaesthetic. I need to find out what I can buy and have a lesson about its use. I also want to buy some anti-tetanus shots and other vaccinations. Now that I have the fridge, I can buy some antibiotics."

"I would guess that Dar General is the best, but they will be the busiest. However, there's a hospital just before we reach the airport; it's Catholic, Cardinal something. They might be able to help. Then at the airport, there's a clinic; they may be up to date with vaccination information. If you want to talk to them, you can use my satphone.

"As the hospital and the Blue Sapphire Hotel are near the airport, you could fly in and back."

"Okay, let me investigate those. It'll take a day or two."

15

———————

Marijke didn't have a chance to investigate the hospital the next day because an eight-year-old boy arrived at her veranda with two cheetah cubs minutes before Ken came to lunch.

"*Bwana*, look at these cubs; they're tiny. How old are they?"

"Possibly a bit more than a week old. The cub's eyes are still closed, so less than ten days."

"But where did they come from, and what must I do with them?"

"The night before last, the rangers surprised two poachers skinning a cheetah they had shot. It was a lactating female, so I told the rangers to search for the cubs she was feeding. As you have the cheetah *mzimu*, the only logical course was to bring the cubs to you, so you are now a cheetah mother."

"What happened to the poachers?"

"Stripped of clothing and boots and pushed off a truck in the most remote spot in the park. I won't allow the rangers to kill them unless they shoot back; taking them to the police wastes money and time, and the rangers agree that if poachers want to walk around in the park naked, we should allow them to do so. They are all men, so the rangers call them skinny elephants. *Tembo nyembamba*."

Marijke laughed. "Do they survive?"

"Usually, but the experience is discouraging if not fatal."

"What milk can I feed the cubs?"

"I don't know, we can look it up on the web; but at a guess, goat's milk is probably closer to that of a wild animal than cow milk. I know wild-animal milk is high in fat."

"Okay. Amali, fetch me some goat's milk. I'll find a teat and a bottle."

A plastic water bottle, half-filled with goat's milk, and the finger cut from a rubber glove with a hole in it seemed ideal. But neither of the cubs wanted to drink.

"Amali, can you melt some butter and mix it with the goat's milk? They might need more fat."

The first cub began to suckle on the third try, and the second one followed suit. *It was just how thirsty they had to be.*

"Amali, we can't put them with the goats and pig; they'll need a separate box."

"Yes, *Bibie*, but what do we do with them when they grow?"

"One thing at a time, Amali. Have one of the boys feed them three times a day and let them sleep in a box."

Three days later, Marijke was feeding the cubs on the veranda, one asleep in her lap, when a thought came from nowhere. *I need help.*

"Amali, I must see the *mganga* in the closest village. I need help."

"*Bibie*, you must ask for the young women who are learning from the *mganga*; there's one in the nearest village and another at the woodcarver's village; they are ready to learn new things."

"How do you know, Amali?"

"They are beautiful, *Bibie*."

"Then let's go this afternoon." *I should have thought of that.*

"Okay, *Bibie*, I'll be ready."

Amali had only a thick staff. Marijke checked that she had her paper bag, and they left the lodge along the path to the village. They expected no danger with less than a kilometre to go in daylight along a well-travelled footpath.

Halfway along the path, they rounded a familiar baobab tree, and

Marijke stopped dead. *Cheetah! I'm face-to-face with a cheetah. I suppose eight metres is face-to-face.*

Amali stopped beside her, every sense on alert, watching the animal for any reaction. When he heard Marijke making blowing sounds, he risked a glance. She was blowing up a bag!

His eyes again fixed on the cheetah; he missed Marijke's movement, closing the bag's mouth in her left hand, and was shocked when she suddenly strode forward and shouted.

"*Scat*, you overgrown pussycat, push off and let us pass."

Amali couldn't catch her but was only a metre behind when the cheetah bared its teeth. Marijke didn't pause; she shouted again, "Go on, *scram!*" Then, she brought her hands together when four metres away and popped the bag. It was too much for the cheetah. Attacked by a billowing multi-coloured dress that exploded, it leaped gracefully off the track into the surrounding bush.

"*Asante-Sana.*" The bemused Amali was sure she had thanked the cheetah for leaving.

"Come on, Amali; we must see the *mganga*. That was a female, and she had milk dripping from her teats. Why was she here and not with her cubs?"

"She might be looking for them, *Bibie*."

"How could she lose them?"

"It frequently happens when other predators take them. Hyenas, vultures, eagles, and foxes do. It could also be a snake. The *duma* must hunt, so leaves the cubs alone for short periods."

"That's a shame; they're so lovely."

The arrangements for one of the young women to help proved easy, and the *mganga* promised to tell the *mganga* of the woodcarver's village that another one was necessary. Amali arranged for some men to come and build a hut for the women to sleep in; they would use the toilet block of the lodge employees and eat in the communal kitchen.

Amali told the *mganga* about the cheetah. She nodded and said, "Of course, *Bibie* was not afraid; they share the same *mzimu*."

They started back, Amali keeping a wary eye out for a cheetah, and when they reached the baobab turn, he said, "Please, *Bibie*, before we go past the tree, let me check the other side."

The path was clear, but as they approached the lodge, Marijke thought she saw movement to one side. "Amali, I think our cheetah is watching us."

"I think so too, *Bibie*."

"Maybe she can smell the baby cheetah's odour on my dress. If she's looking for her cubs, it must be attracting her."

In bed that night, Marijke asked, "*Bwana*, how far away can animals smell things?"

"It varies, but with the breeze in the right direction, some can smell something miles away. Unlike a few mammals and man, smell is the major sense; eyesight is a poor second or third after sound."

Marijke thought, *She must have smelled them or me; I wonder if she would take my cubs?*

Earlier, Amali hadn't been sure *Bwana* would've believed him if he told the whole story, so he'd said to Ken, "A cheetah is roaming around the lodge."

The following day after breakfast, when Ken had left, Marijke fed the two cubs on her lap and called Amali. "I'm going to the baobab just before the cubs' next feeding. I want to see if the cheetah will adopt the cubs."

"*Bibie*, I must fetch my rifle; *Bwana* has ordered it."

"Okay, but stay well back of me, fifty paces."

They set off; she was carrying the two cubs, and Amali stayed back. But only thirty paces.

Twenty metres before the baobab, she stopped, sat down cross-legged, put one cub on her lap, and played with the other on the ground before her, rolling it over and scratching its tummy.

Fifteen minutes later, the mother cheetah appeared silently in front of her, only five metres away. Marijke thought she had timed things precisely, for the cub was trying to suck one of her fingers, and the mother still had milk dripping from its teats.

The mother stepped slowly forward, sniffing the air, studying the cub. At two metres, Marijke turned the cub and pushed it away from her; it took a minute for it to stagger closer to the female, smell the dripping milk, and try to reach a teat. The mother reacted instinctively and lay down, so the cub managed to latch onto a teat and began sucking rhythmically. Marijke gave it about three minutes, then pushed the second cub forward; it wasn't as courageous as the first, so she leaned forward to give it another push.

The mother watched her and didn't budge while Marijke sat back. She could have touched the mother. The mother washed the first cub, *just like a cat and kittens*, and when the second finished sucking, she cleaned it too.

The mother stood, picked up the second cub in its mouth and silently moved away. Marijke recovered the first one, and the mother turned to look at her, then disappeared.

Will she return? Or will she share and leave a cub with me?

Marijke played with the cub for twenty minutes before the mother reappeared and came close enough to collect the cub less than half a metre from Marijke. She turned to look at Marijke again, then left.

Amali had watched the whole episode; all he had to say was, "We can go home now, *Bibie*; she will not come again."

Amali knew he had watched something unique and magical; people would think him a liar if he told the story, so when someone asked what happened to the cubs, he replied, "The *mganga* with the *mzimu* of the cheetah gave them to another cheetah to raise."

Ken asked Marijke directly, "Where are the two cubs?"

"I gave them to a cheetah mother to raise."

"Marijke, please tell me the whole story from the beginning."

She did.

"The paper bag, why do you call it a '*bobbejaan sakkie*'?"

"My parents raised me in the mountains of the Cape. There are baboons everywhere. Some farmers shoot them, others put silver detonators on the rocks in bits of banana, and when the baboons bite them, and one explodes, they leave for weeks; it's cruel because the baboon that bites it gets its head blown off. Baboons are dangerous; they can attack if they think you have food in your bag. Popping a paper bag does the trick, as they know what a bang means. So, I always carried one."

"Do you appreciate the risk you took? A cheetah is not a baboon."

"I know, *Bwana*, they are far less dangerous. People have kept them as pets for thousands of years. I'm a woman, *Bwana*, a female; you won't understand. I could sense the cheetah's hurt after losing her cubs, and I had two I couldn't raise the way they needed raising. I smelled the same as the cubs, like a female cheetah with cubs. She might have been slightly confused, but I felt sure she wouldn't harm me if I didn't threaten."

Ken thought, *Not many people would have had the courage to do it. Why does she not have children? Did she have some taken from her? That might be enough for suicide.*

Ken had her name from her passport; the mountain wine estate was enough for an address. Ken thought, *I don't want to remind her of her past, and it's my fault she left precipitously; I'll try to find out the status quo before bringing it up.* He emailed a Cape Town detective for a report.

That night Ken asked, "Marijke, I have no explanation for what you did with the cheetah cubs except to believe you should have children. Why don't you have any?"

"*Bwana*, I fell in love with the son of another estate when I was seventeen. He was at the same school a year ahead; it was a schoolgirl crush. He was going to Cape Town university to study law because it would help the estate, for his father knew nothing about agreements. When he left, I decided to achieve high grades and chose the subjects I needed to gain entrance to a law school. That was, I think, my first mistake; I chose the wrong career for the wrong reasons.

"When I started law school, the boy already had another girlfriend. I changed my subjects to avoid him and graduated with a specialisation in family and criminal law; I should have changed my degree, but I felt like my high school results locked me into law. That was my second mistake. I should have done something else.

"Once I graduated and began working, I met an accountant called Greg who worked in contract negotiation and we got married. When I didn't fall pregnant, I went for tests, and the doctor said I was fine but that Greg should get tested. That's when Greg told me he was sterile and didn't want children." She thought, *I should have divorced him within a month; he only had sex with me occasionally and left me without an orgasm. I felt like a dirty dishrag and unattractive.*

After a pause, she continued: "I found out that he had a mistress in Johannesburg, so I filed for divorce and moved to a flat alone." *Finding he had a mistress was a relief.*

Ken looked shocked.

Marijke added: "The divorce took two years; the final papers came a month before I met you." *Two years alone, I couldn't look at another man in case he found out and used it to block the proceedings.* "So, Bwana, no kids."

Ken felt sorry for her and struggled to find anything good to say. *I won't ask if she wants kids; she was trying to have a child. For her, it must have been hell.*

Before Ken could react, Marijke changed the subject: "*Bwana*, can one of the rangers drive to three villages on Saturdays and collect some kids in the evening? Then return them after dinner?"

"Of course, Marijke, but what for?"

"I have a surprise for Saturday."

Before dinner on Saturday, Marijke announced, "We have two surprises for you tonight. The first is two of the dishes; instead of plain mashed potato, you have *Irio*, our East African equivalent mixed with corn and peas, and next to it on the table is *Ugali*. This cornmeal cake is the staple of many African countries, with a tomato relish. The second surprise comes after dinner; please don't leave the boma too soon."

After dinner, Marijke and Amali disappeared for a few minutes. Marijke appeared wearing her headdress and announced, "Ladies and gentlemen, the staff sing and dance for you during the week, but we hope you will like our Saturday entertainment. The children of the villages have come to sing for you. They are unpaid. If you appreciate their performance, something in the box beside the office will help with their schooling."

Amali led into the boma sixteen children of all ages; the eldest, a boy about thirteen, had a drum, and the littlest, a girl, was about seven. They lined up in three rows, with the drummer to one side, and then when silence fell, Amali signalled, and the drum began to sing a rippling rhythm.

They sang five songs, all with glorious harmony, and then as the applause died down, Marijke stepped forward and spoke: "The children have another to sing for you; I'm sure you will recognise it, and they have learned the English words, especially for your pleasure. It's a song with three parts and a chorus. Jabali, Asani, and Jasiri will sing the lead parts."

Jabali, one of the tallest boys; Asani, a young boy with an expressive face; and Jasiri, a sweet young girl with a powerful soprano voice, stepped forward, and then with a nod from Marijke, Jabali began.

"*Hakuna matata*, what a wonderful phrase..."

The audience could see that the children smiled, laughed and jigged, enjoying every second wrapped up in the song. Especially when Pumba farted, and the chorus all made the sound. When it ended, every person there stood and applauded for minutes.

"Marijke, that was a fantastic surprise. How did you manage it? I'll bet that box will overflow."

"*Bwana*, I don't have to do much, just an idea, a little push and a bit of help. The village people love doing new things, especially the children. I took a tablet and showed the kids the piece from the film with the song, and once they saw it, I couldn't stop them from singing and practising it. They've already changed the harmonies, and many words are in Swahili. I think it will evolve further."

"Marijke, in three months, every lodge in the park will have kids singing on Saturdays."

She has created a new life, and she's changed mine. I know I love her.

<h1 style="text-align:center">16</h1>

A week later, the atmosphere was sombre when Marijke arrived for lunch.

"What's wrong, guys? Why are you all so miserable, and where's the *Bwana*?"

Amali answered, "Someone shot an elephant, *Bibie*; we think it's ivory hunters. *Bwana* has gone with Lucas to find out."

"Where?"

"About five kilometres upriver."

"Is there any danger?"

"The hunters will be long gone, *Bibie*. Lucas is with him, and the wildlife will have scattered, so no. *Bwana* should be back soon."

The meal continued in silence. Marijke could feel how the rangers felt, and she felt the same way. They heard the vehicle arrive, and Ken entered the dining room. Everyone could see and sense his anger; he was boiling.

"*Bwana*, why are you so angry?"

"Marijke, ivory hunters killed another elephant last night, a cow. It's an endless battle fighting them and such a waste. She was young, and her tusks were small."

"Where are the ivory hunters from?"

"They aren't local; they must come from Dar or somewhere on

the coast, where smugglers can ship the ivory offshore in dhows, although a local person may be involved in guiding each group for a few shillings."

He turned to address the rangers. "Hami, take two others with you and the tractor driver. Fetch the lowbed trailer and the tractor from the shed, collect the carcass, and take it to the graveyard."

Thinking of the colossal elephant, Hami, a short, muscular man, picked two other heavyweights, Erevu and Mwamba, and then they left the table.

"Why do you do that, *Bwana*?"

"The kill is too close to two villages. Unless we move it to the graveyard, the area will be swarming with lions, hyenas, jackals and vultures within six hours, and the danger to the village people becomes too great."

"And what's the lowbed?"

"It's a low trailer with a ramp and a hydraulic winch driven by the tractor. We can haul an elephant carcass onto it."

"And where's the graveyard?"

"The point in the park furthest from all human habitation. It's about a five-hour drive for the tractor; the rangers will return after midnight. The sooner they leave, the better."

Ken didn't eat and hurried off, and then Marijke returned to the veranda to treat the last of the day's patients.

Only two hours later, Marijke's assistant was packing the medicines back in the cheetah boxes when Marijke heard the tractor and saw Ken running from the office, so she dashed down to join him. Lucas was trailing behind. "*Bwana*, what's wrong? Why's the tractor coming here?"

"I can only think of one reason. Lucas, open the elephant pen gates."

Lucas scurried off, shouting for help. "Ambokile, Erevu, *kalamu ya tembo!*"

As the tractor came into view, Marijke could see why the people were coming from everywhere to line the track on either side of the tractor. Behind it was the grey mound of the elephant carcass on the trailer, but fifty metres behind that trotted a small elephant and, running beside it, a baby.

"*Bwana*, how old are they?"

"The biggest is between two and three; the baby is under six months."

"What will you do?"

"When they go past, follow them; the tractor will drive through the pen. We haven't used it for over a year. Lucas will arrange for men to ensure it's strong enough."

They followed the two young elephants as the tractor and trailer drove between two lines of thick posts with bars connecting them, creating a fenced road, and as soon as the young ones were between the side fences, men ran forward and closed off the entrance. Others hurried along to close off the rails behind the trailer as the tractor accelerated down the road; Marijke knew it was heading for the graveyard.

The two youngsters, squealing in anger or fear, tried to push past the bars; the youngest, Marijke thought, was crying.

"*Bwana*, what happens now?"

"The older one can feed itself; Lucas will find fodder for it. It will be good company for the little one, but you're now Mama Tembo. You must feed the baby; they drink ten litres of milk daily."

"Why Mama Tembo?"

"You must watch *Hatari!* The early sixties film starring John Wayne. I think Mama Tembo, in the film, used a goat's milk and mash mixture and put it in the baby elephant's mouth a handful at a time. It will die without milk and will need feeding by tomorrow morning."

"Okay, let me organise things. How long will it need feeding?"

"It's she, and although she will begin to eat the tender parts of the same fodder as an adult after six months, she will need milk until she's two."

Ken checked on Marijke's progress, and by five that afternoon, Marijke had found the right formula from the web and organised a regular supply of ten litres of goat's milk daily. She had a homemade mix of the first ten litres from ingredients she'd found in the kitchen, and had ordered two weeks' supply for urgent delivery along with six months' supply staged over the coming months.

"Marijke, when are you going to feed the baby?"

"In ten minutes, *Bwana*."

"How are you going to do it?"

"I have a hosepipe with a tap in the line a half metre from the end. Lucas will hold the bucket and the hose on the top beam of the pen, and I'll squirt the elephant mixture into her mouth using the tap to control it."

"This I must see."

A crowd watched as Marijke and Lucas tried to feed the baby. The first problem was that the baby wouldn't come to her, so she climbed between the fence bars into the pen. The older elephant smelled the milk and came, but not the baby. Marijke thought of a solution.

"*Bwana*, can you send someone for a sack of yesterday's bread buns? And then persuade the older one to come and eat them from you. You must get him out of my way."

Ken did, and once the older one moved away with Ken to a corner of the pen, Marijke soaked a bun in the milk bucket and strolled towards the baby, crooning gibberish and holding out the bun. The baby was hungry, and the smell of the milky bun drew it closer until Marijke managed to push it into her mouth. Marijke backed away to the fence, took another soaked bun from Lucas, and the baby came eagerly to eat it. Taking the hosepipe, she opened the tap slightly so the milk dripped, pushed the end into the baby's mouth as it chewed the bun, and slowly increased the milk flow. It worked, and ten minutes later, the bucket was half empty and, judging by the overflow of milk onto the ground, the baby had a full stomach.

The tractor returned at two the next morning with the trailer. The guards reported that when returning, they had seen two lion prides and several hyenas heading toward the carcass.

Marijke and Ken repeated the feeding performance twice daily for the next three days and trained a couple of volunteers. On the third day, Ken heard the tractor and went to look. With an earthmoving bucket, it was digging a shallow pool north of the elephant pen.

"Marijke, are you making an elephant wallow?"

"Yes, one of the rangers is getting a hosepipe; I think those two are ready for a bath. I'll try the baby first, then the other will follow."

"Have you given them names yet?"

"The big one is Uhuru; the baby I call Shy."

The next day, Ken watched along with nearly everyone else at the camp and several people from the village as Marijke led the baby from the pen to the water-filled wallow, a bun in one hand and broom with stiff bristles in the other. The baby wasn't interested in the wallow; it wanted the bun, so she squelched into the muddy water to the middle, and the baby followed. While it stood in the middle chewing the bun, she took the hosepipe and sprayed the baby with water. The baby got the idea and lay down, then rolled over suddenly, knocking Marijke off her feet, so the baby elephant and Marijke were sitting in the middle of the wallow. The entire crowd laughed uproariously.

Marijke grinned, took the brush, and began to scrub the baby, who wriggled in delight. "*Bwana*, let Uhuru out."

Three minutes later, she had both elephants rolling around, the dirty water was becoming mud, and one of the young men watching had joined her to scrub Uhuru.

With the help of many willing hands, Marijke managed to squelch her way out of the wallow; the broad grin told everyone she had enjoyed the mud bath.

As she left with Ken, Shy saw her go and ran from the pool after her, expecting food, so they took her back to the pen where Marijke's young crew fed her.

"Marijke, I like you in that condition; I had the urge to come and roll in the mud with you because you enjoyed it so much."

"That would be fun; I can understand why elephants do it. But it will dry hard in five minutes if I don't shower now."

"Okay, we'll go to the bungalow."

"*Bwana*, can you come and scrub my back? I don't usually have mud there to wash off."

"Okay, coming."

Ken thought, *We are behaving like man and wife; I like it.*

"There, it's all clean."

"Thanks, I'll dry myself and my hair; pour me a tonic."

Clean and dry and wearing a loose kaftan, Marijke sat in one of the lounge chairs and said, "The crew can continue feeding and bathing the elephants; I've done my job."

"Not quite, Marijke; the moon will be full in three days."

"What's that have to do with elephants?"

"The period of a near-full moon is when poachers come hunting, so I'll have the scouts out and coordinate with the other lodges. It's also the time that elephants move long distances at night. In the dark of the moon, they stand quietly in the thickets and wait for the night to pass; during a full moon, they will walk continuously, usually upwind, if they can smell no danger. If the matriarch of the herd your babies came from comes to see them, she will come in the early morning after a bright moonlit night."

"Then I'll give Shy her morning feed alone."

"Aren't you afraid?"

Her reply stumped him. "No, it's natural; if the matriarch comes, I'll tell her she can take Uhuru to the herd and come back to check on Shy every month until she's old enough."

Ken came late to bed the following night. *I don't want to tell her; it might bring back the depression; she's done so well up till now that I don't want to destroy her progress. But I must tell her for the sake of the elephants.* He slid into bed and said, "Marijke, we can't keep Uhuru; he must go to a zoo, and Shy will have to go once she's over six months. I shall try to find a zoo."

Marijke exploded; she sat up and almost shouted, "You're going to sell my elephants?"

Oh God, she's angry; it's going to be difficult. "Not sell them, Marijke; give them away."

Ken could see the grim expression on her face and the determination in her eyes as she said, "If you do, then you can give me away as well."

More than difficult. "I don't want to, Marijke; it's not for me, but for them."

Still angry, Marijke said, "Why do you say that? We can look after them here, and the tourists will love having little elephants to look at."

Is it because she doesn't know? "Calm down, Marijke, calm down and listen. Do you know what a forager is?"

She shook her head but replied, "Yes, an animal or person that looks around for stuff."

Ken couldn't miss the sideways movements of her breasts that shaking her head caused. *They're lovely, but concentrate, you fool.* "That's too general; for animals, it's food. The carnivores have no problem; they eat meat with all the salts, vitamins, fats and sugar they need. The omnivores have a slight problem, but most vegetarian foragers have a huge problem."

"Why?"

She's still a furious icicle, but she's listening. "They must eat a variety of grasses, roots, leaves, and other vegetation for the vitamins and minerals they need to survive. The ruminants can do so on a few grass varieties if they're the right kind because they can extract what they need with their four stomachs. The others can't. You've seen the zebra moving along while they graze. Do you know why?"

"Because they've eaten what's there and then move on."

"No, they eat a bit, then move on when they need something different. They don't think, 'I've had my vitamin C; I better find some A.' They feel it."

"Oh, and elephants?"

Finally she's calmed down. "They're the same. They eat fruit, tree bark, roots and small twigs, leaves, grass and some reeds."

"To feed Uhuru, I must collect a whole mixture of vegetation?"

"Yes, otherwise he will die."

"But can't we do that?" *Bugger, I'm waving my boobs in his face again.* She laid back and pulled up the sheet.

Ken felt relief; she had used "we".

"We won't manage it; we don't know what they need. We don't have the time to learn which plants growing here are suitable. Zoos buy a selection of fruits and vegetables and give them all to the elephants to choose from so the zoo learns which ones are necessary for them. Sometimes the elephants pull up small plants and eat the roots. We'd need a hundred people scouring the park for vegetation; the elephants walk dozens of kilometres to feed on different plants."

"So, we must buy food as the zoos do."

"We can't afford to do that, Marijke. Uhuru will eat fifty kilograms a day. Although Shy is easy to feed until she's six months old, Uhuru will fall ill if he doesn't eat a balanced diet."

"Then wait a few days; if the matriarch comes, the problem of Uhuru disappears. And we will have three months or more to solve the Shy problem."

17

―――――――

Five nights later, Ken arrived at one-thirty after a fruitless night scouting for poachers. He slipped into bed beside Marijke and fell asleep at once; he woke as the first birds cheeped, saw Marijke was not in bed, hurriedly dressed and headed for the elephant pen. He had the feeling of something out of place that comes from living in the wild; any change in the daily rhythms of the bush is enough.

In the gloomy early light, he could see Marijke. She had a bag of stale buns and was climbing into the pen; she must have pulled the locking pin from the elephant-house door as he saw it open, and first Uhuru and then Shy came out, trunks in the air, checking the airborne scents. He thought they were reluctant, but Shy passed Uhuru and came straight to Marijke, who stood with her back to the fence. Shy recognised the bag of buns.

Ken searched the nearby bush but could see nothing. Lucas came silently up to him and handed him his rifle. *Lucas knows too.*

Suddenly, a slight movement drew his eyes, and then the shadows coalesced; he saw the outline of a massive elephant just behind the screen of the bush, only twenty metres behind Marijke, watching her. Marijke broke a bun in half and gave one piece to Shy, and the other she threw to Uhuru, who promptly picked it up and put it in his mouth.

Ken watched her and the enormous, unmoving elephant as she broke another bun, and he saw the gigantic shape drift like a ghost silently towards her. He wanted to shout a warning but didn't dare. And then Marijke took out a third bun, *but she held it straight up in the air over her head!* He saw the trunk appear above her and delicately pick the bun from her hand. Then she began to edge along the fence while giving another bun to Shy and Uhuru, followed by another above her head, taken just as delicately. Reaching the gate, she pushed it open, waved another bun in front of Uhuru, and threw it outside. Uhuru followed the bun. Marijke followed and grabbed the gate and pulled it closed; then, she fed Shy another half and turned to look at the matriarch. Marijke had one hand on Shy's head.

Ken heard her voice; he strained his ears to listen as she said, "There, Gogo, you can take your great-grandson; he's ready to join your herd. I'll keep this baby until she's big enough, but you can come and check she's okay every month. Here, have another bun and go before the sun rises."

Ken saw her throw a bun to Uhuru and then reach across the fence to give another to the matriarch before turning. She marched towards the shed, followed by Shy.

He realised Marijke had told the matriarch precisely what she said she would.

Ken and Lucas saw the matriarch herding Uhuru away as they left. Ken returned to bed. When Marijke came, he said, "Well, you've solved that one; I almost had a heart attack. But Shy may still have to go to a zoo in six months."

"If she does, I'll go with her; I promised Gogo I would look after her. Shy would be traumatised by a move, so I must go with her until she settles in."

"Marijke, what else can we do?" *She would probably take a job at the zoo and never return.*

"*Bwana*, we'll grow her food. I'm sure she'll love lettuce and cabbage."

"Then I'll do all I can to help." *I don't want Marijke to leave.*

Later, Marijke asked if they had wire netting at the workshop, and the workshop manager showed her several large rolls.

"What is this for?"

"Repairs to the roofs. The netting goes above the reeds to stop the birds pulling the reeds out to make nests."

Clever birds.

Then she went to see Dhakiya, the linen manager. "Do you have some spare mosquito nets?"

"Only one or two, but we have lots of old nets that have tiny holes; we use them to repair the nets in use."

"Then bring one of those to the bungalow this afternoon with needles and thread, *tafadhali.*"

She returned to the workshop, where she gave orders. "Please, gentlemen, I want a big birdcage, ten metres by four—just poles and rafters covered with netting. Put in a door and inside two small trees for the birds to perch on. I'll need it in three to four weeks. I'll tell you later where to build it after I have spoken to *Bwana*, but you can start collecting poles."

She didn't think about whether she had the authority to order it.

That afternoon, Ken found her on the veranda. "What are you doing, Marijke?"

"Making butterfly nets."

"Is that something to do with the birdcage?"

"I've told the villages I want birds' eggs from any insect-eating species. They'll bring them here for hatching. I'll send each village a roll of this old netting with a sample net. They can make the nets, and the kids can catch flies; a thousand cans and jars are in the shed, still waiting for recycling. They can put the flies in them."

"Only insect-eaters? Why?"

"For the moment. Later, we can have a full aviary at the lodge for the visitors."

"Explain please, Marijke."

"*Bwana*, I spent my first years on a wine estate. Did you spend yours on an estate or a farm?"

"No, my uncle had the family estate; he was the older brother. I was born in a mansion outside Paris with a huge garden but only flowers. Lots of roses, my mother's passion. When I was a kid, I wanted to become a gardener. Our gardener taught me a lot about flowers, but my father wanted me to study finance, and my mother backed him up by saying gardening had no future."

That's something new about him; he, too, had a life he didn't like.

"That explains why this lodge is missing something important. I don't know how to manage a game lodge or a tourist business, but the lodge is like a remote estate; it needs a farm and a community of married workers, where the women and children look after the farm and its animals. I was one of those children until I was sixteen. My mother ruled the house and my father the vineyards."

"Okay, I'll accept that; it seems like a great idea. But why the birds?"

"You said some time ago that there was no farm because the insects would eat everything. That village I visited uses bats to eat them at night, and we have lots of bats now."

"I follow, Marijke, birds in the day and bats at night." *Brilliant.*

"A lot more than that, *Bwana*. I need toads for the insects that lay eggs in the ground, the ones the birds don't reach; mongooses to save the toads from snakes; and jackals that hunt rodents at night."

She added, "*Bwana*, can I tell you what I want to achieve and why?" *I don't want to undermine his authority; it would be better if Bwana gave the orders for the farm.*

"I know, you want to feed Shy."

"No, *Bwana*, the villages have no pumped water, and Lucas said growing food needs a lot of people, which is why his community doesn't grow vegetables.

"Can you choose a piece of ground, I guess about a hectare, for the farm? Then dig an elephant and hippo trench around it?"

"My God! You don't think small."

"Because we must think of the villages around us. You do exactly that, *Bwana*, when you shoot an old lion or drag a carcass to the graveyard. I'm doing the same thing."

"What will you do in the hectare?"

"The villagers will build birdcages with concrete basins to grow plants in. The cages will be about twenty by five metres each. The villagers will surround the whole hectare with a heavy mesh fence and capture jackals, foxes and mongooses to patrol between the fence and the cages to eat the rodents and snakes."

"But why a hectare?"

"I'll recruit the villages; each can build beds to feed their people. The lodge will pay them for the vegetables we use, but we will use the money to pay for cement, mesh, ongoing maintenance and water pumps. The lodge will have healthy food, unpolluted by pesticides, for life. The villagers can sell to the other game lodges or villages if they grow more than they need.

"You can also tell the men who live here that you'll give them the materials, and they can extend their rooms or build houses for their family if, in exchange, their wives and children will help with the farm.

"Now, let's go and talk to them about this."

Ken and Marijke met with the workshop leaders, and Marijke explained to them what she wanted.

"I'll call all the *waganga* from the nearby villages to a meeting here. I ask you to help persuade the *waganga* that what I want is not foolish."

"Lucas, can you tell all the *waganga* within half a day's walk to come to a *mkutano*, a meeting, *tafadhali?*"

"I can, *Bibie*. When?"

"Will five days be enough time? I'll tell *Bwana*. Will you send runners?"

"No, *Bibie*, I'll tell one person from the nearest village; they will tell another, and then they will all know."

Marijke thought, *Facebook and Twitter are poor imitations of the bush telegraph; everything goes viral here.*

The *waganga* came; Ken thought that wasn't surprising as, like all committee meetings he had attended in France, it provided a platform for making speeches accompanied by free food. However, he admitted they could not ignore an invitation from the *mganga* with three *mizimu*.

He sat at the conference listening to the arguments. *It's what I expected: like all homeowners' council meetings, it will fail to come to a decision due to entrenched self-interest, and fizzle out.*

Later in the day, he thought, *Marijke's incredible; I saw her glance at the* mganga *from the mountains. He countered the argument that the birds would not fly at night and eat the pests when he told them about the bats they keep for that purpose.*

As the conference ended successfully, he thought, *Not just incredible, she's a great leader, she has nothing further to do, and the farm will grow into existence from her ideas.*

She described the role her mother had. Now Marijke's taken over that role here, and I'm delighted. She's getting closer to saying yes to my proposal.

"*Bwana*, they'll need sand and gravel, lots of it. Can you fix that truck and maybe buy a bucket loader? And order tons of cement?"

Ken had a warm feeling. *Now she's giving me orders like a wife.* "Yes," he said.

"Meanwhile, *Bwana*, if you're getting lots of sand and cement, I have another request."

"Okay, she may be small, but you'd be surprised how much damage a baby elephant can do."

Marijke asked, puzzled, "What's that got to do with anything?"

Ken explained, "You want to let Shy free in the lodge area?"

"Stop trying to second-guess me, *Bwana*; you'll never manage it."

"Okay." *She's probably right.* "What's your request?"

"I want a small separate building with a view of the river; we'll call it the Elephant Spa."

"Explain, *please*."

"A tiny reception area, with two armchairs for guests and a little desk with a chair, then a room with two wall showers, two massage tables, and a large mud bath like a jacuzzi; I'll add oils and perfumes and disinfectants to the mud and heat it from the same boiler as the shower water."

"Do you think the guests would like it and pay for massages?" Ken asked. *The elephant wallow must have given her this idea.*

"I do, the women will adore it, and their husbands will fall into line."

"How will you find the masseurs?"

"I'll ask the *waganga* for four young women to train."

"But you aren't a masseur, or do you have a hidden talent?"

"I'm confident that if I ask, the *waganga* will find a woman who is a masseur and will come and train them. The women will have a job for life or until they leave the lodge.

And they will marry rangers and have children, and the lodge will be a happy place.

"You build me the spa, *Bwana*, and I'll organise the rest."

She will, just by asking. "Do we have free massages and mud baths?"

She grinned. "Yes, but only if we do it together."

A delighted Ken grinned back. "I'll build that spa at once."

18

———

A month after Ken's request to the Cape Town detective, he received a complete report. It ended with "Reported missing on the twenty-second of February. The police have found no trace, and her file is in the no-action pile awaiting the discovery of a corpse."

Ken knew Marijke's father was dead, but he now realised her mother didn't know if Marijke was alive. *I must do something*, he thought.

He replied to the detective, "Please hint to the police that a taxi driver dropped her at the airport's international terminal the day before the missing person's report. The driver remembers because she had no baggage."

Ken would not learn for many months that shortly after his email, a young police inspector called to see Marijke's mother. Fortunately, her son, Petrus, was with his mother when she saw the policeman's uniform, for she almost fainted and would have fallen.

Once seated, the embarrassed young policeman said, "Mevrou Coetzee, it's good news; your daughter left the country by air on the twentieth of February.

"She went to Nairobi and then to Dar es Salaam. She bought the ticket two hours before departure and had no baggage. The Tanzanian police don't know where she is, but they have no report of her death, and I feel sure she will return one day. We have closed her file."

Ken was so impressed by the meeting with the *waganga* that he said to Marijke that evening, "I've been thinking about poaching. The park residents hunt for themselves, but some help the hunters from outside. I call them the 'sub-contract hunters'; they live in the park, kill for a fee, and give the meat to outsiders. If you can persuade the *waganga* to cooperate, maybe we can make things more difficult for the outsiders."

"*Bwana*, I'll talk to the *waganga*; maybe they can tell me more about the poachers."

After a discussion with the two nearest *waganga* in nearby villages, she asked, and Ken agreed to pay for a feast at a *waganga* conference in a bush clearing away from anyone else. They had no problem with secrecy; by the time the conference met, fifty *waganga* had told the population that they would call the *mizimu* together, so no one dared go anywhere near.

The discussion was intense, and with the help of her two trusted *mganga* colleagues, Marijke managed to expose her idea. After the arguments had completed a full circle, she picked her moment.

"No one has mentioned that the animals we eat have far more unnecessary males than females; I have meditated and thought about this and understand that predators will eat some, so the extra males are for that reason. Has anyone another reason?"

There was another discussion. The *waganga* agreed with Marijke when a *mganga* said, "Lions and leopards indeed prefer to hunt the males."

Marijke added, "I also feel that only the predators and people who live in this area must eat the animals. Others, who live elsewhere, must not have the same right. I thank the *mizimu* of the animals for their generosity when I eat their meat."

They all knew that she did so at the lodge dinners. As she had a cheetah *mzimu*, they accepted it at once. It was straightforward and acceptable: poaching did not include hunting for the village.

"So, we must not allow hunting for money, where others eat the meat. I have visited Dar; there are so many people there that they will eat all our animals, and our children will starve."

It was the final nail in the decision. *Poaching must stop.*

Then, after three hours of arguing about how to stop the poachers, Marijke summed up: "We agree that a group of us go from village to village. At each settlement, we will call on the *mizimu* to devour the *nafsi* of those who kill animals for money. Including those who don't kill but help the poachers."

She accepted the lodge would pay for whatever was necessary, starting with a hundred chickens to sacrifice and safari vehicles to carry the *waganga*.

It took ten days, even with the vehicles transporting the *waganga*, their paraphernalia and food. They loved it.

Ken attended several performances and thought, *If that didn't frighten the hell out of the villagers, nothing will.*

The performance at Lucas's village began with a song of praise to the animals, thanking them for the bounty they supplied. Then there were individual performances when a *mganga* danced and whirled, calling on the *mizimu*.

Marijke was impressive, wearing her most colourful dress, headdress, *jujus*, and the young python coiled around her neck, but she didn't speak; the *mganga* from Lucas's village did.

A young man with a drum held between his knees began a slow but accelerating rhythm before her turn to speak. Two other drummers joined in as the rhythm peaked and cut, leaving silence as *Bibi Mkubwa* raised an ox heart on a wooden platter above her head. Then in the ominous silence that followed, she cried, "This is the heart of a buffalo killed by the poachers. I call on the *mzimu* of buffalo, and all other slaughtered animals to rise from the depths and devour the *nafsi* of these demons who would kill animals for money and take food from our children's mouths."

The assembled *waganga* cried out the same in unison and stamped their feet.

Ken came to fetch her for lunch two weeks later and said, "Marijke, you've done it. The poaching has stopped."

"For a while, anyway, and only the contract poachers, not the outsiders."

"Probably longer than you think; two of the lodges say that a man warned them poachers were coming so they led the poachers into a pre-arranged trap."

"What happened to them?"

"I don't know, but one of the lodge managers told me they did what we do; if the poachers manage to avoid the predators, the experience is undoubtedly enough to discourage their return, but it might give us another problem."

"What, *Bwana*?"

"We go out on poaching patrol every month for eight days around the full moon; sometimes, we are lucky when we hear shots and reach them before they can butcher the animal and flee. Sometimes we have a warning of where they will be from a villager, usually a village where an outsider has recruited a contract poacher. We won't receive these tipoffs any more. So it's back to the patrols."

"Then we must think of another strategy."

A month later, Ken and Marijke, with two rangers and several of the guests, were sitting on the veranda; the moon was full, and a ranger had reported that the elephant herd was approaching. The light was sufficient for them to see the herd milling near the water; some were bathing, and several females clustered in a group.

Marijke remarked, "That's strange, *Bwana*; there's something wrong."

"I think so too." He asked one of the rangers, "Mwamba, I can't see as well as you at night; please fetch the night binoculars."

When Mwamba brought the binoculars to Ken, he said, "*Bwana*, it looks like they are standing around an elephant lying on the ground; it's not moving."

Marijke asked, "Is it sick?"

Ken, binoculars to his eyes, said, "Either that or old. Elephants do die, you know."

"Yes, like us all, but it's still sad."

Marijke took the binoculars and strode to the veranda edge, "They seem to be stroking the downed elephant with their trunks."

"Then it's dead or dying."

"There's also a baby there with them; it's tiny. Have a look, *Bwana*."

Ken looked for nearly two minutes. "It's small enough to be a newborn, poor thing. If its mother has died following childbirth, the baby will be dead in two days max."

Marijke turned to Amali and said, "Please, fetch buns in a shoulder bag and a pail of goat's milk quickly."

"Marijke, I forbid it; those elephants are upset and mourning; any interruption is unwelcome."

"I know, *Bwana*; I'm just getting ready for what will happen next."

"What?"

"Gogo will bring me the baby."

Ken found it unbelievable but then had second thoughts. *I'll bet she's right.*

"How long must we sit here, Marijke? She's not coming."

"After midnight, *Bwana*, when the wind changes."

Half an hour later, Marijke stood up and moved to the veranda edge again, where she felt the first stirrings of the morning breeze.

Amali approached her and handed her the bucket with the milk and the packet of buns. "The matriarch comes."

Ken had the binoculars; he whispered, "Gogo is having trouble with the baby; it wants to return to its mother. Wait."

No one on the veranda moved or made a sound. The crickets stopped chirruping.

As the view of the enormous elephant and the baby she steered in front of her with pushes from her trunk became clearer, Marijke took a bun, dipped it in the pail and waved it in the air. She repeated it three times, stepped off the veranda and paced forward thirty paces. The baby smelled the milk and rushed straight for her.

She fed it three milky buns before the massive bulk of the matriarch reached her, and she raised a bun high, and the enormous trunk took it delicately. Everyone heard Marijke say, "Gogo, I'll look after your great grandchild; you can have her back in two years." Then she handed up another bun, dipped another in the milk and walked back and around the side of the lodge towards the elephant pen with the baby following.

The matriarch returned to the herd, and Ken gave orders to the rangers: "No sleep for you guys tonight. Fetch the tractor and the lowbed. When the herd moves away, you will have a carcass to move before the lions invade us, and I want to know why she died."

The guests said nothing then, although they would talk about it after breakfast. They knew they had seen something extraordinary.

As Marijke slid into bed, she said, "Thanks, *Bwana*, for not getting mad."

"I said you could do whatever you wanted, Marijke, but elephants and cheetahs were not in my thoughts. You're taking enormous risks with wild animals; even if they seem tame, it's only a veneer; they can turn savage in seconds."

"*Bwana*, when I met you on the mountain, I thought you were a nutcase, and later after you brought me here, I decided you're an upside-down man."

"What do you mean, Marijke?"

"Well, you said it's hell here when it's heaven. The people and animals here consider themselves civilised, and the outsiders are the barbarians."

"Now you're talking like a nutcase."

"*Bwana*, two blind people meet by a wall. One says the wall is white; the other says it's black. Which one is right?"

"I don't follow your argument, Marijke."

"A dog bites a baby, and a cheetah walks by. Which one is wild?"

"A guy bumps into another in a bar and is shot or stabbed. Is that civilised?"

"Are you saying it's all viewpoint?"

"Exactly. The animals here aren't wild; they're normal; it's their world. You said it once when you said you didn't want electric fences. They think we are a bunch of savage barbarians, and I think they're right."

"But we don't eat each other."

"Very few of them do; they aren't cannibals—we were until recently. And our consumption of beef, chicken, lamb and pork far exceeds that of so-called wild animals, who only eat what they need.

"I think of elephants and cheetahs as lovely people; their senses are far more developed than our *primitive* abilities, so they sense my feelings, are curious, and don't intend any harm.

"*Bwana*, you would say that Andwele's Tommy has learned it's safe; I say that Andwele's Tommy senses it's safe. Shy and Mtoto sense the same thing."

"Who's Mtoto?"

"Our latest baby."

"Marijke, I must think about what you've said."

"Then think about the barbarians who come to Selous, shoot an elephant with two babies, take tiny tusks and leave a mountain of meat."

Ken didn't reply. *She has a good point there.*

"I'll try to be more ordinary, *Bwana*."

"Don't; the animals will miss you." *And so will everyone here and for miles, especially me.* "And I love you as you are."

Marijke didn't miss that comment. *He said it!*

19

———

Marijke received confirmation from the Mother Superior at the Catholic hospital that she was welcome. She also received a message from the clinic doctor at the airport to say she could come. Ken drove her early Monday to the nearby lodge for breakfast before the plane arrived. Marijke hadn't thought about meeting the lodge manager and his wife, but knowing how women can be far more critical of a stranger than a man, she hoped the manager's wife would be friendly. She needn't have worried; her name was Lindiwe, a Zulu woman from South Africa, keen to meet the *sangoma* from Rufisi Lodge.

Ken introduced Marijke to the lodge manager, a Scotsman with red hair, as Jock, and then to Lindiwe. At breakfast on the manager's veranda, Marijke asked, "Lindiwe, how did you meet Jock?"

"He saved me from drowning off a Durban beach, and when I recovered, he looked so nice I told him he now owned me, and he must take me with him."

Marijke laughed. "I bet that surprised him."

"If so, he didn't show it. He said, 'Let's fetch whatever you want to bring, and we'll go and see the captain.'"

"The captain of what?"

"I learned then he was the chief engineer on a ship and was going to Dar, where he had accepted this job. He took me with him."

That story sounds familiar.

"When I return from Dar, you must come and visit. I need help with my project to increase vaccinations."

Marijke followed the signs in the airport building to the airport clinic and spent the rest of the morning learning about vaccines and vaccination. The young doctor said that if she could come with a cold box just before departure, he would give her a stock of the government vaccines. Still, she would have to buy the tetanus ones at a pharmacy, but he did help by calling the pharmacy that supplied Rufisi Lodge and arranged delivery to the airport clinic to add to the cold box.

After checking in to the Blue Sapphire, she called for an appointment, had lunch, and then at three, took a taxi into the city; she had an address to go to. Marijke felt a little guilty, but when Ken had gone to another lodge for a meeting, she had removed a file from his unlocked filing cabinet and copied the name and address of the notary who sent the annual form for signature by the shareholders.

The office was old-fashioned with no glass doors, only a brass plate with two notary names. She knocked and entered.

The young woman behind the desk stood at once, and her eyes widened as she saw the *jujus* around Marijke's neck.

"Good afternoon; I've come to see Mr Barongo."

"Certainly, *Bibie*. Please come this way."

The office the secretary showed her into was small and neat, and Mr Barongo was younger than she had expected, but she didn't expect his reaction when she entered.

He leapt up and bowed. "*Bibie*, I thought you were a myth. Please sit down."

She did, then said, "I'm sorry to disappoint you. Where did you hear of me?"

"My grandmother is a *mganga*; she lives out in the country, in the village where I was born. I visited her last weekend, and she told us stories about the *mganga* with three *mizimu* who walks with elephants and cheetahs. I thought them too far-fetched to be true."

"Unfortunately, they are true, but within a year or two, I'll probably have the reputation of living on the moon.

"If you know so much about me, you will know I have come from Rufisi Lodge."

"I do."

"Well, I'm not here to ask about the lodge or its owners, but to tell you what help I need and why, and ask if you can do anything to help me."

"Please go ahead."

"First, I have the same problem that many *waganga* encounter because the water the villagers drink is unhealthy. I have many cases of dysentery, diarrhoea, and possible cholera.

"The lodge employees have clean drinking water as we have an expensive filtration plant, but the villagers don't. I have checked on filtration plants; they produce water at excessive purity levels and are costly to buy and operate, even the cheapest ones. However, when I was a little girl, my father drilled a small borehole to find clean water filtered through the earth for drinking. I want an expert to assess the possibility of having such boreholes fitted with pumps and solar panels at each village.

"The second is that there is no definitive list of the snakes, scorpions, spiders and other noxious inhabitants of the Rufisi area. I can only guess at a treatment without any knowledge of the source of the bite or sting. Therefore, I want a zoo of such pests so that people can visit, learn what bites or stings them, and when it happens, can tell me what bit them. Plus, the habitat and behaviour so the people can learn to avoid them. And finally, someone to research anti-venom I can use to treat their bites or stings.

"My reason for coming to you is that I hoped you might propose to the shareholders that they fund either one or both."

"Do you have what you said in writing?"

"I do; I emailed it to you before I took the taxi to come here."

"Excuse me for a moment ..."

"Yes, I have it. *Bibie*, I have several companies and associations in my books. One of them is a charity looking for projects in Tanzania. I'll send your requests to them because they are your best hope. The shareholders of Rufisi are unlikely to make an extra investment; the growth at Rufisi has come from revenue and the shareholders' levies. It has never declared a profit. Agreement from multiple shareholders for a capital injection is tough to achieve, and I cannot tell you who they are, for they dislike being disturbed. Leave it with me, and I'll do what I can. Then I can tell my grandmother I'm helping the *mganga* with three *mizimu*."

He didn't tell the whole truth, a common affliction in the legal profession. He sent Marijke's report to the shareholders, except Ken, and said he had suggested a charity might fund the projects.

The following morning Marijke went to the Cardinal Rugambwa Hospital and spoke to the receptionist, who then ushered her into the office of the Matron, an impressive Catholic nun.

"*Jambo*, are you the Mother Superior?"

"No, the hospital Matron. But you are a complete surprise."

"Why?"

"I was expecting a *mganga* from what you said in your emails, and I assume you are one from the *jujus* you wear. However, it's unusual that you are white."

"Unusual perhaps, but our sisterhood, like yours, is worldwide, and skin tones cover the entire range, although I haven't met a green-skinned member."

The Matron chuckled. "You are a Catholic?"

"My mother is Catholic, but my father raised me as a Protestant in South Africa; today, I don't know how you could describe me except as one who believes in a holy spirit."

"Then welcome to our hospital. You said you wanted to learn how to use a needle on cuts."

"A lot more than that. I want to know what sutures are available in the pharmacies here—the varied sizes, types, and threads, and for what injuries I can use each type. Then I want lessons on how to use them if it's possible.

"Sister, please understand, I'm not a doctor, but when injured people come to me, I must do my best for them, for they will die because the nearest hospital is hundreds of kilometres away. The injuries could be deep cuts, goring by horns or tusks, breaks where the bone exits the skin, and anything else that might need a stitch, especially hands and feet."

"Then I'll call the pharmacist to tell you what's available and bring samples, then our doctor who can tell you when to use them, and finally the sister who teaches the nurses; she has teaching materials—it will take all day."

"I expected that. I can stay until late this evening. I have a room at the Blue Sapphire."

After learning what Marijke wanted, the pharmacist asked, "*Bibie*, how many of each suture do you want? I'll bring two of each. Sealed and sterile, they will last a long time. There are some we don't use often; I can give you a lot more. I can make up a list of the quantities you should buy."

"Do you throw them away after use?"

"No, we throw away the remaining thread, then sterilise them. The vets collect them, buy the thread on a reel, and use them for animals."

"Can you email this pharmacy and place an order? They are delivering a box of vaccines to me tomorrow."

"With pleasure, *Bibie*."

"Then ask for reels of thread. Half my patients are animals."

Marijke wrote down what the doctor told her; beside each suture sample name, she wrote what he recommended, and before she could ask about anaesthetics, he said, "You will need a good stock of anaesthetics and some wide-range antibiotics. Lignocaine and pentothal are your best bets. The sister can show you how to use them. Pass me your list; I'll put an L or P next to each needle. You'll judge the needed time, which determines the anaesthetic dose. The pentothal has a data sheet showing the amount required for a patient mass and the time knocked out. Never exceed forty minutes.

"I'll give you a prescription for the antibiotics; read the data sheets. I'll also add several litres of an excellent antiseptic; if you must use it in open wounds, which seems likely in the bush, carry a bottle diluted fifty-fifty with sterile water and use it liberally. I'll add the sterile water too. Are you flying back?"

"Yes."

"Tell the pharmacy, and they will pack them in ice for you."

"Can you mail it to my pharmacy? They will add it to my order that they are delivering tomorrow morning to the airport."

"I shall. Here's Sister Mathilda; she's our training expert."

Sister Mathilda gave her lessons using synthetic flesh to sew up, showed her how to reattach muscles, and to reconnect the ends of severed blood vessels with microscopic stitches. Then she said, "That's it, except for a lot of practising. I'll find two other nurses you can practise with until you return to your hotel. Come back anytime if you want to check how you're doing, but I'm sure you'll be excellent."

Sister Mathilda returned several minutes later. "Marijke, Mother Superior would like to see you. You can come back after seeing her; to practise."

Mathilda knocked on a door, and when a woman's voice called to come in, Mathilda gestured for Marijke to enter and whispered, "Sister Imani is a little deaf," then closed the door.

Marijke saw a woman she guessed to be seventy with a smiling round face and a calm expression. Then she saw her eyes.

"Marie-Jeanne, please come in and sit down; it's a pleasure to welcome a *mganga*."

"Thank you, Reverend Mother, and it's a pleasure for me to meet one."

Sister Imani's eyes seemed to twinkle. "You have just confirmed what I have heard about you. And I'm not deaf. One of the few advantages of age is the right to ignore things that are said because you are a little deaf."

Marijke laughed. "But you've told me."

"Only because you are a *mganga*. A real one. Not one of the charlatans you can find in the cities."

She continued, "Initially, I trained to be a *mganga*. We might be much alike. I wanted to learn much more than herbal medicines, so I attended a mission school when I was thirteen and then studied to be a nurse, first at a country clinic and then Dar General Hospital. I became the Senior Sister in the surgery wing before taking my vows and coming here.

"Please confirm you were sixteen when you left your *mganga* teacher."

"I was, Reverend Mother. Then I took the wrong path."

"And now you're back on the right one?"

"I think so. I still have much to learn."

"From what I've gathered, you are learning fast. I asked you to come for a reason, if you don't mind me offering advice."

"Not at all. I welcome it."

"What you have learned today could put you personally at risk. A situation that has evolved since I was your age. Sister Mathilda says you will be an excellent surgeon, but an operation without a doctor's qualification carries the risk of an accusation if something goes wrong."

Marijke almost snapped her reply, "So I should not intervene, and let a person die?"

"No, I know you cannot do that. Like me, you have a calling and cannot resist it. I would like to help. The most I can do is to give you a certificate as a Senior Emergency Nurse from this hospital. It will help in all but the worst cases.

"But I also have a piece of advice, one that was given to me when I studied nursing. Never intervene in a serious case without a *mganga* or a doctor present, if possible. Then in front of a witness, ask if the *mganga* or doctor wants you to do the intervention."

"I understand, Reverend Mother. I didn't realise I should do so. Can you explain why?"

"Marie-Jeanne. I won't say you are white. It doesn't matter to me, for you are a *mganga* and a sister, but you are a foreigner in Tanzania. The courts are much less likely to uphold a challenge to a local *mganga* than a foreigner. In the worst case, you might face deportation."

"I can believe that, and I thank you sincerely for the certificate. That will reassure me. But how do you know I deserve it?"

Her reply was cryptic. "There are Christians everywhere, and information has been our church's lifeblood for two thousand years."

Marijke returned to the hotel later than she thought; after other nurses came and helped her practise. One of the nurses said, "I always thought women would be better than men at sewing up a cut; you are as good as any of the doctors here." By nine o'clock that night, she had sewn together four severed artificial arteries.

On the Lodge Air flight back to Rufisi after breakfast, with her box of medicines and the ice box of vaccines and antibiotics in the luggage box under the aeroplane, Marijke had an hour to think. She thought of what the Mother Superior had said.

It took twenty minutes to reach the first conclusion. *I don't have to think about what I want to do; I want to be a* mganga *or a* sangoma *and treat sick or injured people.*

The next one was more difficult; she only decided when the plane descended to the airstrip. *I want to stay here, but if it leads to deportation, I must leave Ken behind. I shall have someone make me an old-fashioned nightie; I must stop teasing him until I decide to risk it or go.*

20

———

After arriving at the lodge, Marijke found Dhakiya, the woman who looked after the linen. She asked, "Do you have any old bed sheets?"

"Yes, *Bibie*, we do," Dhakiya said, pointing out a stack of sheets.

Then Marijke explained what she wanted. They looked through the sheets, chose two, and sent them for laundering.

Two days later, Marijke visited a woman in the nearest village who made clothes for the kids and asked her to make two nighties from the sheets, simple ones without sleeves. After some measurements, Marijke was about to leave when she thought, *Would the little girls like new dresses if I dye that stock of old sheets to a nice colour?*

The seamstress was enthusiastic and said she would ask the mothers and tell Dhakiya what colour the cloth should be.

On her return to the lodge, Marijke told Dhakiya what she had decided and then told Ken.

"*Bwana*, we have a stock of sheets with holes, probably from cockroaches, and they will rot if we do nothing with them. I've told Dhakiya to check all the double sheets and, if possible, cut them to make singles, then have everything left dyed a suitable colour, and the villagers can turn them into dresses for the little girls."

"What colour?"

"I don't know yet; the village women will decide."

Three days later, Marijke collected the nighties, hung them in the bedroom cupboard with all her coloured dresses, and thought, *I'm not sure I can wear them; Ken will be shocked.*

A month later, Marijke had already sewn up four severe cuts using lignocaine as an anaesthetic injected around the cut, a bite from a genet that also clawed the man's leg, and a broken arm where the bone broke through the skin; for that, she had to use pentothal as an anaesthetic.

When she thought about why she suddenly had more severe wounds to treat, she concluded, *Once they know I can treat them, they come here and don't try to reach a hospital.*

She was unsure of her skill using a needle and thread, but using the old ones, she had sewn up over a hundred cuts inflicted on carcasses and over a dozen severed arteries and veins. Her two assistants had practised with her, building confidence with each exercise.

The latest visitor to the lodge impressed Marijke. He was tall and had silver-white hair and piercing blue eyes. Dr Kurt Gruber's military bearing made Marijke think he was a retired German Army officer. Marijke thought Kurt's wife, Helga, dressed smartly, *chic*, even in the African bush. She didn't know the couple were there in response to Ken's letter to the German Embassy, requesting a student doctor to provide medical treatment to the people.

On the fifth day of the Grubers' visit, Marijke sat with them at dinner. They hadn't finished their excited descriptions of their day's game sightings when Lucas came to the table. He spoke in Swahili: "*Bibie*, a warthog has gored and badly hurt a young man; the *mganga* says he bleeds red blood. Can you come?"

"Of course, Lucas. Put the medicine boxes in the Land Rover."

She turned to the visitors and said, "I'm sorry, I must leave you; a warthog has gored a young man, and he has a severed artery. I must go quickly."

As she pushed her chair back, Dr Gruber asked, "Ma'am, if you don't mind an observer, I would like to come. I've never seen such an injury."

"You're welcome, but it will be bloody and messy."

"I can stand it."

"Then come."

After a bumpy but fast drive to the village, the vehicle pulled up in front of the *mganga's* hut. Outside, a young woman stood naked while village women poured water over her head and body, washing away a soapy foam. Inside the cabin, the boy lay on a leather hide; at his head, the *mganga* was crooning hypnotic incantations; his upper left leg was a gaping wound with the white bone visible. A tourniquet made from a twisted hide strip was tight around his upper thigh.

Dr Gruber couldn't understand what Marijke asked, but after a reply, she bent down and eased the tourniquet; bright red blood began to fill the wound, so she tightened it again. He thought it was hopeless; what was needed was a three-hour operation in a fully equipped operating theatre with two surgeons and a large staff.

Lucas came in and set up two powerful battery-powered lights on stands, lighting up the wound; the young woman from the outside appeared wearing a surgical gown and mask, followed by a boy carrying two carved wooden boxes he opened.

The young woman took a bottle of disinfectant from a box, washed her hands with it, donned gloves from a sterile packet, took out surgical masks for her and Marijke and fitted them to their faces, and then put a surgical gown over Marijke's head. Marijke held out her hands, and the young assistant poured disinfectant on them before she gave her gloves.

Dr Gruber approved but still didn't expect what came next. He recognised the label on the bottle of liquid that Marijke took from a sealed packet and was shocked when she poured half of it into the wound. She said something to her assistant, who pulled out a small bottle of what he recognised as pentothal, loaded a sterile syringe with two millilitres, wiped the boy's arm with alcohol and did the injection. Two minutes later, after a murmured request, the assistant put a scalpel in Marijke's hand; she delved into the wound to free up the two ends of the severed artery. Five minutes later, the assistant handed over a curved needle with thread hanging from it, and Marijke began to sew the two ends of the blood vessel together.

She was fast; he had never seen anyone do it as fast, but it took ten minutes for the closely spaced delicate stitches. Then Marijke released the tourniquet. The artery held; he could see it pulsing as he thought, *Now the pentothal will wear off.* After a brief pause, Marijke asked for a different needle and thread and another massive dose of antiseptic, mainly wiped away using cotton swabs so she could see, and she packed the muscles into place one by one with quick knots to hold them around the bone. Every time she did so, the young woman leaned over with a giant pepper pot—Kurt Gruber had no other word for it—and sprinkled the wound liberally with a brown powder. Finally, as Marijke came to the closure, she used what looked like two metal claw hair clips to hold the sides of the wound together while she sewed it up with another liberal dose of brown powder and then a bandage. That was when he realised the boy was still unconscious. *Why hasn't the pentothal worn off?*

Marijke asked the *mganga*, "When did this boy have a tetanus vaccination?"

"Last week."

"Then we shall give him an antibiotic." She spoke to the assistant, who loaded a syringe and injected it into the opposite leg.

Marijke told the *mganga*, "We are done; we must ask the *mzimu* to help him recover." The *mganga* chanted a phrase several times to the boy, and then he began to wake.

"I'll leave him to your care. He must not stand or walk for a month."

As they left the hut, the villagers appeared with bowls of warm water and clean towels for Marijke to wash her hands and arms. Lucas removed the lights, and the assistant packed the medicines in the boxes for others to return to the vehicle. The efficiency impressed Dr Gruber.

As they drove back, Dr Gruber said, "That was a revelation. No doctor in Europe would have done what you did. You are the best emergency medical surgeon I have ever seen operating, and I've seen many on the battlefields. Your team, too, is excellent."

"Thank you, I had no choice; if I had told them to take him to a hospital, he would have died before arrival. That's what it's like out here; we must do the best we can, whether it's for animals or people."

"And who pays?"

"The lodge buys my medicines and medical supplies. The people don't have to pay, but they often give me a gift; I have eight goats and two pigs in my farmyard, and the lodge must have over a hundred chickens. They will not allow me to pay for anything when I visit, and I receive presents like necklaces and dresses.

"Compared to big cities, we are a small community where survival depends on everyone helping each other. I try to do my bit."

"I didn't follow the anaesthetic procedure. When we arrived, what was the village herbalist doing?"

"She gave him a mix of plant extracts. It's part soporific, part relaxant, and a little hallucinogenic; it makes hypnotism easy. As it takes effect, she can hypnotise the patient and convince him to ignore any pain."

"But you used pentothal?"

"I had to be sure he wouldn't move while I sewed up the artery; the shot I gave him was for twenty minutes."

"And what did you dust the wound with as you closed it up?"

"That's a different plant mix; dried leaves ground fine. The powder prevents infection from developing and lasts a lot longer than an antiseptic; it's part antiseptic, part desiccant and part a natural antibiotic, like penicillin fungus."

"But you used half a litre of the antiseptic biocide?"

"A warthog tusk caused that injury; tusks carrying billions of bacteria. I doubt doctors in Germany have warthog attacks to treat. There wasn't time to do much else but pour in enough to kill as many bacteria as possible. The powder should do the rest, and the antibiotic I injected should kill off those that entered the bloodstream. The antiseptic is a fifty-fifty mix with sterile water."

"I understand; I shall remember that the circumstances merit the treatment.

"Can you give me a sample of each of those plant extracts? I want to analyse them and will report the results to you."

"Of course, it will be interesting to know, but they are free medicines that work, so I use them."

"I would have given him a tetanus shot. Do you have that in your kit?"

"Yes, of course, but I asked the *mganga* when he had his last booster shot, and she said she had given him one last week."

"Amazing; what's the vaccination percentage here and in the surrounding areas?"

"At the lodge and the nearby villages, a hundred per cent. Then it gets worse as you go further away, it's the transport and distribution problem. I have encouraged the other lodges, and they call me when they have people to vaccinate. It will never be a hundred per cent because there are always people moving between the city and the country."

"All the vaccinations?"

"All the pharmacies can supply cholera, typhoid, yellow fever and tetanus vaccines. All the children receive the classic multiple vaccines—hepatitis B, diphtheria, tetanus, pertussis, measles, mumps, rubella, varicella, and polio. The government supplies them at the government clinics, but many people don't visit them. I fetch the vaccines from there, so I do them, or one of the *waganga* I have trained does so."

"Amazing." *She's one hell of a doctor!*

"Do you keep records?"

"Not those like you keep in Germany. Most older people, like the *waganga*, can't read or write; they rely on their memories. With reasonable accuracy, the *mganga* can remember and tell me every vaccination she did in the last few years."

"*Mein Gott!* I have learned much tonight."

21

The next evening Dr Gruber sat in the lounge and looked at the vaccination figures published by the WHO, the World Health Organization, on the web. His wife had gone on a game drive with Marijke and others.

When he and Helga had dinner after their return, he asked Marijke, "Doctor, how have you achieved such high vaccination rates when the WHO statistics show low figures for all African countries?"

"Dr Gruber, please call me Marijke; I'll not deny your assessment of me last night, but outside of this reserve, I would be a poor doctor as I have no experience of the common illnesses in towns. I have no medical degree.

"I can tell you what I believe to be the reasons for the high vaccination rate. You would have to live here to appreciate the power and status of a *mganga*, you met one last night, and I'm one as well. We prescribe herbal medicines, but I have expanded my skills. I can do vaccinations as a *mganga*, but I teach the others. Over thousands of years, the *waganga* have cooperated to build a leadership position in their communities; without including them, nothing is achievable. It enhances their status if they do vaccinations. Sending a stranger to vaccinate the people meets resistance as it threatens the *mganga's* status."

"I can understand that. Even in Europe, status is important in the medical fraternity. Is that all?"

"No; when I arrived, I learned of the belief that vaccinations make women and men sterile, something probably dreamed up years ago by the *waganga* to protect their position in the community. I had to reverse it."

"An almost impossible task; changing long-established beliefs takes years," Dr Gruber said.

"I know, but this belief was created only recently, in the last fifty years, when vaccination began to spread out of what you call the civilised world."

"A label you disagree with?"

"Yes, for we who live in this park, ours is the civilised world; you are the barbarians."

Dr Gruber laughed. "Marijke, you are challenging one of the most popular and well-established beliefs of a large part of the world. But I salute you for doing so."

"Thank you, sir; now I shall ask you, how would you challenge the belief that vaccinations cause sterility."

Apart from a few words, Marijke didn't understand the discussion and argument in German that ensued between Dr Gruber and Helga; it continued for several minutes.

"Marijke, we cannot agree on a solution other than some form of education. How did you do it?"

"I used a much older belief that came into existence thousands of years ago to fight the new one and let the *waganga* spread the new idea to support their participation and enhanced status that vaccinations brought. I told you I keep no records; it would not have worked if I had asked them to do so; however, it's unnecessary.

"The people have believed for millennia in a pantheon of spirits influencing their lives and events: some bad, some good, and some personal. I'm a woman with three spirits: a cheetah, a dolphin, and a bird.

"I had only to state that the vaccination holds a small bit of a good spirit that would live in the body and fight any evil spirit that tried to make the person sick, then wait for the belief to spread. I'll admit I can believe this myself because I'm not a pharmaceutical chemist."

"How do you explain a reaction to the vaccination?"

"The evil spirit was already present in the person's body when vaccinated, and the fight for supremacy made him feel ill. He must be glad the vaccination occurred before the evil spirit took over."

Dr Gruber thought carefully about what she had said. "You said the problem with improving the vaccination rate was logistical?"

"Yes; given an easily accessible vaccine store, without red tape, constantly renewed, the *waganga* will vaccinate everyone. Each store needs only one person who knows the different vaccines and can speak the languages of the local areas, possibly a *mganga*."

Helga intervened, "Kurt, I'm beginning to understand. The *waganga* are what we in Germany consider, often disparagingly but with respect and affection, as country doctors. If you think of the *waganga* as doctors, although qualified in a different community, and that they have the same status and ability, then it becomes easier to accept what Marijke is saying.

"They are the doctors who know the name of every person in the community and only the health problems of that community.

"Marijke, it might take Kurt some time to sort out what you have said in his mind, but I believe it already. I'll make sure he does too."

"Thank you, Helga." *It's not often that we have visitors who can understand.*

In bed that night, Helga said, "Kurt, Marijke has incredible courage."

"Why do you say that?"

"Was there a chance the boy would die?"

"Yes, that exists for every operation, sometimes for an unexpected reason. But, in the boy's case, I thought the best that could happen would be an amputation if gangrene didn't develop before he reached a hospital; his leg would have had no blood flow for hours."

"And what would happen if someone blamed her and complained to the authorities?"

Kurt had to think about the question. "In Europe, she would go to prison for practising as a doctor. Here, I don't know; prison maybe, then deportation."

"Does she know that?"

"I'm sure she does but will continue, because she can't stand by and not try to help a patient. She told me, 'I had no choice; we must do the best we can for people and animals.'"

"Is there anything you can do to help her? Like, make her an intern from Heidelberg University?"

"I don't know. I'll see. I shall recommend that the WHO appoint her as their vaccine representative and order analysis of those plant mixtures."

"And what about the letter from Ken?"

"I'll tell the university there's already a doctor here."

A different scene played out in the bungalow while Kurt talked to Helga.

Ken was already in bed when Marijke came from the bathroom wearing one of her new nighties.

"Marijke, why are you wearing a nightie and not a *kikkoy* for the first time?"

"*Bwana*, yesterday I operated on a young boy; a warthog had gored his leg. He had a severed artery and would have died if I had told them to send him to a hospital. Although Dr Gruber said I'm a great emergency surgeon, I know what I did would put me in jail in Europe, especially if anything goes wrong. The Mother Superior at the hospital warned me of this. I don't know what will happen; perhaps I'll have to leave Tanzania, so I feel I should put some distance between us."

Ken felt a terrible tension in his chest as he blurted a reply: "Marijke, no one will ever complain. Did anyone want to send the boy to a hospital?"

"I asked the *mganga*; she said the boy's mother wanted me to operate, and the *mganga* did the hypnotic anaesthetic."

Ken felt relief. "You see, you weren't alone; they'll stand up for you if there's an investigation."

"I know, but the leg might develop an infection, and if the boy dies, sentiment can turn against me rapidly. *Bwana*, I can't sit back and do nothing in an emergency, but don't think I like living with the fear of reprisal."

"Okay, Marijke, but we must think about what we can do to eliminate it.

"For starters, I'll have that certificate from the Cardinal Rugambwa Hospital framed and fix it to the wall of our veranda."

Ken slept poorly that night, as did Marijke; she thought it was because she wasn't used to wearing a nightie.

Once Marijke had agreed on the site and the plan, Ken built the spa. Unsurprisingly fast.

"Marijke, I've finished your spa. Do you want me to fill the mud bath?"

"Yes, with the finest clay the men can collect, twenty centimetres from the top so that I can add water and oil. I'll come and see it the day after tomorrow; I must ask the women to come."

Marijke came to see the finished building. Ken saw her approaching with four women who looked to be about eighteen. With them was a woman of about thirty.

Marijke introduced them: "*Bwana*, this is Adimu, the aunt of Busara, the first of the trainees, and she works as a physiotherapist in Dar. They are both from Lucas's village. The other three are Fadhila, Kanoni and Neema.

"One of the rangers has volunteered to be their first client, and the others will follow. Adimu expects to be here for a week. I've put them all in the spare cottage next door. They'll live with my assistants when their training ends and Adimu leaves."

Ken welcomed them and left with Marijke.

"When do you put the oils and perfumes in the mud?"

"I'm going this afternoon after the first massage lessons."

"Can I come?"

"No, we'll all be naked or near naked; we must be in the bath to mix up the mud until it's right."

Ken heard from the rangers, who had been willing patients, that the massage and mud bath were fantastic. When the week ended, Marijke said to him. "Tomorrow, *Bwana*, we're going to the spa; it's our turn and their final exam."

When the two masseuses left the room and closed the door, Marijke said, "Right, *Bwana*, into the mud."

As they both slithered in naked, Ken said, "Marijke, that massage was fabulous, and this is certainly relaxing."

"Roll around, *Bwana*, like an elephant; feel the mud sliding over your skin, and rub it all over you." She showed him how, then sank below the surface and came up with her head covered in mud. "Now, your turn." She grabbed him and ducked his head below the surface.

He came up, holding her in his arms. *I would kiss her if she didn't have a face covered in mud.*

She thought, *It's the first time Ken's held me naked in his arms. It feels nice but slippery.*

"Okay, *Bwana*, showers."

"Is that all?"

"For now, yes. You must decide how much the clients will pay for this experience."

Although Ken raised the spa price four times in the next two months, it remained fully booked. He was about to increase it further when Marijke said, "*Bwana*, don't increase the price; separate the mud bath from the massage room, and we can double the turnover. And add a second mud bath; then, we can change the mud without shutting the spa."

"Okay, Marijke." *She now says "we" all the time. Can I ask her to marry me again?*

22

———

"*S*et *fire to Rufisi Lodge, and kill anyone you can, particularly the lodge manager and his wife.*" That's what the assassin's client had said. As he sat in the pickup on the way to Nyerere National Park, the man remembered the meeting clearly. The leader of the bushmeat trade had called him in and, after telling him who the mark was, had added, "I'll supply flares and an AK-47."

The assassin had set a high price for the job, and it satisfied him, thinking it would finally allow him to retire.

The pickup dropped him at the roadside five kilometres from the park entrance, then turned and drove off as he melted into the bush. He planned to camp five kilometres from the lodge at sunset, so he had eight hours to walk twenty kilometres. Something he thought would be a gentle stroll.

It was the first time he had left the city, and he found the going hard; thorns tore at his clothes, his feet sank into holes, and the AK seemed heavier as each hour passed. He saw no animals and was surprised at the silence.

He didn't know that the crickets stopped chirruping for several hundred metres around him, only starting again long after he passed. He hiked in a pool of silence, and as he advanced, the silence followed him. The animals heard the silence and moved away. The movement, once begun, didn't stop; perhaps they moved slower, but they moved, and their expansion sucked in others until, like the ripples in a pool when a stone drops in, the movement spread for kilometres. Then, like ripples rebounding from the poolside, the predators began to move towards him, the hyenas in the lead.

It took him ten hours to reach his planned camp, where he lit a small fire, unwrapped a steak, and grilled it on a stick over the flames. He didn't know that every predator downwind for kilometres would smell the odour of the meat and could pinpoint his position. He had chosen the date because a narrow crescent moon would rise two hours before first light, giving him enough time to cover the five kilometres to the lodge; he would be there on the edge of the lodge area as soon as it was light enough to plan the next steps.

He unrolled a plastic sheet for sleeping in and lay down. The pool of silence shrunk, and the two hyenas a kilometre away slunk closer, as did three cats and two jackals. However, the man had no experience with being assailed by mosquitos and gnats that came in swarms, nor of the hundreds of ants and insects that came to investigate, crawling up his legs or arms from the ground.

Sleep was impossible, so he stood, and the pool of silence grew; the hyena stopped moving but didn't retreat. Patience was their chief asset.

He laid down again after wrapping the cloth around him, carefully arranging his plastic sheet and stoking up the fire. The pool of silence shrunk; the hyenas, cats and jackals moved closer. The jackals knew the hyenas were there; they would stay back but close enough to dash in and bite a chunk from any available prey.

He had no choice but to wait for the moon. Sleepless, he held the AK over his knees until the light from the rising moon made it possible to move. He could see no further than the light of the flames, and his fear began to grow; the assassin huddled over the fire when he heard the hyena howl or the sharp jackal bark from another direction.

It took him longer than he had thought to reach the lodge, and the light was brighter when he arrived. He could hear the first stirring in the lodge area, the sound of a shower, and the chopping of wood for the kitchen stove. Someone might see any move into the open to set fire to a reed roof. He decided to wait, try to shoot his target, and set fire to the lodge's reeds in the ensuing panic.

He didn't know how close the hyenas were, only five metres away behind a bush, waiting patiently for an opportunity. He didn't see the cat, even closer, in a different direction, and the jackals hiding in a third direction—waiting. He concentrated on his target, the AK held in front of him.

In the bungalow, Marijke shook Ken twice. He mumbled, "What is it, my darling?"

She didn't react to the endearment. "*Bwana*, there's danger. Something's wrong."

He came awake instantly, swung his legs out of bed, and whispered, "Don't switch on a light." He pulled on a pair of shorts and picked up his rifle at the door. Marijke didn't bother with underwear; she slipped yesterday's dress over her nightie and closely followed him as he moved through the lounge and eased the door to the veranda.

The assassin saw the door ease open and raised the AK. He was aiming. He almost pulled the trigger but saw a second shadow behind the first, so he waited. He would shoot both.

Three things happened almost simultaneously. Marijke shoved Ken forward and fell on him. The assassin heard the hyena cackle and then a growl as the cheetah's jaw closed on his leg, tearing half his thigh away. His finger closed on the trigger in a reaction, and the AK fired three times before it fell to the ground. He died when a hyena tore his face off in a single bite.

Ken heard the bullets fly overhead, only a metre above, so he rolled over to protect Marijke and asked, "Darling, are you okay?"

"Yes."

Lucas whispered from the bungalow, "*Bwana*, crawl inside."

They did, and Lucas said, "I think the hyenas are eating him; they're having a scrap with jackals. But stay here until everyone is up; there may be more."

Forty minutes later, a tracker told them the story. "The man came early; he was alone, I followed his trail, and there were no other tracks for a kilometre. I shall go much further to check. He was a city man; otherwise, he would have known both the hyenas and the *duma* were close. He was a man of the night; the sun had never shone on his skin.

"He stood at this place and waited. Then a *duma* attacked, so the hyena did too. You can see the *duma*'s track with the hyena's track over it. He died because the hyena took his face. The jackals came, and they and the hyena carried away parts of the body.

"This is his bag."

Ken looked inside it. "Nothing but a bunch of flares; he must have intended to set fire to the lodge and shoot anyone that moved."

"Not anyone, *Bwana*," Lucas said. "I think you and *Bibie* were the intended targets."

"Possibly. Wipe the flares, the AK, and the knife with an oily rag, then put them in the gun store. I shall photograph this, then we must bury the rest of the body somewhere so animals can't dig it up and no one can find it. We are not responsible if a man wants to walk in the park and a hyena eats him. Forget him."

"Marijke, let's have breakfast."

"*Bwana*, where did the man come from and why?"

"I think one of the bushmeat chiefs hired him, one of the dregs of Dar. He had zero bush experience; the hyenas would have tracked him for kilometres. I don't know why the cheetah came, but I suspect you do. But tell me why you pushed me. It might have saved us both."

"Because the cheetah told me to."

"You can't mean that."

"I do; I have no other explanation. Have you ever thought someone was behind you? Looking at you?"

"Yes, several times; it's uncanny."

"I woke feeling someone was watching us, and as we stepped out on the veranda, I felt it so strongly I reacted and pushed you down. Just like when you spin around suddenly and then find no one there."

"Well, I'm glad you did. But why did you say the cheetah told you to?"

"When I gave the cubs to the mother cheetah, she could only carry one, so she left one with me. Before entering the bush, she turned and looked at me, and then I was sure she was saying, 'Look after the other until I return.' So, I did, and she came back. It was a similar feeling.

"*Bwana*, I don't have second sight, but I know the *duma* are my friends. If they thought that man was dangerous, it wouldn't surprise me. But something else does."

"What, Marijke?"

"Oh, bugger, you've gone backwards."

A bewildered Ken asked, "What do you mean backwards?"

"When I woke you, you asked, 'What is it, my darling?'"

"I must have been dreaming about my dog; Gracie was a lovely spaniel."

Marijke grinned at him, "You weren't dreaming after the bullets flew over us, and you asked, 'Darling, are you okay?' It's in times of stress that the truth comes out."

Ken surrendered: "Alright, my darling, you win; that's how I feel. Do you want me to use 'darling' all the time?"

"No, just in times of stress. Is an attack like this unusual, and if so, what brought it on?"

"I guess because you and the *waganga* have stopped the sub-contract hunting. I never considered it, but city people are behind the bushmeat business. Like the assassin, they know nothing about the bush. Compared to the cost of hiring a local sub-contractor, city thugs must be expensive to hire and far less efficient. Stopping the local sub-contractors has made the bushmeat business far more costly, so you've made a dent in their profits."

"So, they are likely to try again?"

"I think so, but they will re-organise and send in hunters from the city. Untrained and inexperienced, they'll spray anything that moves with an AK."

"So what action are we going to take?"

"Well, to begin with, I'll order the water sprays for all the reed roofs. I should have done it long ago; I did intend to, but the reeds were green and not a fire hazard. I'll talk to the workshop crew. Do you have a suggestion, Marijke?"

"Geese. They are the best watchdogs around. They would have heard or sensed the hyena and jackals and made a terrible din."

"Where do we put them so nothing can eat them?"

"In with the chickens or the goats."

"I'll find out where to buy some."

"Then, *Bwana*, let's meet with the rangers for some ideas. I have one."

23

____

The email, addressed to the lodge for the attention of Doctor Marijke Coetzee, was a mystery.

Dear Dr Coetzee

At the request of the WHO, I shall be visiting Tanzania with two security agents to assess our vaccination programme. Can you please reply to the above email address when accommodation at Rufisi for two or three days is available?

Regards
Dr Elisabeth Calmette-Poussin

"*Bwana*, who is Elisabeth Calmette-Poussin? Is she a relation of the Louis de La Vallee Poussin, who dedicated a book to you?" Marijke explained that she'd seen the inscription in the book *Les Animaux de Selous.*

"I don't know. Look up 'Elisabeth Calmette'."

"I'll look her up on the WHO site."

"God, the internet is slow today. Okay, Elisabeth is four years older than me and has a degree as a doctor and a master's in medical management from Brussels. She joined the WHO, implemented small clinics in Rwanda, and became a consultant to the WHO for

169

hospital management. Her father is Gaston Calmette, an epidemiologist and WHO consultant; her mother, Rosemary, is a doctor."

"Marijke, that's strange; why is she coming here to assess vaccination?"

"I don't know, nor do I know why she needs two security agents. We'll ask when she gets here. Send her two or three dates. She'll need a cottage and another with two beds for the security agents. The agents' cottage should be as close to hers as possible."

The white helicopter with the WHO logo was the first chopper Marijke had seen land in front of the lodge. After the three passengers moved from under the whirling blades, it rose and flew off, leaving their baggage on the grass. Marijke, Ken and Lucas came forward to meet them.

Marijke welcomed them: "Good morning, I'm Marijke; welcome to Rufisi." *Elisabeth is beautiful*, Marijke thought.

Elisabeth wore Arab clothes and a headcloth, and Marijke and Ken thought she must be Muslim.

Elisabeth took Marijke's hand as she replied, "I'm Lisa, and I've been looking forward to meeting you." She turned to Ken. "You must be Ken Phillips."

They shook hands as he said, "I am, and I'll add my welcome to Marijke's."

"Let me introduce my guards to you; they both speak Swahili."

Once Ken and Marijke had shaken hands with Ahmed and Muammar, Ken introduced Lucas as the assistant manager, then added, "Please come to the lodge veranda."

When they were all seated, Marijke noted: *Muammar is sitting in the corner.*

They ordered drinks, and Marijke asked, "I looked up your profile on the WHO site; why is a consultant in hospital management doing a vaccination check?"

"My father would normally have come, but he's had dengue fever; he caught it in Chad, and my mother won't let him go anywhere until she thinks he's fully recovered, so she called me and asked if I could do it."

"That makes sense, but I have something to confess; your email labelled me 'Doctor Coetzee', and I'm not a doctor."

"Aren't you a *mganga*? A well-known one? That's what Doctor Richter in the WHO Dar office told me."

"Yes, I am. Perhaps too well known."

"Well, in my book and that of the WHO, you are a doctor. In Katanga, a province in the DRC, many of the *waganga* have registered as doctors."

Amazed, Marijke said, "I'm surprised; I didn't know that."

"The WHO started a training school in Lubumbashi. It teaches *waganga* and their assistants how to treat medical cases in the countryside. We've been phenomenally successful, and with a bit of WHO pressure during their Ebola crises, the government has allowed a new category of doctors who attended the school and received a diploma. They cannot receive payment for their services, so charities or the WHO fund most of them, but they can receive gifts from grateful patients. There is an act under discussion."

"If only the Tanzanian government could do the same."

"I doubt they will; the universities in East Africa award degrees. But if you need it, spend a month at the Lubumbashi school and earn a Katangese doctor registration certificate."

Ken asked, "Lisa, your guards look like Omanis. Is that where you live?"

"How did you guess?"

"Years ago, I hiked the Frankincense Trail and recognised their dishdashas. Your dress, I can't pin down."

"Quite right, Ken, my husband is Omani, and since I had my first child, he won't allow me to take any risks."

Marijke asked, "How many do you have?"

"Three, but he wants five; the first two are twins, a boy and a girl, the third a boy."

"That's marvellous; I've wanted children for years."

Ken thought, *Me too, but only since I met Marijke.*

Marijke said, "Lunch is in the dining room in half an hour. If you want to freshen up, I'll take you to your room."

"That would be great."

As soon as the two women were out of earshot, although Ahmed followed them at a distance, Lisa asked, "Are you going to marry Ken?"

It took Marijke by surprise. *She's straightforward, but Lisa's a doctor, so it's typical.*

"He's asked, and I want to, but there are two problems, so I feel deep down I might have to leave."

"Tell me; sometimes it helps to talk about them."

"Lisa, I was on Table Mountain, about to commit suicide, when Ken stopped me and brought me here. I have thought about why I reached that depth of depression. I was in the wrong job and wanted to become a mother. I divorced my husband for playing around; he was sterile.

"If I stay at Rufisi and marry Ken, we will have kids. The lodge is not a place for raising children. I can change things to make it a happy place to raise children by bringing families to live here and work on a farm, so that problem *is* solvable. But the other is not.

"Ken loves Rufisi. If I land in trouble with the government because I'm not a doctor, they'll deport me, and it will kill him if he comes with me and me if he doesn't, and what happens to the children? If I don't solve the problem, the fear of deportation will grow until it wrecks our marriage."

"Then visit Katanga and earn a registration certificate. With the local people and the WHO behind you, I'm sure you will be okay."

"It's certainly a solution. Lisa, here's your cottage; come for lunch in half an hour, then I'll take you to see the elephants."

"You have elephants here?"

"Yes, two babies; you'll love them."

After lunch, Marijke took Lisa to the elephant pen. When Lisa saw Shy and Mtoto, she exclaimed, "They're lovely!"

"The bigger one is Shy, and the baby is Mtoto."

"Why are they here?"

"Mtoto was a newborn calf; his mother died from a prolapsed womb after childbirth. Ivory hunters shot Shy's mother. We trapped her and her brother Uhuru in the pen when they tried to follow their mother's carcass. They would have died without my care."

"Why, and where's Uhuru?"

"I gave him back to the herd. The matriarch came for him, and I told Gogo she could come for Shy in eighteen months. Elephants need milk for the first two years, and a mother elephant can only feed one when lactating."

"Gogo?"

"That's my name for the matriarch, her great-grandmother."

"You told her to come back in eighteen months? Will she remember?"

"Of course, she comes around full moon every month to check on both of them, and we chat."

"And Mtoto?"

"I couldn't fetch him because the elephants were mourning his mother. I had to wait half the night until Gogo brought him to me to look after."

"Marijke, it sounds unbelievable."

"Ask anyone at the lodge; they'll tell you it's true. I think of the animals as nice friends, and they sense it. Gogo knows I mean no harm. So, she won't harm me."

"All the animals?"

"I don't have much contact with the others, apart from those who sense the lodge is safe. They come for a while, like the warthogs, gazelles, and other buck. We have a mongoose family that gets rid of snakes; bats and birds that eat insects; and a fox family. The cheetahs are friends. The scavengers and other carnivores are different; they ignore people unless it's an injured person."

"It sounds a bit like Eden."

"To Ken and me and all who live here, it would be if we could eliminate the poachers. Ask Ken about the poachers; he's been here over three years and can tell you more than I can. Let's return to the lodge for tea after you freshen up, and you can ask me about vaccines."

Over tea, Marijke repeated what she had said to Dr Gruber but added some extra information: "One of the problems with vaccines is cold storage. Leaving the vaccines with the *mganga* is a waste, as once they are hot, they deteriorate. An ice box is okay for someone who goes to a village to vaccinate some people, but the people are often not there.

"If I could obtain for each *mganga* a small chest freezer like those sold for campers, with a solar panel to plug in, it would solve the problem."

"Marijke, I can recommend the WHO appoints you as their vaccination representative in Tanzania; it will give you an official status, and you could ask for freezers."

"That might be useful."

"Then think about going to Katanga. Can we visit one of your villages tomorrow and speak to the *mganga*?"

"Of course; Lucas can drive us to his village, or we can walk to the closest one."

"I have boots; let's walk, it'll do me good to exercise."

"Just one thing: I'm known as the *mganga* with three spirits, and the people call me *Bibie*."

"I'll remember."

They strolled with the two men close behind as Lucas described what they could see to Ahmed.

Marijke could tell that Lisa was impressed by the cleanliness of the village. Lisa asked why the young children carried butterfly nets, and Marijke explained they were catching flies to feed insect-eating birds used to help with pest control. When they met the *mganga*, Lisa was further impressed when, before any introduction, the *mganga* said,

"Welcome to our village, Doctor Lisa. It makes me happy to see you here."

"Have we met?"

"No, I have family in Rwanda; one of my nieces told me about you. She runs one of the clinics you built. The *mganga* everywhere know of you."

"Thank you, I didn't know my fame had spread this far. *Bibie* has told me of the problem with vaccinations because there is no cold storage. Can you tell me anything else?"

The *mganga* thought about it, then said, "It's our problem, Doctor Lisa; we do not like going to towns and cities to collect anything, and finding someone to go is often difficult."

"Why don't you like going to towns and cities?"

"There are too many people there; the *waganga* become confused, for there are many evil thoughts, and we would rather avoid it. So, to do the vaccinations at the right time, someone must bring us the vaccines."

On the walk back, Ahmed marched about thirty metres ahead and Lucas behind an equal distance. They had passed the baobab when Ahmed stopped until the others caught up, and then he said something in Arabic to Lisa.

She repeated it in Swahili, "He says he has seen an animal that has spots; he thinks it's a cheetah."

"That's alright, let me walk a pace ahead; I'm sure it's a friend of mine that's come to check I'm okay."

An amazed Lisa thought, *How can a cheetah be her friend?*

Marijke set off, and the others followed. Lucas smiled; he enjoyed seeing the reactions of strangers.

As they reached the lodge, Lisa asked, "Marijke, how did you know it was a cheetah and that it wouldn't harm you?"

"One of my three spirits is the cheetah. They are all my friends; they know my smell, and also Lucas, Amali, and Ken, so they don't investigate, but you and Ahmed are new, so one of them came to check that I was okay. Two weeks ago, we had an assassin come to set fire to the lodge and kill Ken and me. The poaching gang sent him because we've stopped all the local people from helping them. A cheetah attacked him as he tried to shoot, and two hyenas finished him off."

"My God, so no one else was hurt?"

"No one. We've now put water sprays on the reed roofs and geese in with the chickens and the farm."

The WHO helicopter came the following day to collect Lisa. Before it arrived, Marijke had a chance to ask Lisa for her reactions over coffee.

"Marijke, I admire you for everything you've achieved here. I'm sad to leave, but I know you'll continue your good work and help the people long after I go. I hope you and Ken manage to settle."

"It has been a pleasure having you here, Lisa. Yes, I hope so too. *Bwana* and I have a lot to overcome."

"If there's anything I can do to help, please contact me." Lisa thought, *I won't say I'll draft a report recommending her and send it to Doctor Gruber, the man behind my visit. Maybe he can help her.*

"Thanks, I will." Marijke felt Lisa's offer was warm and genuine. She asked, "Are you looking forward to going back home?"

"I'm sure my husband, Leo, is missing me."

"Does he also work for the WHO?"

"No, the World Bank. He is Prince Asad bin Rashid al Said, but people outside Oman know him as 'Leo'. His father, Louis, is a financial advisor to investment companies and a consultant to the International Finance Corporation. Leo has continued to build the family's fortune, but he's an adventurous soul and likes investing in unusual business ideas."

"Like what?"

"Well, for starters, he was instrumental in Oman getting its first satellite. He has also built a factory that supplies generic medicines. He's an enigma; he doesn't even have a phone. He has shares in small gold mines in Africa."

"That's impressive," Marijke said.

A thought struck Lisa: *I must tell Leo about Marijke and her work here.*

He could help, especially with the poaching problem. He might be able to supply satellite intel to help them intercept the poachers. And I'll also tell Grandad; he's a co-owner.

The helicopter flew in and touched down. The two women said their goodbyes, and Marijke watched the chopper leave, thinking, *What a remarkable woman and family. I hope we'll meet again.*

24

____

The workshop team built the first farm bed. At least, they expected to do that, but they were surprised when several young men from the villages came to mix cement and make blocks for building the growing trays. Everything worked as planned; the toads were happily at work, and the mongoose family delighted with their chicken-egg diet while waiting for a snake or something else. The foxes ate the mice, shrews and crawling insects with enjoyment.

The first lettuces didn't grow as they should have, and Marijke noticed the reason.

"*Bwana*, come and look at the farm."

"Okay, Marijke, what do you want to show me?"

"The lettuce."

Lettuces had sprouted in the first farm bed, and the first leaves were thrusting into the sunlight.

"That's fantastic, Marijke. Why did you want me to see them, except to say, 'I told you so'?"

"Because I have a problem."

"What?"

"Look at the drainage pipe at the end of the bed, *Bwana*. It should be dripping water, but it's dry. The soil the men have collected is clay, the same ground that turns into sticky mud when the rain comes, the stuff deposited by the river in flood, so it doesn't drain. I need to mix it with sand and gravel. The lettuces have no air around their roots.

"But I need a layer of stones first, and we don't have stones; do you have a solution?"

"Let me think about it, Marijke. We might have to truck them in from the mountains."

A few days later, while Marijke and Ken were having lunch, she asked, "*Bwana*, what are you doing so mysteriously at the workshop?"

"Building a rock maker."

"What's that?"

"Come and look."

When they arrived at the workshop, and Marijke saw the machine, she said, "*Bwana*, it's a drum that turns on wheels, like a concrete mixer."

"Yes, but without blades inside to stir up the mix. The men have a little sand, cement, and clay that they'll shovel in, add a little water, and we'll see if it makes balls when it turns."

"That's smart, *Bwana*; I hope it does."

Two days later, the drum was turning, and Ken began experimenting. After another two days, if the angle was right and the clay/cement/sand ratio correct, balls two centimetres in diameter trickled from the drum's low end.

He made the drum longer, and it produced a steady stream.

One night, a rat squeezed through the fence and ate half a dozen lettuce.

"*Bwana*, the rats are too much for the foxes. I have two jackals; I must use them."

"Foxes and jackals can't jump high; divide the fox run into two, using a fine mesh, with jackals on the outside.

"How are you doing with the insects?"

"So far, so good. The marigolds and the other plants and herbs do an excellent job. I'll try citronella outside; maybe the animals won't eat it. The toads do a decent job."

"Are you ready to expand? The netting and mesh for the fence are due in a week."

"Then I'll have the *waganga* build more beds."

"You haven't had a visit from the elephants or hippos yet."

"No, but the tractor has almost finished digging the trench around the farm. Once the villagers have the food, they'll have the motivation to line the outer wall with blocks to stop it from falling in."

The meeting with the rangers to discuss poaching took place on the bungalow's veranda.

"Okay, you want to know what I want to discuss. Since Marijke and the *waganga* have stopped the contract hunters, our tip-offs have dried up. The dry season will end soon; we can expect the poachers from the cities to come in a last all-out effort when the moon is bright—what do we do?"

The discussion ranged over possible strategies while Marijke listened, and then she asked, "Can I say something?"

"Go ahead, Marijke."

"Everything you've said up to now consists of ideas to stop the poachers from getting to the animals. You know it's an almost impossible task; some will always bypass you. What if we change it around? Don't try to stop them from getting in but from getting out."

The conversation after her statement was polite to not-so-polite refusal. "They'll still hit the animals we want to protect." And similar phrases.

Before Marijke could reply, Ken, who had said nothing but had a visible frown, said, "What exactly do you mean, Marijke?"

"You said it after the assassin came. You told me the meat poachers had sent him because we had made a dent in their profits. If they can't return and they lose the meat, their guns and maybe their pickups, it will make such a big dent that there will be no profits.

"They all come in pickups, don't they? If you can disable the pickups before they return to the city, and the villagers can dismantle them, which I'm sure they will enjoy, then coming to hunt becomes an expensive business and a long walk home."

"So, how do we do that?"

"*Bwana*, in Cape Town, the car parks have spiked traps to puncture a car's tyres. How about a massive chain with spikes we can pull across a road? Blow several tyres, and they must walk."

The roar of laughter, as the rangers pictured it, changed the mood of the meeting entirely.

"Okay, everyone, but how do we know which road? We can't put one across every dirt track entering the park. Marijke, can you solve that?"

"I looked at the map. There's the principal road from Dar and the one from Morogoro that joins it near the park's official entrance. The one from Fuga is unlikely. During the days around the full moon, put a watcher with a radio or satphone before the park entrance, and he can warn us of an unknown pickup. Put a chain a short distance, say two hundred metres, or as far as possible before any forks in the track, along those you consider the most likely routes they'll take from the main one. Then position a watcher from a village with a radio every two or three kilometres. You'll know where the poacher turned in, say between watchers three and four, and a tracker will find the trail under the moonlight. Then if it doesn't have a chain, go with a truck and lay a chain; the poachers will most likely leave the way they came. The nearest village can have the meat and dismantle the pickup."

One of the rangers asked, "What will they do with their rifles?"

"Probably hide them," Marijke answered. "A tracker will find them and must bring them here for storage.

"*Bwana*, you must buy the chains, the satphones and the radios. When we're ready, I'll tell the *mganga* the villages can hunt pickups and poachers!"

"Marijke, you have us all thinking differently; well done. Don't you have any crazier ideas for trapping pickups?"

"Only one, *Bwana*; if we had a big digger, I would suggest digging a pit trap to catch a pickup. Like a homemade glooper."

It brought another roar of laughter.

"That might be fun. Meanwhile, I'll buy that chain; there must be a forge and blacksmith in Dar, possibly near the port."

"Don't visit Dar, *Bwana*," said Marijke, "everyone will learn what we are doing. Is there nowhere else?"

"I don't know; we need a place like a shipyard. There's Mombasa."

"That ship on the lake, where was it built?"

"Kigoma; I don't know if a forge and blacksmith are still there."

"Then find out."

"Would you like to visit? I can ask Lodge Air to fly us there. We could also take a trip on the *Liemba* steamer."

"That would be fun, *Bwana*; maybe we need a holiday. Find out if it's worth going. Maybe we can go fishing; what's the fishing like?"

"I'll tell you when we're there, Marijke." *Even three days with Marijke and no worries will be heaven.*

Ken thought about the poachers and remembered Louis Poussin, who had come for a week and stayed two, for he had loved Rufisi. He remembered discussing finance with him and had discovered he had a portfolio of hundreds of minor investments. Ken had found it interesting that Louis held all his shares through proxies, allowing him to remain unknown. He also knew that Louis had married a woman named Soraya, the daughter of Oman's finance minister and granddaughter of the Sultan. As Louis was a lodge shareholder, the only one Ken knew anything about, Ken thought it reasonable to expose the problem to him, so Ken composed an email, told him what they intended to do, and asked for any suggestions. He added that he had a partner, that her name was Marijke, that the chains were her idea, and why.

Five days later, Ken received a reply from Louis Poussin:

Dear Phillipe,

I've heard only good things about what you and Marijke have achieved at Rufisi. I appreciate that the problem regarding the poachers remains and that you need all the help available. Catching poachers isn't something I do very often, but I asked my son, Leo, to look into this. He helped Oman get its first satellite, so he was able to upgrade the software to enable you to track the movement of vehicles in your vicinity by day and night. At night, you'll be able to spot their headlights. A live satellite view is available at http://www.omansat.images.com. You can access coordinates by hovering your mouse over any map area. If your internet connection speeds are too slow, we can send a satellite dish to help you access the site.

Best,
Louis

Ken read the email in amazement, looked at the site and the map, and replied that a direct satellite link would improve things enormously.

Four days later, a man arrived on a Lodge Air flight, installed the satellite dish, connected it to a black box and a monitor, and left. Ken had a live view of the park and an additional keyboard and mouse. Placing watchers along the road was now unnecessary. Even without the spiked chains, they had enough warning and directions to catch poachers at the next full moon; Ken organised another meeting.

"Okay, guys, we now know the exact position of any poacher vehicle that switches off its lights. You can spread out, and I'll call the nearest ranger. He must walk and shoot out the tyres if he can find their vehicle."

Lucas remarked, "But they will still have killed."

"I don't want you guys in a shooting war if it's unnecessary; once they learn they can't return by truck, they'll stop coming."

Erevu added, "Okay, *Bwana*, then I want a headlight on the back of our wagons to reverse at high speed. We'll be safe behind the Lexan windscreen if they shoot at us."

It worked; they collected four poacher pickups and sixteen Ak-47s, but one poacher team left a guard on their vehicle the following full moon. The rangers shot the guard when he fired at the rangers.

When they reported back, Ken thought, *We need those chains, for this could become a war.*

Marijke finished bandaging her last patient, a young girl with a severely burned arm who had fallen into a fire.

"Now, keep that bandage clean. Come back in two days, and I want to see the bandage the same white as it is now."

"Yes, *Bibie*."

As Marijke turned to put her scissors in the box, she saw Ken walking towards her from the office. *He's mad at something. I hope it's not me.*

"Marijke, you can't go on collecting goats. We must eat them."

"Why?"

"We've more than enough for the elephants' milk. We're feeding the goats for nothing."

"And the baby antelopes? How about the warthogs?"

Ken threw his hands in the air, "Okay, I'll take back what I said. You can work out another solution."

"Amali, can you tell all the villagers that we have too many goats? I know they want to show how much they appreciate my help, but can they find something else? Otherwise, we'll have leopards or lions coming to feed, and cheetahs are no match for them."

Amali passed on Marijke's message, and the *waganga* discovered, by asking the Nairobi *mganga*, that her *juju* held a blue gemstone. It wasn't long before a patient gave one to her.

"*Bwana*, is this tanzanite? Is it valuable?"

"That's an uncut stone, Marijke. The colour is lovely, but without a loupe, I can't tell whether it's clear or flawed, and I have no idea how it will cut and polish; only an expert will know."

"Is it legal to own it?"

"It's probably from a tiny mine; they come from a small area south of Kilimanjaro airport—just a couple of guys with spades digging in a hole in the ground. If you don't try to sell the stone or take it out of the country, it's okay. Smugglers took a lot of stones out of the country in the past; these days, there are still many stones, genuine and imitation, used as a bartering currency. A miner may have dug up this stone years ago."

"Okay; if they give me more, I'll make a collection."

25

————————

The mail sent over by Jock included a large brown envelope with a Heidelberg University stamp on the front. When Marijke saw it, she thought, *My analyses.*

The analyses were there: two computer printouts with rows of chemical names, complex chemical formulas and quantities, most of them incomprehensible to Marijke. She thought, *I'll have to search the web for those chemicals.*

The letter in the envelope explained the included thirty pages of text, with interspersed blank spaces carrying a number and a question to answer. The letter, signed by Professor Dr Gruber on the university-headed paper, was short.

Dear Marijke,

The two analyses are of the medicines you use. As you rightly said, they have proved highly effective, so the university requests your approval to apply for patents in your name. Can you please suggest names for them? The attached documents are in the form of a thesis that I will submit with the patent applications. Please use a separate sheet/s of paper for each numbered space, and fill them with the requested information. Number them accordingly. Please feel free to add anything you think might help. Explain where indicated your experience of herbal medicine and the extent of your knowledge. If you have photographs of the growing plants and their leaves in a fresh and dried state, please include them in an attachment.

My thanks and our warmest regards,
Prof. Kurt Gruber, Doctor of Medicine.

Marijke visited the *mganga* the next day and returned with dozens of photos of the plants. Ken had received a reply to his query about chains from the Kigoma docks, and she planned to take the documents and pictures with her to complete.

Marijke packed a small case for her and Ken, and they boarded the Lodge Air aircraft at Jock's lodge. They stayed at the Hilltop Lodge for three nights on arrival at Kigoma. They had a cottage to themselves with a glorious view across the lake; Ken saw the manager and handed over a packet of brochures about Rufisi and Nyerere National Park.

Marijke thought the exceptional service was because they were managers and probably at a special rate. She had never asked Ken about money, for he never mentioned it; she believed Rufisi did well.

They had a late salad lunch on the cottage terrace looking over the bay, and Marijke asked, "*Bwana,* you promised to tell me about the fishing."

"The fish are plentiful here. The lake supplies a quarter of a million tons of protein to the people each year. One of the fish species is a giant cichlid, up to a metre long. The biggest is the *Lates,* called the Nile perch; it can reach two metres in length and a hundred kilograms, although there are the usual fishing stories of one that is even bigger."

"And no one has caught it?"

"No, although hundreds say they've hooked it, and it always breaks their lines. They call it '*Nyirakuru*', which means 'grandmother' in the local Kiha language, and say its mouth has a fan of fishing lines trailing from it."

"I thought fishhooks rusted through quickly, so the fish were soon rid of them."

"In seawater, but this is a freshwater lake. The hooks must rust through eventually, but it takes much longer."

"Then I want to catch it."

"Okay, but we must first visit the old shipyard where the manager says they have the old chain. We must say the chain is to keep elephants out of the lodge; the mention of poachers might end up in the wrong ears."

A taxi took them there, and the driver agreed to wait.

The man in the office, about sixty years old, Ken guessed from his greying temples, greeted them enthusiastically with a broad smile. "You must be Mr Phillips; I have so few visits from strangers, it can only be you. I'm Joseph Makame."

"I'm Ken Phillips, and this is my partner, Marijke."

So, I'm Ken's partner now; he's promoted me.

"A beautiful *mganga* is doubly welcome to my office. Just coming to visit me has made my day." The man bowed.

Marijke smiled at him. "You are a handsome man; the ladies must adore you. How many children do you have?"

"Seven, *Bibie*, and all boys. They are with me in my business." He grinned.

Ken laughed. "That's one way of keeping them out of trouble."

"Yes, and they don't go on strike!"

They all laughed, and then Mr Makame said, "You said you wanted an old heavy chain in your email. How much do you need, and how heavy? We have many chains in the yard, most old and rusty. The chains used for the *Liemba* launching are still here."

"I guess about eighty metres, cut to six-metre lengths; I must see it to decide what will be best."

"What do you need it for?"

"I want to weld spikes on it and lay it down to stop elephants coming into the lodge area. More than a six-metre piece may be too heavy to manage with our vehicle winches."

"Then let's go and look." He took heavy gloves from a rack behind him, saying, "In case you want to touch a piece, I'll bring a pair of gloves."

Mr Makame took them to more than a dozen heaps of chains in many sizes and states of corrosion. "Those are the heaps with at least eighty metres of chain. Don't worry about the rust; we have heavy grinders, and a man can clean six metres of chain—just the spots to weld it—in three hours."

Ken replied, "Let's go back to look at two of the heaps I think are suitable."

At the first heap, Mr Makame said, "This is a forged iron chain, made decades ago; I don't think it will weld easily. Let's look at the other one. Which heap was it?"

Marijke pointed and said, "It was over there somewhere."

"It's steel, probably anchor chain, and there are over eighty metres. It will weld easily."

"How heavy is it?"

"It will take twenty men to carry six metres, about a hundred kilos a metre. Plus, of course, the spikes you want to add."

"Our vehicle winches can manage that, so this looks like a good choice."

"Right, I'll flag it."

It amused Marijke when he took a small spray can of paint from his jacket pocket and sprayed several links on the top of the chain pile white. "See, I'm as good as a football referee," he said.

"Now, let's go back and see what you need for spikes. We have a pile of steel reinforcing bars; our business makes reinforcing cages for construction, with the occasional steel building. We have hundreds of offcuts."

When they returned to the workshop, he sent one of his sons to cut off a piece of chain with three links. His son left with a grinder and a long cable. Ken asked, "Is there power in the yard?"

"There are still several power points that work; we keep them working for when we need something. Let's look at the rebar."

It took over an hour to learn about different rebar qualities, choose the right diameter bar, cut four pieces, and have the eight ends sharpened to points.

By that time, the three links of the chain had arrived. Mr Makame's son had cleaned the sides of the links.

They stood at a workbench while Mr Makame asked, "How should we weld these spikes to the links? Will one on each link do?"

"If they form a cross, giving four spikes, I think so," Ken answered. "Can you tack weld them in place, and we can see how the chain lies?"

The son took them away to weld. Marijke used the wait to ask, "Where does the biggest fish in the lake live?"

"About an hour's boat ride south of here. All the fishermen know of her. You could ask one to take you. It's unlikely you'll see her, but if you have a short rod, line and a hook, the fishing for the smaller cichlid is good at that place. She hangs out there because of the fish."

The son returned with the spiky chain piece, and Ken and Marijke were enthusiastic: "That's perfect."

Mr Makame asked, "Have you any welders at the lodge?"

"Yes, in the workshop. Why?"

"Then I propose we cut you twelve chain lengths, clean them for welding, and make up a cross for every link. It'll be easy to ship if we don't weld the spikes to the chain.

"I'll include welding rods with the box of crossed spikes. How do we ship it to you?"

"It's about a ten-ton load," Ken replied. "Can you find a transporter with a ten-ton truck?"

"I can, but sending it by rail to Kidatu might be better, and you collect it from there. The trucks here will not have four-wheel drive."

"*Bwana*, if the chain goes by rail, send it via Dar and the Tanzam railway to Fuga. We can send the tractor and the lowbed to Fuga to collect it."

"That's a great idea, Marijke. Mr Makame, can you arrange that?"

"Return in three days; I'll have the shipping documents ready for your signature. The railway will shunt a rail wagon here; we still have a siding."

"That's fantastic; what must I pay you, and how?"

"I won't charge you for materials except for the welding rods; the rest is all scrap. I'll work out a labour cost and deliver an invoice to your hotel. Where are you staying?"

"Hilltop."

"The invoice will be at Hilltop early tomorrow morning; if you call me and say okay, we'll start work immediately. The bank details are on the invoice."

After effusive thanks, Marijke and Ken left to eat a late lunch at the hotel.

Over lunch, Marijke told Ken, "That was successful, and thanks for my promotion."

"What promotion, Marijke?"

"You introduced me as your partner."

She doesn't miss a trick. "That can mean many things: professional, tennis and others."

She smiled. "But as I don't have a share in the lodge and we aren't playing anything, I think it has the other meaning."

"I won't deny it, Marijke; I proposed, you haven't accepted, but it's how I feel."

"*Bwana*, we need to take some precautions while handling that chain. If it weighs a hundred kilograms a metre and one of the men drops it, the spike will go straight through a foot. You'll have to buy some heavy gloves and safety boots."

"You're right, Marijke; if they have them here, I'll buy them in Kigoma."

"What will we do now, *Bwana*, for two days?"

"Have you any things to do?"

"I want to visit the hospital, buy a box of vaccines, and then visit a pharmacy to top up my medicines and tetanus shots. And I need to buy more sunscreen and skin creams to stay beautiful for my *partner*. I can do that tomorrow. What must you do?"

She'll find a way to use the word "partner" for weeks.

"This is a good place to buy some steel cable, blocks and slings. I think we'll need them to manage the chains. I'll ask a supplier to deliver them to Mr Makame for inclusion in the box of crosses, and I'll ask about safety boots and gloves."

"Then the day after, can we go fishing?"

"Why are you so keen on fishing, Marijke?"

"Until I grew up, I often fished in the streams for trout, the dams for black bass, and a few times in the sea. It was a happy time for me. I want to do it again. And I'd like to see *Nyirakuru* if possible; maybe my dolphin *mzimu* is inviting me."

"There are no dolphins here, but tomorrow afternoon we'll go to the quayside and see if someone will take us fishing."

"Okay, I'll make an appointment for tomorrow evening with the hairdresser. This afternoon I'll try to complete the patent application data."

"*Bwana*. I have names for the medicines—'Rufigipan' for the anaesthetic and 'Ganganamide' for the antiseptic. But this document is far more complicated than I thought. It's like the legal briefs I once wrote; I suppose applying for a patent is much the same; I must persuade a judge to award it. It'll take me a week. I'll have to complete it at the lodge because I need the *mganga* to help with the anaesthetic; I don't know the dosages for patients with different masses."

26

The boat was long, not very wide, and built with bent planks that joined in a pointed front and back. The two fishermen with paddles sat at either end, with a small outboard that Ken thought perched precariously on one end. Ken and Marijke sat in the middle on small boxes with the fishing rods that Ken had bought and a bucket of Kapenta, the Lake Tanganyika sardine.

They had a pleasant ride for an hour to the bay, where the fishermen said the fishing was good, and then they baited their hooks and cast. It was peaceful; Ken relaxed, the fishermen lay back at either end, and Marijke relapsed into childhood memories until a fish struck.

"*Bwana*, I've caught one!"

"Then bring it in."

He could see she knew what to do as she reeled the fish in, then lifted it into the boat, where the fisherman at her end removed the hook and baited it again.

She cast again, then sat back, looking over the water. "*Bwana*, is that a crocodile over there?" She pointed.

Ken asked the fisherman behind him, who replied, "No, the crocodiles wait out of the water in the daytime unless there is something to eat. We can go closer."

They used the paddles and drew closer. "It's a huge fish, *Bwana*."

Ken asked a fisherman, "Is that *Nyirakuru*?"

"If it has many lines coming from its mouth, yes."

"*Bwana*, it's *Nyirakuru*, but it's sick or dying. It looks skinny, and it's lethargic."

As the boat drifted slowly closer, Marijke leaned out. "It has so many hooks and bits of line in its mouth that it can't possibly catch fish. I think it's starving."

"That may be, but it's still a monster."

Ken didn't notice Marijke turn, lift the end of a rope in the boat, and rapidly make a noose with a slip knot. As she turned back, he exclaimed, "What will you do?"

"I'm going to catch it."

The fishermen watched, bemused; they had never seen anything like this. As the boat drifted alongside the fish, she leaned over to put the noose around its head, but her movement tilted the overgrown canoe suddenly; Ken and the fishermen had to throw their weight to the other side to avoid the boat filling, and she lost her balance and fell head-first into the water. Ken reacted as his side of the boat almost reached the water, throwing himself back again, where, finding the rope still on the gunwale, he grabbed it and looked over to see Marijke surfacing. "Marijke, do you still have the rope?" She raised a hand with the rope in it. "There are crocs here—quick." He pulled her to the boat.

"Keep the boat balanced," he shouted to the two boatmen as he grabbed Marijke's hands and pulled her from the water until she collapsed in a soggy heap at the bottom of the boat. He was furious.

"Of all the damn stupid things you could do, that was the worst. You deserve ..."

The voice from the heap stopped his angry tirade. "Later ... Is *Nyirakuru* still on the rope?"

"You put the noose on her?"

"Yes, before she moved away."

Ken pulled the rope in and gently pulled when he felt the weight.

"Yes, she's here."

"Then pull her beside the boat and remove all those damned hooks."

I won't argue with her now. Ken removed his multitool from its belt pouch and opened the pliers.

"Marijke, I can't remove the hooks and hold *Nyirakuru* simultaneously. I don't think she'll like me pulling her head up."

Marijke sat up. "Give me the rope." She moved slowly to the side of the boat as the boatmen balanced it, then leaned over behind Ken. "She's almost dead, *Bwana.* I'll lift her head a bit. Can you cut off the barbs outside without her mouth coming right out?"

Ten minutes later, he had cut off the barbs protruding through her mouth and, with the pliers, had worked the hooks out. The fish only protested once, and the rope stopped her. "There, the hooks are gone."

"Can I see?"

"Yes, I'll move back so you can."

Marijke looked—*she will die unless I feed her*—then said, "*Bwana,* give me the bait bucket."

The two fishermen, who had already concluded that their passengers were utterly crazy, now saw the woman grab a handful of Kapenta from the bucket and feed it into the gaping jaw of the fish.

She fed the entire bucket to *Nyirakuru* and then slipped the rope off.

The fishers heard her Swahili clearly: "There, *Nyirakuru,* you are better now; you can swim away and catch some fresh food and have many more great-grandchildren."

The fishermen paddled away, and *Nyirakuru* followed until the outboard started.

Marijke removed her dress, wrung the water out and put it back on. "That must do for now."

Back at the quay, Marijke disappeared into a market stall that sold women's clothing and reappeared in a new dress with her old one a damp bundle. At the hotel, the receptionist said the hairdresser would wait until she was ready.

When Marijke returned to their room after a shower and visiting the hotel hairdresser, she asked, "*Bwana*, do you want dinner now, or will you tell me what I deserve first."

"Marijke, I said it in the heat of the moment; I was terrified because the lake has huge crocodiles, and I had visions of you being eaten alive."

"*Bwana*, I'm sorry; I didn't think of the boat tipping. I only thought of helping that poor fish when I saw it." She grinned at him. "You helped, so thanks. You would only have lost a *partner*."

She's repeated it; now I feel guilty. "No, I would have lost the woman I love."

Wow, he said it. "Then I'll never to do it again. Let's go for dinner."

When they checked out in the morning to sign the shipping documents and then go to the airport, a beaming manager gave them a painting.

Surprised, Marijke accepted it, but before she could ask him anything, the manager said, "A local artist painted this for you when he heard what *Bwana* and the *mganga* with the three *mizimu* did to help *Nyirakuru*; he captured it in a painting. The hotel has waived your bill, and we've ordered another painting to hang in the lounge. Thank you for visiting us. You have a visitor waiting outside."

When she saw the aged woman waiting for them, she recognised a *mganga*. Ken did, too, and felt charmed by a delightful smile.

"*Bibie*, we cannot let you leave without a *juju* from the fish of the lake who are grateful that you saved *Nyirakuru*."

She lifted a *juju* from her neck, and Marijke bowed to allow her to place it around her neck. "I thank you and all the *waganga* of the lake communities for the honour you do us."

Six days later, Marijke gave the envelope with the patent data to the office with instructions to take it to Jock's lodge for the next Dar flight.

Ken received notification that the chains would arrive at Kuga in twenty-four hours; he thought it must be a record for Tanzania Railways. He sent the lowbed and tractor, and two days later, the shipment arrived. A week later, the chains lay in twelve rows beside the workshop with a wicked-looking array of spikes on each chain.

Marijke was with him when they inspected them.

Ken remarked, "Anything that drives over those will have shredded tyres."

"So, we must make sure the poachers drive over them."

"I'm sure the guys can hide them under leaves and brush."

"It needs more than that; I have an idea. There are boxes in the lodge store marked 'Xmas decorations'; I'll look at them."

"What are you up to now?"

"I'll show you later."

Marijke fetched a cardboard box that had carried cans of food from the kitchen, then had the workshop paint it black. When the paint was dry the following day, she cut eyeholes and stuck squares of paper covered in glitter on the inside of the holes. That night she hung it from a tree in the dark alley between the lodge and the boma.

After dinner, she said, "*Bwana*, come with me." She led him into the alley with a torch shining on the ground and then raised the torch so the light shone on the box. Ken grabbed her violently and pulled her to him. "Marijke, lion!"

"Oww! Let go; it's my eyes box."

He didn't let go. *I like holding Marijke like this.* "What the devil is an eyes box?"

Marijke shone her torch on it, and the eyes swung away, then back again. "I made it to draw the poachers' attention from the road and perhaps make them accelerate."

"Well, I'll call Lucas and the rangers to look at it."

After the rangers had seen it, Ken called a meeting on the bungalow veranda. "Marijke, this is your idea; please explain it to us all."

"Okay, you're going to lay a chain across the road. First, pick a place as far as possible along a road into the park. At the end of a straight stretch and just before a corner."

"Why?"

"I'm trying to think like a poacher; I'm driving, I accelerate on the straight bit, and then I can see the corner; I'm going to slow down, but I see the eyes in the headlights in the bush ahead. It distracts me; I don't look at the road, and 'bang', we should puncture all four tyres. Then, after they've gone, we find where they hid their guns, then move the chain so that we flatten another two or four tyres when they return for the guns.

"*Bwana*, will they try to fetch their pickups?"

"I doubt it; they probably steal them."

Lucas said, "If we have ten boxes with only one eye, they will think it's a herd of buck. I think it will work well."

Marijke asked the cleaners to help.

"Marijke, we must agree on something before the poachers come."

"What, *Bwana*?"

"I'm going with the rangers this time; I'll supervise chain laying in the park. I want you to stay in front of the satellite image to feed us the poachers' movements."

"Why?"

"Because I shall spend all my time worrying about what crazy stunt you will pull next; I won't be able to do my job."

He's worried about my safety. That's nice.

"So, you'll leave me here to defend myself alone?"

"No, I'll do the same as we've done whenever the rangers go on poaching patrol. Hire five men from the villages who know how to use a rifle to guard the lodge."

"Okay, but put a light outside, on the lodge wall where the guards can see it. Put the switch inside the office where I'll be sitting. If I feel there's something wrong, and I switch it off, they must look out for an attack."

The chains were all in place four days before the November full moon on the first; the rains had held off, and only a few light showers had dampened the ground.

Although muddy, the roads in the park were passable. Seven chains were on the tracks Ken and the rangers had agreed were the most likely to be used; the five others were in five safari wagons with winches, cables, and extra villagers. The experience they gained while laying the seven gave them the confidence to install the others in an hour each. They all wore heavy safety boots and gloves.

As night fell, with all the crews grouped around the vehicles at the lodge, Ken said, "Okay, Marijke, you have your satphone. Call me if you see a vehicle on the road. We'll take our positions, guys, no park radios; the poachers listen in. I'll SMS your satphone with instructions. Call me if you have a problem. We can't expect them much before midnight."

No poachers came that first night, but on the second night, Marijke sent an SMS: "Five vehicles driving along the road." She tracked them as they approached the park gates, but they turned off before the gate and circled the gate buildings three kilometres away before rejoining the road.

Ken relaxed when she reported they had turned off the road at five of the seven tracks with chains. *They are together; they each have a sector.*

They began the clean-up early. Three vehicles had blown all four tyres on the chain; one had skidded sideways when the front tyres burst and had one blown rear tyre. The last only spiked the front tyres; however, the driver had tried to reverse out, and the rear had sunk to the axle in the mud.

The tracker collected twenty AK-47s, and the crew pulled chains across the tracks leading to the poachers' gun caches. Then they told the villagers to take what they wanted and break the rest. When the villagers finished with the vehicles, the hulks were lying flat on the ground.

Only one vehicle came to collect the guns, and the driver and passengers had to walk when the spikes destroyed four tyres. The same night, three other poachers' vehicles came, but as they used tracks with no chains across them, the rangers had to pull chains across the exits. Two were within sight of the main road; the poachers accelerated when they saw the road, and the chains punctured all four flat tyres. The third saw the chain; it was far from the main road before splitting into two on the way out, and the pickup slowed and then stopped.

Four men descended, looked at the chain, and decided to pull it to one side with a towrope.

After attaching a rope to one end of the chain and the front of the pickup, they tried reversing; the chain moved a fraction, but the spikes dug in as an anchor, and the vehicle's wheels spun. The driver told the three others to lift that end of the chain. They did, the pickup reversed, a man slipped, and the chain fell. A spike pierced the soft sports shoe of one man, and he screamed in agony as it thrust through his foot. In the quiet night, the rangers half a kilometre away heard his scream.

The poachers managed to lift the chain, but the man fainted as they pushed the foot down to release it from the spike; then they tore up his shirt, tied it around his foot to stop the bleeding, and put him in the back with the dead animals. That was when they found themselves staring at the muzzles of four rangers' rifles. The poachers had left their AKs in the cab.

Mwamba brought the rangers' safari wagon, and Ken called for another vehicle.

They transferred the injured poacher, and Mwamba drove him to the clinic at Mambwe. They tied up the other three in the back of the first safari wagon, and after leaving Ken at the lodge, the rangers unloaded them, naked, in the middle of the park.

Another fourteen AK-47s swelled the gun cache, and the villagers had a feast after pillaging the vehicles.

"*Bwana*, all the poachers took a bypass around the park entrance. Can you find it and put two chains across it? One near the beginning and another just before the end?"

"We can; that's a great idea."

"I'm also getting a feeling, *Bwana*, that while you are out there, the lodge is vulnerable; perhaps we need a chain across the road. The poachers might send a vehicle or two to roar down the road to the lodge and shoot whatever they can see."

"Let's drive it later to see the best places."

"Marijke. You once suggested a pit trap to catch poachers; this place looks ideal for digging one. If the front of the vehicle drops into it, they'll never pull it out, and our guards will make life hell for them if they try. We can fill it in during the day and dig it out at sundown."

"Okay, pull a chain across the road just after the turnoff and another close to the workshop. Leave that one visible so the poachers stop where the guards can see them. There may be more than two vehicles."

"You're a great military strategist, my love."

"No, that's common sense." *He called me my love.*

27

———————

The mail arrived with the irregular post delivered to Jock's lodge. The big white envelope with a WHO logo had a brief note pinned to it. Jock thought it looked important, so he ordered his driver to deliver it to Rufisi.

When it arrived at Rufisi Lodge, the driver brought it straight to Ken. Inside was a formal document on heavy paper; it looked ready for framing.

Under the WHO logo and heading, it said:

The World Health Organization appoints Doctor Marijke Coetzee as the WHO representative for vaccination management and control in Tanzania.

H.G.Richter
Dr H.G. Richter
WHO Director for Tanzania.

When Ken read it, he left the office immediately and took it to Marijke, who was watching an assistant bandaging a small boy on the bungalow veranda.

She saw his excitement as he said, "Marijke, I have something for you; look."

She read it and said, "That's marvellous, *Bwana*, but it doesn't make me a doctor. It might help if someone comes to ask questions about my status."

"Marijke, I thought you would be thrilled."

"In a way, I am." She thought: *But it's still possible for someone to accuse me of illegal practice and for the government to deport me.* "It means recognition for what I've done, although there's a lot more to do, and it gives me the authority to ask the WHO for help, so I'm glad."

Ken stated, "I'm going to frame it immediately and hang it next to the nursing certificate."

It was not a hunting moon, but Ken said, "I think this is the last night we can expect poachers; the following nights will be too dark for them, and then it will be far too wet; I'll collect the crews and go out early."

Twelve men in three vehicles came with the waning moon early in the evening. They weren't hunting game; they planned to drive straight to the lodge at full speed, shoot everything that moved and set fire to whatever would burn.

Marijke, sitting in the office after sunset, with the door locked, had the dark satellite view in front of her and glanced at it every minute or two while she paged through a magazine.

The screen was still black when she looked after page thirty, but when she looked again after page thirty-two, she dropped the magazine and picked up the satphone. "*Bwana*, three vehicles. They must have come to the park in daylight and waited; they've just switched on their headlights."

"Okay, Marijke, tell me where they turn off."

Five minutes later, she said, "*Bwana*, they've turned into the road to the lodge, all three."

Ken could hear the urgency in her voice. "Right, Marijke, we're coming," he said.

A minute later, the rangers and their vehicles were tearing through the bush towards the lodge, not an easy thing to do at night. Ken moved onto the plain where he could drive faster; Lucas had to hold tight in the bouncing car.

God, I hope we make it in time, Ken thought.

The three vehicles accelerated once they turned into the lodge road; only two of the twelve men had been to the area before. They knew what happened to poachers, so they prudently rode in the back of the third pickup. The driver of the leading vehicle was convinced he had a clear road to the lodge, didn't notice the chain, drove straight over it and came to a stop with four shredded tyres.

The satphone in the dashboard holder squawked. "*Bwana,* they've stopped where the first chain is."

Thank God, it'll delay them.

Ken didn't answer; he couldn't take his hands off the bucking wheel but said to Lucas, "Answer."

"Okay, *Bibie,* we are coming."

After checking the vehicle, the poachers found a way to push through the bush to one side of the chain, and twenty minutes later, the two pickups had passed. The four men from the wreck split into pairs and joined each of the remaining two pickups.

The noise and lights were enough for the hyenas to lope in their direction.

"*Bwana,* one must be damaged; two have started up again," Marijke reported.

"Understood, *Bibie,* we are coming soon."

Ken clung to the bucking wheel. *I wish it were sooner; she must be terrified.*

As the leading pickup saw the light on the lodge's wall, it accelerated, and the driver shouted, "Target in sight," then switched off his headlights. Then the lodge light went out, and he didn't re-establish night vision before the nose of the vehicle dropped into the deep trench and hit the far side. The rear end flipped up, and over; all four men in the back fell out, and then the pickup fell on top of them, crushing the driver and his mate in the cab.

The last pickup saw the wreck in its headlights and two pairs of headlights approaching the lodge from the river, so it did a rapid three-point turn and drove away from the buildings. The hyenas moved in.

Ken screeched to a halt by the lodge, leapt from the safari wagon and rushed into the building, rifle at the ready. There was no one. *I hope she's in the office and okay.* He called, "Marijke, are you there?"

He noticed the outside light come on—*she must be okay*—then hammered on the door. "Marijke, it's Ken."

He heard the lock click open, and Marijke stepped out. His reaction was automatic. He took her in his arms. "Darling, I'll never leave you alone like that again."

Marijke thought, *Now I know he loves me.*

After a minute, she said, "The second vehicle ended in the ditch, and the third turned back as you came. The last I saw, it was almost at the first wreck."

"Bugger them; I just want to know you're okay."

"I'm fine; there may be a lot of injured men out there."

"I don't care about them."

"*Bwana*, the men must be waiting for orders; I'm okay; let's go and see them."

"No, I'll go. You lock yourself in again; I don't know if poachers are still around."

"Okay."

Ken sent the rangers to check out the first truck; they returned to say the hyenas were having a feast and wouldn't leave unless they shot them.

The third vehicle reached the one with blown tyres and tried to make its way around it; the driver thought he was doing well until a large thorn tree, with roots damaged by the two vehicles that had passed earlier, fell on top of the pickup. In the back, a mass of dense, long thorns trapped the four men who had to use both hands to keep the thorns away as they tried to climb out; their AK-47s lay on the pickup floor. The driver forced his door open against the thorn-tree branches, and a waiting hyena took a chunk from his thigh when he stepped down. His scream was enough for the passenger to remain inside. The four men from the back tried to escape; climbing back into the thorn tree might have been a better choice because none survived.

The passenger was still deciding if he could leave the cab when an elephant stepped in front of the headlights and sauntered away; shortly after, a cheetah crossed in front of him. He chose to stay there until somebody came.

The satphone spoke: "*Bwana* if you can hear this, the last pickup has stopped to one side of the first wreck. I think it's stuck there."

"Okay, Marijke, we'll wait until daylight. I'll come and fetch you. Guys, we can sleep and clean up in the morning."

When Ken and the rangers with the tractor behind reached the two vehicles, the man in the cab was a gibbering wreck, suffering from dehydration. They gave him water, and he rambled about attacks by monsters, elephants, lions and hyenas. Ken let him go.

"If he can hitch a lift into Dar and tell that story, it will be worth it."

The graveyard now had more than elephant bones; rows of stripped pickups rusted in the open.

A week after the last attack, Ken came to the veranda mid-morning. "Marijke, why is there a hydrologist coming to visit?"

"What's a hydrologist?"

She's avoiding the question. "I'm sure you know; they go around drilling holes to measure the water levels."

"Well, we certainly don't need one; water surrounds us. But how do you know a hydrologist is coming?"

"I've received an email from an organisation called 'Water for the World', saying they want to do a hydrological survey."

"I've never heard of them."

"I looked at their website; they've been looking for water in Ethiopia, Afars and Issas, where they have no water as it's a volcano. I don't know why they would come here."

"Probably sick of drilling dry holes; at least here, they can guarantee water wherever they drill. A bit pointless, though. Are they going to pay for lodging?"

"Yes, the hydrologist and a crew of four. They've asked for a parking space for their truck and equipment."

"Then give them Mongoose Cottage at the east end with the separate road and parking. It's the smallest. And arrange rooms for the crew with Lucas. When do they want to come?"

"Three weeks to a month from now."

"Tell them they're welcome but send them a picture of our tractor with four big wheels. They must bring a tractor if they come before May. Too soon, and our tractor would have to pull them from the mud daily."

Ken was still suspicious. *Now she's giving orders and trying to avoid more questions. I'm sure she knows something.*

Two days later, Ken came to the veranda again. "Marijke, this time, I'm sure you're involved."

"With what, *Bwana?*"

"This request from a professor at Dar University for a night's accommodation."

"Is he studying hydrology?" *Avoiding again*, thought Ken, *but I've trapped her this time.*

"No, biology."

"So, what makes you think I have something to do with his visit?"

"Because the email says, 'An evening when your wife is available.'" *She can't avoid that!*

"Then he must have the wrong lodge; you aren't married."

And she has! "Marijke, if you don't give me a straight answer, I'll take you inside and spank you."

"Ooh! Please do; my masochistic desire has been dying for that to happen since Nairobi. Have you brought a whip?"

Ken grinned. "Then I won't; waiting is the most painful."

Marijke pouted, "Damn, I got that wrong," and then she returned the grin. "I did tell someone I needed a zoo of creepy crawlies, but I don't know what the professor has come to do."

"I'll tell him he can choose his day. We have an empty room for two weeks; I blocked it for *your* hydrologist."

The professor came three days later. Marijke dressed in one of her most colourful *mganga* dresses, with her *jujus*, and she spoke Swahili. Ken thought she had the professor at a disadvantage, for the professor had heard rumours about her.

When he stepped from the safari vehicle that brought him from the airstrip lodge, he greeted Marijke: "*Habari za asubuhi, Bibie*; are you the *mganga* with three *mizimu?*"

"Good morning to you, Professor; I am. And this is my husband, Ken."

"How does a white South African woman become a *mganga*? You are unusual."

At least he didn't say impossible.

"Not at all; I have colleagues in the same profession, of all colours and nationalities worldwide. In Africa, most are dark-skinned, but they are mostly pale elsewhere. In South Africa, they call us *sangomas*; in Australia and other places, shamans; in Europe, witches and wizards have been so for thousands of years. I'm born and bred African, and I love this country and all of Africa."

"Then I understand. My brief says you have specific requirements concerning 'creepy-crawlies', although that's hardly a scientific term. Can you tell me more?"

"Please come to the lounge; we'll have a drink, and I'll tell you."

"Professor, I'm a *mganga*; my only interest is the health of the people in the area. I treat many people, especially children, for bites, stings and snakebites. They and I do not know enough about what we consider pests; it doesn't help when a child says an evil spirit stung him. I have found no reference in the technical literature with a list of what lives in Nyerere Park.

"I can guarantee cooperation from the villagers, and my husband can build a zoo close to the lodge to your specifications. We need one or more students to capture and research examples of what lives in the park. The people and I must know what they look like and their names. We need to learn the habitat and behaviour of these creatures so that people can learn to avoid them, and I need to know which are the best antidotes to their venom and treatments for the bacterial and viral load from their bites or stings."

"That is biochemistry, a different department."

"Biochemists may be participants, but it begins when we know what caused the sting."

"And you see this as a long-term operation?"

"Several years, with a sign that says University of Dar es Salaam, Departments of ...."

"The participating departments are up to you.

"I hope to welcome students in their final year of degree and postgraduate studies. And read with interest the theses they present for their degrees."

"*Bibie*, I shall see what I can do."

"Then please, join us on a game drive tonight and tomorrow morning before your flight back to Dar."

After the professor had left the following day, Ken was grinning when he said to Marijke, "So, of course, you know nothing about him; he came to the wrong lodge, and it turns out I'm married."

She smiled back. "That wasn't a Freudian slip; it was on purpose. The professor thought we were married, and he said so, so I didn't want to confuse him."

"If I was a lawyer, I could convince the judge that referring to me as your husband twice is acceptance of the marriage proposal that you convinced the judge I made."

"*Bwana*, let's clear the air a bit. I want to stay here all my life, and I know I want to marry you, but I must sort something out before I say, 'Let's do it.' I had one disastrous marriage; I cannot afford another. Give me a bit more time."

"No pressure, Marijke. I promised to wait, but thanks for the honesty."

28

Ken was in the workshop when the hydrologist arrived, so Marijke met him first. She was impressed as soon as she saw his vehicle, a double cab Unimog with a satellite dome on the roof and a machine in the truck bed that she assumed was for drilling boreholes. The wheels and tyres seemed huge, and the logo on the door showed a drilling machine and the name "Water for the World".

Marijke thought, *We don't have to worry about that truck getting stuck in the mud.*

The suntanned man who climbed down from the high cab had blonde hair, blue eyes, and an athletic build. *He must be a swimmer or surfer, and the girls on the beach would adore him.* When he said, "G'day, you must be Marijke Coetzee. I'm Dan Culver," her guess seemed correct. *Australian.*

"I am. Welcome to Rufisi; you're far from Australia."

"Nah, it's just over the water. Although I've seen no sheep, you have a nice station here."

"You won't; the lions would eat them all."

He laughed, "Same as dingoes back home. Well, it's a pleasant change from Ethiopia. Before getting this job, I thought I would return to drill in the outback."

The front passenger and three men from the back seat had also climbed down. "Ma'am, this is my crew; we're all Aussie. Pete, Joe, and Clive are all engineers; they operate the drill rig."

Marijke shook hands with all three, and then Dan said, "Fred here is Native Australian; he finds the water, although he didn't do well in Ethiopia."

When Marijke shook hands with Fred, he bowed, and she looked directly into his eyes when he stood up. He didn't look away, and then he winked, and Marijke thought, *He recognised me as a* mganga, *a shaman, and that's a secret between us.*

"Where can we park the rig, and where can we put our swags?"

"Go down the road the way you came about two hundred metres: there's a side road to the right. If you drive down, you'll find two cottages and parking. They're yours while you're here. When you have everything sorted, walk up the path with the 'Lodge' sign and join us and the rangers for lunch."

"Thanks, we will do, ma'am; we'll see you there."

Ken was walking back from the workshop when he saw the Unimog leaving and Marijke standing in front of the bungalow, so he came over. "Who was that, Marijke?"

"The hydrologist and his crew; I have sent them to their cottages and invited them to lunch with the rangers."

"Okay, I'll come too. What's the hydrologist like?"

"His name's Dan Culver. Dan's an Australian with an Aussie crew of four: Fred, Pete, Joe, and Clive. Fred's a Native Australian. Dan's about our age and looks like an Aussie surfer from Bondi Beach; suntanned, sun-bleached hair, blue eyes and the build to go with it. He looks like a guy I knew who thought he was God's gift to women. He's a contract driller."

"Okay." *He's only been here a few minutes, and she knows everything about him.*

Lunch with the rangers was a distraction from the daily routine as the rangers asked questions about Australia; when one asked about the outback, Marijke thought that Dan loved the open spaces and desert from the way he described them.

He treated his job with humour: "I have the kind of job where you don't have to come right all the time. I reckon I'm allowed ten dry holes for every hole where there's water—" he laughed, then added, "—although, in Ethiopia, it was more like fifty dry ones. Looking around, I don't think we'll have that problem here."

Ken asked, "So why did you come?"

"A job is a job, and the client who gave me the rig said I had to find clean drinkable water. Looking at the herds on the plain, I suspect that might not be so easy."

"Why not?"

"Well, what we had to drive through on the way here is heavy clay, probably damp until the bottom of the layer. That water won't filter into a bore, so we must find water below the clay. We can't sense it from above because of the clay, so the only way is a core drill, and I have no idea how far we will go. If we hit solid rock, it will mean a dry hole."

Ken, interested, said: "Five kilometres from here, we have a sand pit. It's deep now; there's a visible sand and gravel layer. One of the rangers can drive you over if you want to look at it."

"That's a dinkum idea. Can we go this afternoon?"

"Sure. Amali, please take him. Dan, if you're back by five-thirty, you can take a game drive with Amali; it'll give you a bigger picture of the land around us. Then we have dinner in the boma at eight-thirty."

Marijke changed tables to sit with Ken and Dan at dinner, and Ken thought, *Is she attracted to him? He does tell exciting stories.*

"Visiting your sandpit was worth a lot of time. I'll core-drill five holes in a line between the pit and here."

"What will that tell you?" asked Ken.

"If the sand and gravel layer is everywhere, I'll learn the depth and thickness, and notably how much water will come from a metre of gravel. I'll also send a sample for purity and bacterial analysis."

It looks like he'll be out of here quickly. Thank God. "Will you leave the rig out there?"

"Yes, we'll take our swags and camp beside it."

I want them gone, not dead. "Dan, you know nothing about the African bush or its dangers. I'll lend you a pickup and a shotgun. Come back here every night; you can leave one man to sleep in the rig's cab with the gun.

"An elephant might try to push the rig around, or a pride of lions climb it. Stick the muzzle out the window and fire a shot into the air, and then they'll leave."

At the dinners in the boma on the following evenings, the amount of time Marijke spent talking to Fred miffed Dan; it wasn't Fred but Marijke who did the questioning. Ken was pleased.

Fred told her about the Australian desert, his life there, and the aboriginal peoples' respect for the denizens and their spirits. On the fourth night, she asked, "What's the significance of the necklace you wear?"

"It's my manhood talisman; the shaman gave it to me after I did my first walkabout alone. However, I realised afterwards that I was far from being a man. I had to try several jobs before I learned what I was good at and wanted to do."

The walkabout is like Ken's hike, a jump into manhood. "I understand."

"I know you do."

On the sixth night, the rig returned, and Dan reported, "I have all the data, and I can drill a test well; the question is where?"

Marijke replied, "At a village. Lucas and I will take you there tomorrow if you don't mind a walk."

I knew she was behind this, thought Ken. *She wants clean water for the villages. I hope that's all she wants.*

As they strolled to the village, Marijke asked what Dan would do. He explained, then added that the bore and pump size would depend on the number of villagers.

Marijke introduced Dan to the *mganga* in the village, and they showed him around the settlement.

Finally, Dan said, "I think anywhere here is as good as another. Where do you want the tank? We'll drill as close to it as we can."

Marijke described the proposal to the *mganga*. She carefully emphasised one point: "Someone with authority must control the use of the main tap water. It's for drinking and cooking. You can use the overflow for anything, but wasting the main tap water will mean nothing to drink."

The *mganga* agreed to have the borehole near her hut and the tank close to it where she could see who used the water.

Then Marijke asked Lucas, "How can we learn the number of people living in each village that needs clean water?"

After a brief discussion with the *mganga*, he replied, "Here live one hundred and thirty-two, *Bibie*. The *mganga* will tell all others to send their numbers to the lodge."

Marijke told Dan, "If you allow for a few extra visitors and some population growth, I think the well here must feed a hundred and seventy people."

A week later, the first village had a bore with a plug, and the rig moved to the next one on the list. Dan returned nightly to the lodge and seized every opportunity to talk to Marijke. The settlements could boast a capped bore at the rate of three villages a week; of course, many more wanted the same thing. Then a truck arrived with pumps, piping and tanks and returned to Dar for more. Ken, Marijke, Lucas, and Dan were at the first village to watch the team install everything; it was quick and easy. When the first water poured from the tap, the visitors could see the joy of the villagers. The party that followed would be a happy memory forever.

Dan still returned to the lodge every night. He knew his contract would end in ten days and was hoping for an opportunity to propose to Marijke. He sensed his chance on the night of the full moon when he saw Marijke leave the boma, so he followed her to the lodge veranda and found her alone, looking out over the plain.

Dan thought she was magnificent, the woman of his dreams who would live in the open spaces with him.

He approached her quietly, but she heard and turned to face him.

"Marijke, I have something to ask you."

It startled him when she replied, "I know, Dan."

"Then you know I love you, want to marry you, and take you to Australia."

"Yes, I know it's the truth, but the answer is no."

"Why?"

"I don't love you, Dan, but even if I did, I would say no, because I can't leave my family."

Marijke had seen the elephants arrive. *They've come to convince me to stay.*

"I didn't know you had family here."

"Wait, watch, and you will see them."

Marijke stepped off the veranda and strode towards the herd, and Dan saw three massive elephants coming to meet her. He thought of running to Ken to tell him, until Fred's voice came from a dark corner: "Don't worry, boss, they are *Bibie*'s family."

When Marijke returned, walking beside a colossal beast, heading for the gap beside the lodge and the path to the elephant pen, they heard her voice. "I've cut down on Mtoto's milk to make him eat some greens; he's doing great."

Dan left a week later when a replacement and crew arrived to continue the work.

Marijke spent the next week thinking of Dan's proposal. *Saying I didn't love him was honest, but maybe I lied when I said I couldn't leave my family; it was easy to avoid the thought, but I might have to. If I do, will I be able to find a way to return? Or will I have to jump again, and create a new life, in a new place, like the Australian outback?*

29

It was after Dan left that Marijke finally made up her mind. She requested an appointment with the medical department at the University of Dar es Salaam. The reply came two days later, and after dinner, she left the boma and sat on the bungalow veranda, waiting for Ken. When he arrived, he was surprised to see her there. "Marijke, I thought you had gone to bed."

"I couldn't, *Bwana*; I must tell you something, then I'll go and sleep in Jackal Cottage; it's empty tonight."

Ken felt a tight knot building in his gut. "Marijke, why?"

"After I tell you I have to leave Rufisi, you won't want me in bed beside you."

The knot became agony. Marijke could see it on his face.

"It's not because of you, *Bwana*, but because of what may happen if I stay; it will destroy both of us. Please understand; I must make this decision, not because I want to, but because after making decisions that messed up the first ten years of my adult life, I cannot make a mistake again."

"What will happen?"

"I know if I stay, I'll marry you because you love me, and I love you, and then we will have children because I want children, and so do you. But I'm not just a woman who can have kids and manage a household. I've learned who I am and what the real me needs to do. I've learned due to you and your patience."

In a strained voice, Ken said, "Explain some more, Marijke."

"I want to do what I'm already doing, being a *mganga* and fixing up sick people. Maybe it's me, maybe it's because I've learned late, but I can't help it. If I stay, I cannot avoid doing it. And in a year, or two, or three, when we have a son, daughter, or both, someone will accuse me of practising as a doctor, and I'll go to jail, or the government will deport me. Then what happens? If I go and leave the children, I'll step off a mountain. If I go with the children, you might do the same thing. And if we go together, both of us leave the life we love, and it will destroy our marriage. So, a decision to stay might ruin more than one life."

Ken said, his voice hoarse, "That will never happen; no one will bear witness against a *mganga*."

"I know, but what if the patient is a visitor from Dar gored by a hippo when visiting family here? I'll never refuse to treat such a person. The complaint will come from the family in Dar. The risk is too great; it may destroy the lives of you, me, and our children."

The pain was excruciating when he asked, "So, what will you do when you leave?"

"I must decide what to do. I could visit Katanga for a month and become a registered doctor there. That might be enough; I don't know. I might be able to sign up for an online degree at a university somewhere in South Africa, America or Europe. I don't know how long that will take or how often I might need to take a practical course.

"I don't know, and I must go and find out. It's no good trying to do so from here. I'll start by going to Dar and the university there."

Ken felt desperate: "But you are a doctor, Marijke; Dr Gruber said you were. You have a WHO appointment that says you are."

"I have no degree, and no court in Tanzania will recognise me as one; that's what matters."

I must do something. Is this the end of our relationship? Ken's anguish was visible. "Marijke, what can I do? Is there any way I can help?"

"Don't cry, *Bwana*. Remember, we're in hell, and hell is not pleasant. I won't walk away and never call. I'll tell you what I'm doing every day.

"I must visit Dar, where I can talk to the university to see what qualification I can get and talk to Cape Town university too. I'll call the WHO office and see what else I can do."

"How about calling Lisa Calmette? Maybe she can help."

"That's an idea; I'll add it to my list. I'll also call Dr Gruber. He's promised me the patents on the plants."

Ken seized on the chance. "Why not wait here until the patents come?"

"*Bwana*, waiting won't solve anything. And patents are not a doctor's degree. I've decided, and I must go."

"Okay, Marijke. When?"

"Tomorrow. Lucas can take me, then do the lodge shopping. I'll send you a note with him on his return."

She slept in Jackal Cottage. Ken stayed on the veranda, despair in his heart and unable to think, hoping she would return. He slept in the chair.

In the early morning, Ken stood dejectedly before the bungalow while Lucas fetched Marijke's suitcase. She had packed it the day before. He joined her when she came from Jackal Cottage with a large cloth bag. "Marijke, please, call me immediately if you have any problems or need help."

"I will, *Bwana*; when I know what I must do, I'll tell you, and you can tell the *waganga*. Look after Shy and Mtoto. You might have to tell Gogo in a month."

As Lucas drove off, Ken waved a dispirited wave. *I don't know if I can tell Gogo.*

The Blue Sapphire Hotel was familiar. She told Lucas to shop for the lodge and return to the hotel in two days. Then she ate her dinner alone in her room, deep in thought. *Am I about to jump again? Will I come back? Can I become a doctor?*

Marijke woke in the morning thinking of Ken. *He must be hurting, but I must be strong.*

The appointment at the university was at ten, where she met the medical school dean. After a lengthy interview, he concluded: "*Bibie*, the lodge employees and their families recognise you as a *mganga*. The *jujus* you wear prove that to me. I know you have treated them for various accidents and illnesses, and that's acceptable, but that doesn't make you a doctor. Our degree takes four years, the last spent outside the country. Registration as a practising doctor will take two more years in the field.

"I'm sorry; I would like to help you, but we have no facilities for part-time study, so I suggest you look elsewhere. You could try Nairobi or South Africa."

"Sir, are you aware that in Katanga, many of the *waganga* who have completed a course at a medical college have registered as doctors, although they cannot receive payment for their services? The Traditional Medical Practitioners Act has been in place in Zimbabwe since 1982. Revised in 1997, it allows for registration as a traditional medicine practitioner, and South Africa is studying such an act."

"I know this, *Bibie*, and in Tanzania, such legislation is under consideration, but I'm afraid it will be several years before it is complete and implemented. You can continue to practise as a *mganga*. Still, as the others do, you must rely on the *waganga* for protection against malpractice, not the law that regulates qualified doctors."

Nursing her disappointment, Marijke had lunch at the hotel and thought, *Do I have the courage to go further than Dar? Do I want to? Shall I visit Katanga? At least that will be quicker. Perhaps that's the next step.*

After lunch, she asked the travel agent in the lobby about flights to Lubumbashi. She would have to route through Nairobi or Johannesburg, and she wondered, *The* mganga *who gave me my first juju said I would return, but I won't be going to buy a wedding dress. Does that mean I should go via Johannesburg, or not at all?*

Marijke had no appointment that afternoon, so she visited the WHO office.

When Ken awoke to wonder how Marijke was, he didn't go for breakfast. He didn't feel hungry but did manage a shower and a change of clothes, and then he left to see the elephants and sat on the fence bar. Shy and Mtoto came to him, hoping for a bun, but he hadn't thought to bring some. Shy tried to search his pockets, and it made him feel better to say, "You'll have to wait, Shy; I'm sure Mama Tembo will be back to feed you soon."

The elephants trotted off when the two boys came to feed them, and Ken ambled to the farm. *This farm is due to Marijke; I don't know if it will continue without her supervision.*

Ken couldn't raise the energy to do any lodge work; instead, he worked through his options and drafted emails. He asked for help for Marijke. Ken wrote to his father, Hendrik; Louis de La Vallee Poussin; and Lisa Calmette. He intended to send them once he had read Marijke's news.

A large envelope addressed to Marijke arrived with Jock's driver in the afternoon, but he didn't open it. He couldn't.

If I open it, I'm admitting she won't come back.

He had dinner in the boma that night, unusually silent. The rangers thought he was missing Marijke, as were they all.

Ken thought, *Lucas should return tomorrow night.*

Ken slept badly.

Is it better to know or not to know? At best, she'll tell me she will be away for a month or six weeks as she will visit Katanga.

The following day he still couldn't work. Instead, he waited in the office for Lucas to return with the promised letter from Marijke.

After desultorily trying to check the accounts, he fell asleep at his desk.

The distinctive sound of the double cab's engine woke him; he stood up slowly and advanced dejectedly to the office door. He wanted Marijke's letter, but at the same time, he didn't. *What will it say?*

A secretary at a desk near the front door of the WHO office took Marijke's name and then asked her to wait when she asked for the representative. While waiting, she sat on a comfortable couch and read a brochure on WHO operations. Although she had never met the representative, he had signed the letter with her WHO appointment document.

"Dr Coetzee, I'm delighted to meet you."

The man's greeting surprised Marijke. "Dr Richter, the pleasure is mine, but I'm not Dr Coetzee, just Marijke Coetzee."

"Don't you know yet?"

"Know what?"

"I think we must visit my office. Please follow me."

His office was spartan, with a large photo on the wall of some thirty young men wearing academic gowns, lined up in three rows, with a building in the background that Marijke thought of as Teutonic. When she stopped and looked at it, he said, "My Alma Mater, Heidelberg University. I'm sure I've aged a bit, but I'm the third from the left in the second row."

Marijke looked and said, "I can see the resemblance, but age has made you more handsome."

"Thank you. You flatter me. Please sit down."

Once she did, he said, "Before discussing vaccinations, let me clear up our minor disagreement regarding your qualification. A week ago, I received an instruction from Professor Gruber of my university; he's the head of pharmaceutical medicine and consultant to the WHO."

"Is he Dr Kurt Gruber, who visited our lodge four months ago?"

"The same. The instruction told me to send the enclosed letter and documents to you. I kept the originals due to the risk of loss and made the copies I sent. Let me give you the originals."

They must be the patents.

He opened a large brown envelope and handed four sheets to her; one was a large vellum sheet, another a handwritten letter, and the last two provisional patent certificates.

Completely bewildered, Marijke read the vellum sheet to learn that Heidelberg University had awarded her a doctorate in pharmaceutical medicine.

She said nothing, feeling dazed, and then read the letter.

Dear Marijke,

The degree is the least I could do; Helga entirely agrees. We both hope that you and Ken can attend the graduation ceremony and we can meet again.

My thanks and our warmest regards,
Prof. Kurt Gruber

"So, Dr Coetzee, you *are* a doctor," Dr Richter said.

"It seems so." *Although I still can't believe it. That must be why my patent application seemed like a thesis. He intended to help me.*

"Then I offer my congratulations. I hope you will accept the offer to attend the graduation ceremony in Heidelberg. It's on July the twenty-third."

"I'll try and convince Ken." *That shouldn't be too difficult.*

"Good, now about vaccinations."

Marijke dug in her handbag. "I have my report on the vaccination rate here and a request. I need someone who will fit into my system and travel to each *mganga* to decide who should carry a stock of vaccines for other *waganga* in the area. The chosen *waganga* must have small solar-powered chest fridges to store the vaccines—a simple system, with a panel, a wire, and a refrigerator plug, like yacht fridges. They'll stay cold all night after a boost during the day.

"The person must speak Swahili and, if possible, one of the local dialects. Although the person I request must set up new vaccination stores, I need another whose sole task is to count the unused vaccine doses and report the numbers to you here. It will be up to you to arrange to restock the refrigerators."

"And how do we prove how well we are doing without records?"

"It will take time, but once the number of cholera vaccinations delivered, with an annual booster cycle, is the same as the population, we'll be at one hundred per cent. And the same for all the others. I do note that expired vaccines must be returned to you here."

"Simple and effective, Doctor. I shall send this proposal to the WHO, and as Professor Gruber is a consultant, I shall send him a copy. I'm sure approval will come quickly.

"Now you have that degree, Doctor. Will you be registering in Tanzania?"

"No, I have no intention of practising as a doctor and charging for my services. I'm not sure that the degree alone would be acceptable for registration; years of hospital practice are a requirement. I'm a *mganga*, and my help is free of charge."

"In that case, registration is unnecessary; in an emergency, you have the right to take the necessary steps to save a life."

"Dr Richter, I'm returning to the lodge tomorrow morning. Do you have your wife with you in Dar?"

"I do; why?"

"Could you join me at the Blue Sapphire Hotel for dinner tonight to celebrate my new status? Say at seven-thirty?"

"Let me call my wife," he smiled. "Yes, it will be a pleasure. We'll see you then."

30

―――――

"Lucas, take me to a pharmacy and a shop selling beauty products for women, and then we can return to the lodge, *tafadhali*."

"Certainly, *Bibie*. I'll be glad to leave this madhouse."

"I agree with you. The peace of Rufisi is heaven compared with Dar. Have you nothing else to do?"

"Only to collect the stores I ordered yesterday; the supplier said he would have the cartons ready by ten."

They weren't. They had a snack at a sidewalk café and left at twelve.

Ken opened the door, expecting to see Lucas, and staggered backwards when Marijke threw herself at him and wrapped her arms around him. His reaction was unthinking; he held his arms around her tight. Then she kissed him. He had to take a deep breath when she broke off the kiss.

"Darling, you came back!"

"Yes, and you'd better kiss me again."

"I didn't kiss you; you kissed me."

"Okay, now it's your turn."

When he broke from the kiss, he asked, "Darling, why did you return?"

225

"When I reached Dar, I remembered something. In Nairobi, you promised to torture me, and you never did. Then you promised to kiss me, and you never did. So, I returned to give you another chance."

"Nothing else?"

"Lots of reasons that are less important."

Ken took her by the hand.

"Where are we going?"

"The torture room."

"I must shower, Bwana; I have dust everywhere, even between my toes."

"Okay, my darling, I'll shower after you."

When she left the bathroom wrapped in a towel, he entered it. She dried herself, hung the towel on a chair and was about to climb into the bed when she smiled, turned to the cupboard, removed six *kikkoy* and wrapped them around her, one on the other. Then she sat on the bed.

Ken came out naked, saw her, and when she stood, asked, "Darling, what are you wearing?"

"Six wrappings *Bwana*. I need unwrapping. The new me is a virgin; I feel like one, and you are my first."

Ken took her in his arms.

Ten minutes later, in bed, she thought, *I feel like the cheetah on the box; I remember he caressed the wooden chest like this; I want to twitch my tail.*

"*Bwana*, I bought a packet of condoms in Dar."

"Why?"

"In case you wanted them, I'm fertile right now. I haven't used a contraceptive in years."

"I don't. Do you?"

"No."

Then she surrendered to the feelings. She felt the accumulated tensions of the last few days draining away, and a sensation of warm relaxation invaded her as she thought, *I should have done this a lot sooner.* Then from the depths came something new that she had never felt before, a tension not in her mind but in her body that began to tingle under Ken's caresses, and she wondered, *Is this how a cheetah feels?*

The tingling grew and became waves of ecstasy, and she felt herself lose control and stop thinking as they coupled. *We're flying!*

A lot later, she thought, *I did twitch my tail, and I've been wrong all my life; sex is fantastic.*

"*Bwana,* did you fly?"

"Yes, my darling, with you in my arms."

"I hope you like children."

"When will you know?"

"Three weeks minimum."

"I hope it's positive; I want at least two children. Will you marry me?"

"Yes, *Bwana,* Rufisi is where I've landed; I belong here, with you. Do you have a letter for me?"

"How do you know? I didn't open it. I thought it was like admitting you wouldn't return if I did."

"I received the originals of the documents in it at the WHO office in Dar. Fetch it and read it."

He did, and when he read the vellum certificate, he thought, *My God, she deserves every bit of her success.*

"Marijke, this is fantastic; we must go."

"If you insist. But I don't have any smart clothes."

"Neither do I. We'll go three days earlier to Paris, buy clothes and then go to Heidelberg."

"That's marvellous, but I don't want to visit Paris."

"Where do you want to go?"

"Back to Nairobi." *The old* mganga *said I would.*

"Mama Keita can find me everything I want. I'll be uncomfortable in European clothes, and so will my *mizimu.* I'll buy a wedding dress as well."

"Tell me when, and I'll arrange for Lodge Air to fly us via Kilimanjaro to Nairobi. Would you like your family to come to the degree award? I'll invite mine."

"*Bwana*, with any luck, I'll be visibly pregnant by then. The shock will be too much for my mother."

"Okay, I have another solution. We'll make love again; we'll invite your family and mine to our wedding in three months. The villages will make it unforgettable, and our parents can attend the award ceremony."

"Why do you want to make love again?"

"Because I want to, as often as I can. I'm going to make up for the lost time. My love, you know my name; why don't you use it?"

"You told me to call you *Bwana*."

"Well, I'll take it back."

"Too late, dearest; you'll be *Bwana* until I die."

"You just said dearest."

"Oh, I'll use that and others when we are alone."

"Okay, my darling."

"That's better. Why are you waiting? I want to twitch my tail again."

"Like a cheetah?"

"No, like a woman."

Ken took her in his arms.

...

"*Bwana*, I've worked it out."

"What, my love?"

"You mustn't say 'my love' too often; then it becomes ordinary."

"Okay, dearest."

"Not dearest or darling either. Keep those for when it counts."

"Okay, what have you worked out?"

"The degree ceremony is in July; hopefully, I'll be six months pregnant by then, so it's okay to fly. I want to marry, say, two weeks before the degree ceremony so that it could be our honeymoon. We can tell our parents about our marriage in May. That gives us six months to prepare everything between now and the beginning of the dry season."

Her mother still doesn't know where she is.

"Darling, your mother doesn't know where you are, even if you are still alive. It's almost Christmas. We don't need to delay telling them, so why don't you tell her? It should make it a happy Christmas for her."

"I'll sleep on it. In your arms."

When they awakened the following morning, later than usual, Ken asked, "Darling, how will you tell your mother?"

"I don't know; I haven't thought that far." *I never will if he keeps running his hands over my tender bits.*

"I have a suggestion. Write your mother a letter. Then I'll send it to my father and ask him to have someone from his Cape Town office deliver it personally and gently break the news. The carrier can tell your mother he was here on holiday, and you gave him the letter. The Cape Town office can arrange her flight if she comes alone, and we can meet her in Nairobi. If your brother comes, we can meet them in Dar."

"Okay, but how about your father?"

"Don't worry about him; he'll arrive by plane or helicopter from Dar."

Marijke wrote the letter. It wasn't as easy as Ken had thought; she had to do it four times. In the end, this is what she wrote.

Dear Mama,

This letter must be a shock to you. I'm sorry I didn't write sooner. My life ended with the divorce, and thanks to a ~~maniac lunatic~~ marvellous man, I started a new life in Tanzania. We are getting married and want you and Petrus to join us, if you can, at ~~the~~ our celebration here in the Nyerere National Park. I have asked a visitor to ~~the~~ Rufisi Lodge to deliver this to you personally because there is no post office within two hundred kilometres and only a muddy track. Our wedding will be on the third of July.

Love, and we wish a Happy Christmas to you and Petrus.
Marijke.
PS. It'll be a big party, a ~~hundred~~ thousand guests lasting a week.

After showing this version to Ken, she wrote it without the corrections, and put the address on the envelope: "Mrs Marie-France Coetzee, Avalon Estate, Hermanus, South Africa". Ken sent it to his father with a cover letter.

Dear Papa,

The latest news. I'm engaged to marry a fantastic, incredible, beautiful woman called Marijke Coetzee. I'll confirm the date when it's fixed, but we have tentatively agreed on the third of July. She's a doctor, and you'll love her.

The marriage will take a week, for we have a thousand guests and it will take place here at Rufisi Lodge. Marijke hasn't seen her mother for months. Can someone from the Cape Town office personally deliver the included letter to her and gently break the news? And if she needs someone to arrange her flights, have the office do so? We will meet her in Nairobi or Dar es Salaam.

Love, Phillipe.

A driver took it to Jock's lodge, and the following evening the pilot handed it to a courier at Dar airport. Three days later, Ken and Marijke sat puzzling over an email.

Hi son.

Congratulations on growing up at last. I wouldn't miss your marriage. I shall personally deliver the invitation to Marie-France and bring her with me.

Dad.

"Is your dad in Cape Town?"

"I don't know, but how did he receive our letters if he is?"

"A personal assistant in France opened it and emailed the contents?"

"I don't think he would allow an assistant to open personal correspondence."

"The only solution is that the letter reached him just before he was due to leave for South Africa."

"That sounds possible, but we will have a problem if they arrive now."

"Why, *Bwana?*"

"The single rooms are fully booked; we've only Hippo, the family cottage, to give them. It's the Christmas holiday season."

"It has two bedrooms."

"But they would have to share the bathroom. My father will accept if I explain the problem; how about your mother?"

Marijke thought about her mother; she had the image of the house in the Cape in her mind. She was about to say her mother would be upset when the picture changed; she saw the path before the baobab and the cheetah male in front of her, and then the female brushed by and joined the male. The picture she saw was crystal clear; the female rubbed her cheeks against the male before jumping into the brush with him following.

"Marijke, are you okay? I asked if your mother would object to sharing a bathroom."

Marijke hadn't realised she had stopped breathing; her breath exploded. "I was about to say she wouldn't share when the cheetah *mzimu* came to tell me it would be okay."

"Okay, I'll block the room for them." *That's a weird reply. I wonder what got into her.*

And Marijke thought, *We'll find out when they arrive.*

They didn't know that Hendrik d'Yquem opened the letter from Marijke and froze in shock. Then after recovering, he turned to his computer and checked the history of the Avalon Estate and its owner. Originally named Eagle's Nest, it had a chequered history of failed crops and owners until Johannes Coetzee, an estate owner near Stellenbosch, bought it.

When he died, his second son, Gert Coetzee, inherited the estate and made it a success by introducing grape varieties that he had studied in France at the Chateau d'Avalon estate. Gert had married the French estate's daughter, Marie-France. When he returned to the Cape from France, Gert had renamed Eagle's Nest to Avalon. Gert had died two years ago, and Petrus, his son, was now the owner.

Now sure of her identity, he sent the reply to Ken, then sat trying to calculate how old she was, for he remembered her well. *She was only a year younger than me, maybe eighteen months, so she will now be fifty-eight. She married at about twenty-one, so Petrus, her son, might be a max of thirty-seven and Marijke a minimum of twenty-eight.*

Then he called his flight crew and left for Cape Town.

At breakfast the following morning, Marijke asked, "*Bwana*, we'll learn why your father will deliver my letter when they arrive. If my brother comes, where do we put him?"

"Mongoose Cottage, Marijke; it's often empty. I should remodel it."

"Let's do an extension to Mongoose Cottage; I'll have a look and see what needs doing. Have you still got the tents that were here originally?"

"Yes, they're in the workshop store, but I don't know their condition. Why?"

"Don't build those two new cottages you planned. We need a private safari camp; put all the tents together in a semicircle in a clearing beyond the spa; under the big tree and hidden away. The guests can have private dinners there if they wish; then we have accommodation for two families, and when it's available, we can put our professional visitors there."

"That's a great idea; I'll look at the site today." *She talks as if she's already my wife. That's great.*

While Hendrik spent fifteen hours in his jet on the way to Cape

Town, with a stop at Sao Tome for fuel, Ken looked at the campsite, and Marijke checked Mongoose Cottage.

Then two days after she had said yes to Ken, Lucas came to see her.

"*Bibie*, the *mganga* in the woodcarver's village says there is a problem, and he wants to see you."

"Please tell Amali to bring a car and take me there."

"I'll take you, *Bibie*; when will we go?"

"Now, if you are free." *It must be essential for Lucas to volunteer.*

Half an hour later, they arrived at the village, and Marijke entered the *mganga's* home. The *mganga* greeted her gravely, and Marijke asked, "*Baba*, what is the problem?"

"*Bibie*, I asked you to come because I must warn you. I have heard from two villages that a government man has visited. The *waganga* in those villages say that he asks about you and what you do; we do not know why. We have learned little."

Marijke felt a lead weight building in her gut. *It's not over; will I have to leave before my marriage? Will it never end?*

"What have you learned?"

"We think the leader of the poachers has complained about you being here; he may be paying money to stir up trouble."

"What have the *waganga* told him?"

"We do not talk about each other, *Bibie*, so they have said that you are a *mganga* with three spirits and that the *duma* and the *tembo* are your friends; they have also told the people he has an evil spirit in him, and they must not talk to him. They must send him to the *mganga*."

That might stop him from getting information but will drag things out for months. I can't afford that; it must be now if the government will deport me.

She took a deep breath. "*Baba*, tell all *waganga*; they are to tell him to come and see me if he wants information. They should also tell him that I'm a nurse from the Catholic hospital in Dar, that the World Health Organization has appointed me to improve vaccinations, and that I have two university degrees; one is in medicine from Germany."

"I shall do that, *Bibie*. If you have problems with this man, the *waganga* will act."

I won't tell Ken, at least not now.

31

The phone rang in the big house on the Avalon Estate outside Cape Town. "Good morning, Avalon Estate. Can I help you?"

"Possibly, I'm a helicopter pilot; I must bring a gentleman to your estate tomorrow morning at about ten. Is there a place to land a helicopter, and do I need permission?"

"There is a place, sir. Helicopters occasionally land on the front lawn. I must ask the master for permission."

"Okay, can you do so? I'll wait ...."

"Sir, the master says you're welcome."

"Thank you. Goodbye."

The tall, slim, handsome man with a mane of silver hair surprised Petrus, who, on hearing the helicopter, had come to the front lawn to greet him.

"Good morning, sir; welcome to Avalon."

He extended a hand, and the visitor shook it as he said, "You must be Petrus. I'm Hendrik d'Yquem. I'm pleased to meet you."

"Yes, I am Petrus, sir. Have you come to taste our wines?"

"I would love to do so; I know the varieties you grow here well and would like to compare them with those in France. But I came to see your mother as well as you."

235

"Do you know her?"

"I did, forty years ago. I didn't know Marie-France was here. I have news of your sister."

"Marijke?"

"Yes."

"Good or bad?"

"Good, nothing but good."

"That's a relief. Let's go into the house, and I'll have someone call her. Do you prefer tea or coffee?"

"Coffee, please."

The news that a gentleman had come to see her surprised Marie-France, but she chose her best day dress, touched up her makeup, and brushed her still-luxuriant hair. The maidservant didn't mention the visitor's name, but when she stepped daintily into the lounge and he stood, she stopped dead, the blood leaving her face. Hendrik stepped forward in case she fainted, but with a considerable effort, she remained upright and said, "Hendrik! What a surprise."

"Can I give you a surprise hug, Mousseline?" He spread his arms.

"Of course." She moved into his arms and thought, *They still feel the same!* "No one has called me that for decades."

After a time that seemed too short for both, Hendrik let her go, and Petrus said, "Mama, he has news of Marijke."

"*Marijke!* Where is she, and how is she?"

"She's in Tanzania, at a game lodge in the Nyerere National Park. I haven't met her, and I only know she has a medical degree from Heidelberg University and is about to marry my son. I have a letter for you from her."

"Then give it to me, but there's something wrong: my daughter has a degree in law from Cape Town university."

"Well, read your letter first."

Marie-France did, then passed it to Petrus. "Well, that sounds like my daughter, but she's been gone a little less than a year, so she can't have a medical degree."

Hendrik grinned. "Then you must come with me and find out.

When I heard my son would marry her, I checked out what I could and found you. Then, I spoke to a professor of medicine at Heidelberg University, Kurt Gruber. He met Marijke at the lodge and told me she's the finest field surgeon he's ever seen, and if Kurt says so, it's true. He also said that she's the WHO-appointed expert on vaccinations in East Africa and has patents filed for some potent medicines."

"My God, it doesn't sound like the Marijke I last saw. If it's true, then something incredible has happened. I'll come. Is your wife with you?"

"She died five years ago, Marie-France, suddenly. She was older than me, but it was still a shock to me, especially my son."

"I can understand that. Gert died two years ago, and I'm only now over it, and I have Petrus to support me. Was your son with you?"

"At her death, yes, but then he disappeared for nearly three years until Phillipe finally told me where he was."

Petrus asked, "Mama, when did you meet Mr d'Yquem?"

"Before I met your father, Petrus. He was the grandson of the next-door estate's owner. We were at the same school for years. Then he disappeared to study in Paris, and a year or two later, your father came to study wines in the area, and I met and married him."

"So, he was your old love?"

"My first one, Petrus," *And I gave my virginity to him between the vines on the hill.*

Hendrik added, "Mine too; I was devastated to hear you married."

"I'll bet, devastated for the two minutes between the blonde and the redhead. Who owns the estates in France now?"

"I do; I bought Chateau d'Avalon when your brother drove it into the ground and declared bankruptcy, and I bought ours from my uncle when he did the same. They both do very well; they have Rothschild's Estates on the label, and when I left the finance world, I became a producer of fine wines."

"Now I know you haven't changed. You were always the smartest kid in the school."

Petrus asked, "Are you a Rothschild, sir?"

"In a way. An arranged marriage to join two estates was quite common in the past. My grandmother was Baron Rothschild's daughter and married d'Yquem. Their son was my father, so Baron Rothschild was my great-grandfather, but all rights disappeared when my grandmother married d'Yquem.

"However, I can take your mother to Tanzania. I know how busy it is on a wine estate when the harvest is due, so if you only want to take a few days off, come when you can; you can fly to Dar and take the Lodge Air taxi."

Marie-France made a snap decision. "Hendrik, can you stay the night? I'll pack what I need and come with you tomorrow. I must see my daughter."

"Mousseline, I'd love to; I'll see the pilot and arrange it. We can fly to Dar tomorrow."

They switched languages without either of them noticing; it was so natural. As the helicopter approached to land at Cape Town International Airport, Marie-France said in French, "Hendrik, *ce n'est pas le terminal international.*"

He replied in French, "No, it's the VIP terminal; I have my jet here."

And they continued in French.

"*Incroyable.* Wow."

"Suddenly, I feel forty years younger, Mousseline."

"Why?"

"Because you are speaking French."

"Hendrik, now you mention it, I do too."

Five and a half hours later, they entered the VIP terminal building at Dar es Salaam to clear immigration.

"Hendrik, do they know we are coming?"

"Yes, I sent my son an email. We will land at a nearby lodge with an airstrip, and they will meet us there."

"They must be excited; I wonder what they expect."

"My son will discover you are a young and beautiful copy of your daughter, just a year or two older, and your daughter will discover I'm an ancient copy of my son. One look, and she may change her mind after seeing what my son will be like when he gets older."

"You're very flattering, Hendrik, but don't run yourself down. You're still young, fit and vigorous. Your suntan makes you handsome; remember, I like older men."

"I remember, but it's only eighteen months."

"At seventeen, that's a tenth of the past lifetime. You were an older man."

Hendrik grinned at her, "Well, certainly old enough."

She blushed and said nothing but thought, *Hendrik remembers.*

"The air taxi pilot should be here any moment."

Fifteen minutes later, they climbed into the Lodge Air Taxi, Hendrik carrying the huge bouquet the pilot handed them.

"Welcome to Selous," the pilot said, "The office says you are Ken and Marijke's parents. They are a fantastic couple. The flight will be an hour, for this is a slow but safe aeroplane."

"Ken? I thought his name was Phillipe?"

Hendrik replied, "It is, but after he left home when his mother died, he visited countries where the surname comes first. When he gave his name as Phillipe d'Yquem, he became Monsieur Phillipe, and d'Yquem became Ken; Phillipe told me that he introduced himself as Ken Phillips in English-speaking countries."

"Does your daughter speak French?" asked Hendrik.

"She did, but she's probably out of practice unless they speak French with each other."

"Well, we'll learn in an hour."

Marie-France thought as she buckled her seatbelt, *I must be crazy. I'm looking forward to this meeting with more pleasure than I've felt in months. I think it's because Hendrik is with me.*

Hendrik thought, *Our children will be even more shocked than us to learn we were once in love.*

As the Cessna Caravan stopped on the small, paved square in front of the thatched two-room building at the airport, Hendrik opened the door, lowered the step and helped Marie-France down as Ken and Marijke approached. Marie-France looked up once her feet were on the ground and saw Marijke. The delighted grins on both women's faces told Hendrik and Ken what would happen next, and seconds later, mother and daughter were in a tight hug.

Hendrik offered his hand to Ken. "Do we shake hands or hug?"

"I think a hug is in order, Papa."

The two men embraced, then turned to the women. Ken said in wonder, "They look like sisters."

"Marie-France has changed only a little since I first met her."

"Papa, have you known her for a long time?"

"Since I was eighteen, Phillipe. She was my first love."

"*Mon Dieu*. Let me introduce Marie-Jeanne."

"I thought her name was Marijke?"

"She told me that the kids she played with as a child shortened it, and she has been Marijke ever since."

"Then she will be Marijke for me."

Ken had to break up the two women, who still had an arm around each other. "Marijke, can I introduce my father, Hendrik d'Yquem?"

"Of course." She stepped straight up, hugged him, and kissed both cheeks. "You have me confused, Monsieur; I'm not sure which of you I shall marry."

Hendrik looked at her affectionately, thinking, *She's like Marie-France when I last saw her at twenty.*

"I'm sorry it won't be me; your mother will always be my first love."

"*Mon Dieu*, I shall hear the whole story from her. *Bwana*, come and meet my mother."

Ken stepped forward and embraced Marie-France, who hugged him tightly.

"I'm as confused as Marijke; you look so alike I may marry the wrong woman."

"Your confusion won't last," said Marie France. "Welcome to our family."

"And you to ours. Let's move out of the sun while the staff load the baggage and freight in the truck. Unless there's an objection, we'll take the open safari wagon for the short drive to our lodge."

Once in the airfield building, where a white-coated waiter served them iced champagne and lemonade, Hendrik turned to Ken and said, "Marijke looks like she belongs here. Does she always dress in such colourful dresses and wear those amulets?"

"She does; she must have a hundred dresses of unusual colours, all gifts from the people. The villages compete to dress her. The amulets are *jujus*; she's a *mganga*, and they are part of her regalia."

Marie-France had heard and asked Ken, "What is a *mganga*?"

Marijke replied, "A *sangoma*, Mama, the same."

"And you are one? That's unexpected. Are you important?"

Ken replied, "The most famous and important woman in the province; if I don't marry her, I must leave the country."

Marie-France thought, *He's exaggerating, but that's because he loves her. I'm content.*

Hendrik's thoughts differed. *He wrote that she was fantastic, so it's probably all true; after all she has the degree and the WHO appointment.*

32

The drive to the lodge brought forth oohs and aahs from Marie-France as Marijke pointed out the game to her mother. Hendrik was impressed by the game density; it was far higher than the photos and reported figures he had received when he learned Ken would stay at Rufisi. He had investigated the ownership of the lodge and found Ken had one share; then, unknown to Ken, he had bought up the available shares through one of his companies. Then he'd given instructions that the lodge should never be short of funds, for he had thought, *Hidden help is more effective than a gift; no one can force him out now. And the forty-five per cent owned by Louis Poussin poses no danger.*

As they drew up in front of the lodge, there was another surprise for all four. The small group of singers and dancers that usually welcomed the lodge's guests had swelled to over a hundred, all dressed for a party.

"Phillipe, is this normal?" Hendrik asked.

"No, Papa, we have a small group of ten with a drummer to welcome our guests. It's spontaneous; I have nothing to do with it. You and Marie-France are VIP guests, so they are showing you how much they appreciate your coming. Please, let's sit in those chairs and enjoy the show. I think you'll be surprised."

Ten minutes later, after the men performed and sang a welcome song and dance, which Marijke explained included a plea to the *mzimu* for their health and happiness, the women filed in, chanting. Marijke told her mother, "Mama, I need to join them." She did, and both parents watched, awed, as Marijke blended into the crowd of women, singing and dancing with them. They could see how she enjoyed it.

"Phillipe, you can never take her away from here. She belongs; she's a part of this country."

"I don't intend to leave, Papa. Our graves will be here."

Hendrik replied, "It's good to know where you belong."

"Papa, they will offer you some presents; you will receive a fly whisk made from strips of animal hide. Please accept and carry it while here; it symbolises wisdom and confers status, like getting a degree in Europe. It's also useful. Marie-France will receive a dress or two; encourage her to wear them in appreciation."

"I don't think she'll need encouragement; she surprises me daily."

"Marijke amazes me too."

When the ceremony and the giving of the gifts ended, they moved inside for lunch. The table where the rangers sat had an added section, and Ken was astonished when Marijke spread their family of four between the rangers around the table.

Hendrik thought, *A brilliant woman; I'm beginning to realise her quality.* Then he settled down to eat and ask the rangers about their jobs and how they liked working at Rufisi. By the time the meal finished, he knew that they considered the lodge the best in the country, a pleasure to work at, and believed Marijke was almost a Goddess. One said, "To work at a lodge where the mistress walks with wild cheetahs and elephants is something we cannot do elsewhere. Rufisi is magical. I shall stay here."

Hendrik thought, *It's an exaggeration, a metaphor, but I'm feeling something I've never felt elsewhere.*

Marie-France was more interested in her future son-in-law and learned that every adult called him *Bwana*, but all the children called him *Baba*, meaning father.

"Isn't that unusual?"

One of the rangers replied, "Yes, but '*Baba*' is also a word that applies to a highly respected man, a grandfather. We may call him '*Bwana*', but he and your daughter look after us. The children call her '*Mama*'."

Once the lunch was over, Ken said, "I'm afraid you took us by surprise, and because of our bookings, all we have available is Hippo, a two-bedroomed family cottage. I felt sure my father would not object to sharing, and I asked Marijke if her mother would, and she replied that her cheetah spirit recommended it. So, I suggest Marijke shows her the cottage while I show my father around the lodge."

Marie-France thought that an excellent idea; she had many questions for her daughter.

"Let's start at the beginning, Marijke. Why did you come here?"

Marijke gave her the whole story, from Table Mountain to the doctorate.

Then Marie-France asked, "Have you lived with your *Bwana* all this time?"

"Yes, Mama, but he refused to have sex with me; he said I had to be free to decide what I would do in my new life. He took me to bed when I told him I had decided to stay here."

"That's a fairy tale."

"It is, Mama, even more of one than you can imagine; I'm sure you will learn why in the next few weeks."

"Will you have children here?"

"Yes Mama, I may be pregnant already."

Ken showed his father around the entire lodge and proudly showed him the enclosed hectare plot where food plants, with a corner of flowers and a pond of toads, grew in raised beds.

"This is massive, far more than the lodge needs," said Hendrik.

"It will grow. It's self-sustaining, costs nothing, and might feed thousands."

"How can it cost nothing?"

"The land is free, the water is free and pumped with solar pumps, and the farmers renew the seed by collecting it from selected plants. The workers change the soil regularly, so fertiliser is unnecessary. Marijke taught the *waganga*; each has a section and competes for the best crops. The labour is free as they have the food in exchange, and the lodge pays for the food it uses, but the money goes to materials for maintenance and expansion. I'm going to apply for a bio label for the lodge.

"Marijke organised the whole thing."

"How can one woman do all this?"

"Not one woman, one *mganga*. She only has to say what she wants, and they do it."

"How is that possible?"

"I cannot explain it, but you will learn. Let me take you to your cottage. I've arranged an introductory game drive at five, and dinner is at eight after our return."

After the game drive, sundowners on a low hill near a part of the river filled with a mass of hippos under the nearly full moon, and then a sumptuous dinner, they all retired to bed. At least, Ken and Marijke did.

"Darling, I think the day passed well; I love your mother, and my father is impressed with the lodge, particularly your farm."

"It did go well. It was a shock to learn our parents knew each other when they were young, but they seem to be getting along well."

"They are. Let's sleep; I'm tired, and we have another long day tomorrow."

Marijke and Ken had no idea how well they were getting along. At that moment, after a cool shower and wearing only pyjama shorts, Hendrik had gone to sit on the veranda of their cottage with an iced drink in his hand, overlooking the river and the riverside plain where under the three-quarter moon, hundreds of hippos were grazing and grunting.

Marie-France came from the bathroom wearing a diaphanous

peignoir; seeing him sitting there, she came to join him. While she absorbed the view and listened to the hippos, she said nothing.

It was Hendrik who broke the silence. "There is a peace and happiness here that I haven't experienced in years."

"I feel the same. Those hippos are noisy, but the sounds make the silence between grunts far more intense than a lack of sound."

"I never thought of it like that; it's a bit like the hill of vineyards under the moon, where the wind rustles the leaves occasionally, and the occasional hoot of an owl breaks the silence."

They sat a bit longer, and Hendrik said, "Much as I would like to sit here all night, I think we should go to bed; it's been a long day."

"Hendrik, do you remember those nights in the vineyard, in our special place?"

"How could I ever forget, my dear?"

"When years go by, can we ever recapture them, or must we just live with the memories?"

"I believe the past is past; all that stays is the memories. But our children have found another path. You cannot resurrect the past, but creating a new life is possible. It might be easier when you're young, but it must be possible at any age."

Marie-France took a deep breath and said, "Hendrik, could we create a new life—together?"

"I don't know, Mousseline, but if we open the window to hear the hippos, we can try."

He stood and took her hand, then as she swayed towards him, he took her in his arms and kissed her.

...

"I heard the owl hoot, Hendrik."

"I know; I heard it too."

At the breakfast table, Ken thought Marijke gave him a few inquiring looks, with an odd grin and smile; however, he didn't understand. Then, when his father said, "Marijke was telling us about your poacher problem. Can you summarise what the problem is?" he forgot Marijke's odd grin.

Ken told him about everything they'd been through.

Hendrik frowned, "*Mon Dieu!* It sounds like a full-scale war. It's a problem that needs a radical solution; I must think about it. What kind of hunting is the worst?"

"Rhino horn to start with. The rhinos are almost extinct here, so we have removed the horns of the remaining three. The horn is only hair, so the rhino suffers no pain. Radioactive tracers didn't work.

"Elephant and hippo ivory is the next; the poachers are contract hunters working for a criminal organisation. The damage they do is enormous when they kill females, particularly lactating females. Marijke will take you to meet her orphaned baby elephants we must raise for up to two years."

"In a way, you haven't stopped the hunting by destroying the vehicles. But you've made it unprofitable because they must pay for new trucks, even stolen ones. So, they've stopped. I'll think about it.

"Marie-France, do you want to brush your teeth, or can I use the bathroom?"

"Go ahead, Hendrik, I'll follow; then Marijke can introduce us to her elephants."

Lucas arrived. "*Bibie*, a boy with a bad cut is at the bungalow. The nurse wants your advice."

"Mama, come with me; I must look at a bad cut, then you can visit your cottage. I'll meet you back at the lounge."

Marie-France watched; she couldn't understand what her daughter said in Swahili but understood that Marijke was teaching her young assistant as she checked the movement of the badly cut finger in every direction for a severed tendon. The authority and competence displayed by her daughter amazed her.

After Marijke and Marie-France watched the assistant put in the deep stitches, Marijke said, "Now sew up the outside and use lots of the magic powder. Then bandage the finger and tape three fingers together; he must not use them for ten days. Ask the *mganga* if the boy is up to date with tetanus. If not, vaccinate him."

Marie-France accompanied her as Marijke stood and left the

veranda. "Don't you want to wait until it's all sewn up and bandaged?"

"The only way to build up confidence in what she does is to leave her to do it; showing confidence in her is important."

Marijke met Ken on the way to the lounge. He asked, "What were those grimaces you made at breakfast?"

"You can stop worrying about how well our parents are getting along."

"Why?"

"Because they slept in one bed last night."

"Is this one of your visions?"

"No, the maid told me."

Ken laughed. "Marijke, it makes me feel happy; how about you?"

She grinned at him, "Well, as she looks like me, and he looks like you, it's an approval of our life together."

When Marie-France arrived at the bungalow, Hendrik was still there.

"Hendrik, I think my daughter knows about last night."

"I'm not surprised, my darling; we forgot to mess up the second bedroom. We must decide whether we sneak off and marry or ask them to make it a double wedding?"

"I think we should let them have their wedding, but we could ask them to let us marry an hour earlier."

Marijke had a question for Lucas.

"Lucas, do you know anything more about the man asking questions about me?"

"Yes, *Bibie*, but he hasn't returned after visiting three villages."

That's even more worrying than a visit to see me.

"Well, if you hear anything, tell me please; I told the *waganga* that he should come and see me."

33

The following day Ken rose at his usual six but returned to tell Marijke, "The rangers caught a poacher, and two others escaped, so we have a problem."

"Why?"

"If he doesn't leave the park, the others will tell the police we have kept him locked up, and we'll have the police here. If we let him go, he'll just come back, so we have no choice but to take him to the police and lay a charge, but they will let him go and never process the charge."

"Where is he?"

"The rangers are bringing him here."

"Then I must talk to *Baba*, I don't know if he can do it, but I have an idea."

Lucas drove her in a safari car, and she returned an hour later. "*Bwana*, tell the rangers to take him to the *mganga* and then wait—it should be an hour to an hour and a half; then to take him and *Baba* to the police where he will make a confession to the police, reveal the identity of the other two, and lay a charge against them."

"Marijke, how is that possible?"

"Hypnosis, *Bwana*. *Baba* must convince the man under hypnosis to tell the truth; the suggestion will force him to do so. *Baba* will go with the rangers as he's unsure how long the suggestion will last once the man wakes, so he won't wake him until they arrive at the police station. I think it will last a long time, for he will tell him when under hypnosis that an evil spirit will consume him from the inside out if he tells a lie."

"The surprises never stop happening with you around. I'll tell them, then join you and our parents for breakfast."

Four days later, it was the night of the full moon.

After dinner in the boma, Marijke announced, "When the moon is bright, we can see the animals come to the water from the veranda. We like to sit and watch; please join us. If the elephants come, it will be late before we sleep."

They sat among the paying guests as a group, and Hendrik was surprised the full ranger complement had gathered at one end of the veranda. Then he thought, *I suppose this is routine; the rangers must go with the guests to their cottages, and if it's a time when the animals are moving, it makes sense.*

They sat with night-vision binoculars, although the water's edge was only a hundred and fifty metres away. They watched the varied species come to drink, avoiding the hippos who ruled the area, remaining clustered in their groups. They saw two hyenas come to drink and then leave. The chirrup of crickets, the grunt of hippos, and the distant roar of a lion filled the night air.

Then one of the rangers said, "*Tembo.*"

Ken said, "You can't see the elephants yet; it's a different vibration in the air. Live here long enough, and you can feel the rhythm of the bush change."

The elephants came, clustered by the waterside, bathing and drinking. Then Marijke said, "I can see Gogo. That's Uhuru beside her."

"Then be careful, my darling."

She smiled at him. "Thanks, *Bwana*; I won't be long."

Everyone, except the rangers and Ken, was amazed when Marijke stood and strode from the veranda towards the elephants.

Marie-France exclaimed, "Where's she going? Isn't it dangerous?"

Ken replied calmly, "She's going to say hello to her friends; she'll be back soon."

They saw the matriarch and a shorter elephant walk towards Marijke, and when they met, it seemed the matriarch caressed her head with the tip of her trunk, and the smaller one came for a scratch or caress. Then suddenly, the matriarch raised her trunk in the air, stepped to one side and appeared to push Marijke towards the elephants, who were closing ranks, moving the babies to the centre of the herd.

A ranger said, "*Simba.*"

To the right, two lions appeared, walking towards the water.

Marie-France asked, agitated, "Where's Marijke?"

"With the baby elephants in the middle of the herd, the adults guard them and her; she'll be alright."

The elephants were moving slowly away from the lions, keeping the herd in a tight group with the enormous elephants on the lions' side.

Hendrik asked, "How's she going to return?"

"Watch, there's no hurry; the lions will leave."

Another ranger, with binoculars, said, "The *duma* has come for her."

"What's a *duma*?" asked Hendrik.

Ken answered, "A cheetah. One is walking towards the elephants on the opposite side to the lions."

"Why?"

"The *duma* is no danger to the elephants, and vice versa; they ignore each other so they can walk close, unlike lions which will kill a small elephant. Marijke will see it, join the cheetah, and then walk back to the road with it. Amali, take the baggage buggy and collect her."

Hendrik and Marie-France were both stupefied. Then Hendrik whispered to her, "It was no metaphor; the ranger said this place was magical, and he was right. If I can help to spread the magic, I shall."

Marijke arrived, flushed but happy. "*Bwana*, Gogo knows I'm pregnant."

"How can she know that?"

"Odour, or sense, she caressed my tummy; perhaps she can hear a heartbeat."

Hendrik and Marie-France tried the spa. They hadn't discussed the previous evening; the enormity of it left little to say. Up to their necks in the mud bath, Marie-France said, "I feel a little like an elephant."

"Me too, but I want to caress you like an elephant."

Marie-France chuckled. "Please do; they like it. I think I shall too."

"So, what do you think of your daughter now?"

"Something marvellous has happened. Your son seems part of it, but it's beyond me; I can only accept what I saw. Marijke wants to visit Nairobi to buy a wedding dress. I'll go with her and buy one too. Will you fly us there from Dar?"

"Of course, my love; say when. Did you notice that our bed cover has changed?"

"No, what is it?"

"A vineyard scene with grapes."

"Then let's have a shower."

Hendrik removed his satphone from his suitcase and put it on charge. That evening he sent a message to Louis Poussin, asking him to call. Then he told Ken and Marijke before dinner, "I've asked Louis Poussin to call; you've met Lisa, his daughter-in-law. As Louis is a significant shareholder in the lodge, you should ask him to your wedding."

The call came the following morning as Hendrik finished breakfast.

"Good morning, Louis; good of you to call."

"Good morning, Hendrik. What are you doing at our favourite lodge?"

"A long story. My son is here, so I'm visiting."

"About time. Phillipe's done an excellent job with that lodge. Is it a special occasion?"

"Indeed it is; he's marrying a fantastic woman, and I'm marrying the woman's mother."

Louis laughed. "Hendrik, I'm not surprised at his marriage. Marijke is incredible, but I didn't know you had met her mother."

"That's a long story too. Have you met Marijke?"

"No, but Lisa knows all about her and has told me about her."

"Then let me pass the phone to Marijke."

"Good morning, Dr Poussin," Marijke said.

"Marijke, forget about the titles; call me Louis. Have you called to invite us to the wedding?"

"Yes, Louis, we'd all be delighted if you could come with all your family."

"Then message me the dates, and I'll arrange it. What would you like as a wedding present?"

"It's a silly idea, Louis, but Phillipe dreams of the day rhinos with horns walk on the plain in front of the lodge, and I would love some giraffes."

"Why's it silly, Marijke?"

"Because Phillipe says the rhino-horn poachers will take them out in less than three months."

"Then I'll talk to my son about it. My regards to all. Bye."

"Bye, Louis."

When Marijke put down the phone, she asked Hendrik, "Poussin or de La Vallee Poussin?"

"Why do you ask?"

"Louis de La Vallee Poussin dedicated a book to Phillipe; it's in the lounge bookshelf."

"The same man, Marijke. I'll be surprised if his son Leo knows his father dedicated a book. I'll enjoy telling him."

Marijke received an email from Dr Richter.

Dear Marijke,

I feel I should give you this news. A man from the Ministry of Health came to see me today. He had a list of questions about you and your qualifications. I answered truthfully and ensured he understood you were a *mganga* and not practising as a paid doctor. I asked questions, and he told me the Ministry was only investigating a report they received from someone outside the government. He assured me the Ministry has no intention of interfering in the excellent work that you are doing, particularly in the vaccination field. I believe you will hear no more about this.

Dr HG Richter

Marijke had almost forgotten about the man making the inquiries, so the email brought back the worry and the thought, *Will I ever marry?*

34

Three nights after Marijke walked with the elephants and the cheetah, Gogo came to see Shy and Mtoto. Marijke knew Gogo would be in the grey morning light at the pen.

There was one difference that morning. When Marijke offered a bun to Gogo, instead of taking it, Gogo caressed her back, so Marijke turned and saw, held in the elephant's trunk, a sprig of brush that Gogo offered her. She took it and said, "Thanks, Gogo; I'll try to understand why you've given this to me."

Back at the bungalow, when the first rays of sunlight gave better light, she examined the gift. A half dozen dried sticks with dried leaves or flowers along each length. *They look like dead lavender.*

When Ken came for breakfast, she asked about it. He replied, "I don't know what it is, darling; you'll have to ask Lucas or a *mganga*."

Later that day, she found a *mganga* from a distant village at the farm and learned the answer.

"It's the plant that the *mzimu* never leaves. It is dead, dried out because it has had no water. But its *mzimu* will never leave it. Even after years, the *mzimu* stays there. If you put it in water, it will grow green again."

"Where does it grow?"

"In the hills, high, in dry, rocky places."

255

Marijke wondered, *How did Gogo get it? That's a mystery I'll never solve.*

She asked a botanist at Nairobi University and sent a picture. The reply said, "*Myrothamnus flabellifolius*, sometimes called the resurrection plant."

Then Marijke knew why Gogo gave it to her.

They stayed at the Norfolk Hotel in Nairobi. Hendrik said he had a business meeting, so the two women took a taxi to the market. Marie-France was surprised at the reception; it appeared everyone there knew they were coming. Mama Keita was beaming; her two daughters were there, and an older woman, a dressmaker, took Marie-France to another stall to choose a wedding dress.

Marijke wasn't the least surprised.

Mama Keita grinned at her when she said her wedding dress had to be 'loose'.

"I know, *Bibie*, the Elephant told me. She will come in three days."

For four days, they returned each morning to try on the dresses at various stages and had snack lunches in the market.

Each day was different; Marie-France didn't see anyone organise them, but small groups of young or teenage children came and performed songs and dances.

Marijke observed her mother and thought, *My mother hasn't realised, but she's absorbing the Swahili words as I did.*

On the fourth day, Marijke was delighted with a new rendering of *Hakuna Matata* in Swahili, and then the market fell quiet as the old *mganga*, who she had met on her first day in Nairobi, supported by two young women, came to the stall.

When Marijke saw her, she went at once to her and repeated her first curtsy, but one much deeper.

Marie-France was surprised. She was about to say something when she realised a crowd of people, jammed in every available space, was watching and something special was happening.

Then Marijke said, "Great Grandmother, your child has come with your gift."

She opened her bag and removed the dried sprig of Gogo's gift. "Great Grandmother, I brought you a gift from the elephants to carry with you." Then she placed it carefully in the old *mganga's* hands.

The *mganga* said, "I need only one *juju* to guide my way. I have looked for someone worthy to receive my *jujus*, and only you have the approval of the elephants to carry the *mzimu* of the Great Elephant."

With the help of an assistant, she took two *jujus* from around her neck and gave them to Marijke. Marijke put them on and then looked into the lovely eyes that smiled at her as the old woman said, "I thank you; I know the elephants approve of my choice. The time will come when you must choose a successor and pass on the *mzimu* of the Great Elephant; choose carefully. Perhaps your daughter will be worthy."

She knows my baby will be a girl. "Great Grandmother, the *mzimu* will be safe with me."

"I know; listen to the advice of the wise eagle."

Then the old lady turned, and the women helped her away.

After a pause, Marijke asked Mama Keita, "What is her name?"

"The Great Elephant. We will call her that until she dies, but you are now The Elephant."

"No, I mean the name she had as a little girl."

"Asatira."

Marijke and her mother returned shortly afterwards to the hotel; a second taxi carried their clothing.

A week after the Nairobi trip, Hendrik told Marie-France, "If you can tear yourself away from your daughter, how about us going to France? I can show you Chateau d'Avalon and my old estate, and we can decide where we want to live."

"Hendrik, I think Marijke and Phillipe need some time without us cluttering up the country, so I agree, but are those the only two estates you have?"

"How did you guess?"

"We could walk between those estates, Hendrik, in case you've forgotten. We didn't need a jet."

"I haven't forgotten, and I do have three other estates. One is in California, another in Australia, and the third in New Zealand. That's how I justify the jet, although when I don't use it, others do."

"Then take me to see them all, Hendrik. We agreed to forget the past and build a new life; perhaps we should do it at one of those."

"Okay, let's tell the kids. We'll come back before the marriage."

After they left, Marijke made another decision: *I can't marry unless I'm sure the government will never deport me. I must visit Dar and ask.*

First, she told the *mganga* in Lucas's village and then spoke to Ken.

Before Amali and Marijke had gone half a kilometre from the village, a runner left there carrying a message to the *mganga* at Jock's lodge. At Jock's, the *mganga* saw Lindiwe, who handed her a Satphone. The *mganga* called her daughter, a *mganga* in Dar, where her husband worked. The bush telegraph in Dar is fast, for it works by telephone. Every *mganga* heard the message within two hours, including the Mother Superior at the Cardinal Rugambwa Hospital. She knew who to call, and she had direct access. She called the Minister of Health and told him what she had learned.

"*Bwana*, I want to visit Dar for a day or two."

"Why? And do you want me to come too?"

"I have to go and see the health ministry man investigating me; I don't want an unwelcome surprise before or after our marriage." *If there will be one, it will be better to cancel the wedding.*

"Do you know who he is?"

"Not right now, but Dr Richter will find out. I'll call him."

Two days later, leaving a worried Ken behind at Rufisi, Marijke landed at Dar early enough to meet Dr Richter.

"Dr Coetzee, I have an appointment for us at the health ministry at three. I see you have two extra *jujus*."

"They are the spirit of the elephants, Doctor. Are you coming with me?"

"Yes, I'm determined to give you whatever support I can."

Dr Richter realised within seconds of entering the Ministry building that all the workers in the building knew The Elephant was visiting. Her head up and back straight, Marijke displayed her determination; she wouldn't leave without an answer, so she swept in—like a queen into a throne room—to spontaneous applause.

The Minister was waiting in the hall and greeted her respectfully with a bow.

"*Bibie*, I'm the Minister of Health; meeting a leader from our health community is a pleasure. Please come to my office."

An official Dr Richter knew, responsible for vaccinations, led him to a different office.

Trying not to display her amazement, Marijke followed the Minister, who ushered her into his office, indicated two armchairs, and said, "Please, we'll sit here."

The meeting was short, for the Minister knew why she had come.

"*Bibie*, I must apologise if my staff inconvenienced you in any way; there was no malice in the investigation. It was a formality necessary to dismiss a complaint. I assure you that the Ministry knows it has much to thank you for."

"Thank you, Minister; what you say is a great relief."

"*Bibie*, I understand you will shortly marry; as a mark of respect for you and the Great Elephant *mizimu* you carry, I'll request that home affairs offer Tanzanian citizenship to you and your husband. I hope you will accept. It will reassure the people of Tanzania that you and the *mizimu* will never leave us."

"Minister, thank you. I shall never leave, nor will my husband."

Ken was waiting when Marijke returned with a giant soft toy; unusually, it was a stuffed cheetah, and she was grinning when she stepped from the plane.

"Darling, where did you buy that toy?"

"A girl I'd never met brought it to me at the airport. She and a group of friends made it for our baby daughter."

I'm already lost the way things are happening; now strangers are giving us baby toys! Ken thought. "How did your meeting go?"

"I'll tell you later, *Bwana*, but we'll have Tanzanian passports in a month or two."

It was too much for Ken. He said nothing.

Ken and Marijke were hard at work building the planned cottages and tented camp when a man arrived from South Africa, two months before their marriage, at the beginning of the dry season. Ken had received an email that said he was coming from South Africa to assess the lodge and the park for the WWF, the World Wildlife Fund.

"*Bwana*, why's he coming?"

"I don't know, Marijke; maybe we can earn a WWF label for our website."

Marijke wondered, *I hope it's something else, and Bwana will have a massive surprise.*

When the man arrived, he introduced himself as Piet van Tonder. It shocked Ken to the core when Piet said, "I need to be sure you have suitable facilities to receive five white rhinos from Umfolozi."

"Five rhinos!"

"Yes, four young females ready to breed and a bull in his prime."

"But who's sending them here?"

"I don't know; all I know is someone is organising the shipment, that this is the destination, and that the guarantees for the rhinos' security are satisfactory. I need to approve what they will eat here and agree with you to build a pen for the first month, with a smaller pen in one corner for the first ten days."

Marijke thought, *Louis must have asked his son to arrange all this!* She assured Piet, "We have a thousand men ready to build whatever you want."

Piet hadn't missed the *jujus* around her neck and guessed what she said was true.

"Okay; first, where will they graze?" asked Piet.

Ken, still dazed, replied, "With the hippos between the lodge and the river."

Marijke, thrilled, thought, Bwana *will live his dream!*

"If the hippos graze there, the grass must be suitable for rhinos, but I'll take a sample back to check; they might need a salt lick."

"Lucas will show you your room, and then we'll meet you on the lodge veranda."

Later, over a drink, Piet explained to Ken and Marijke what they would need to do to keep the rhinos. He detailed the rhinos' grazing needs, how they should build the pen, and how he would fly them in.

"You're going to *fly* them here?" Ken asked.

"Not much choice. We can bring the bull on one flight and two females each on the next two flights. The C-130s will be at half-load with little fuel. Trucks, trains or a ship will be too slow; the rhinos will have no exercise and go off their food. But we must ensure there are a thousand metres of airstrip."

"We'll take care of that," Ken said. "But how do we transport them from the airstrip to the lodge?"

"What about the lowbed?" Marijke suggested.

They looked at it in the workshop, and Ken explained why they had it.

"Well, if it can carry an elephant, it'll manage a rhino," Piet said. "Send me photos of it with the ramp up and down so we can design the crates."

After Piet left, villagers from kilometres around came to build the pen and prepare the airstrip for the landing. They were ready and waiting in anticipation for the first rhino.

Ken had received detailed instructions and the arrivals schedule, so he was waiting on one side of the airstrip with Marijke and the lowbed when the C-130 touched down and braked to a halt, then lowered the tail ramp. A vehicle resembling an airport tug with oversize wheels, but painted in military camouflage, crept down the ramp, pulling an enormous crate; four men in uniform with "WWF" on the back, one driving and the others guiding, watched the movement of the container.

Although a complex process, the crew successfully transferred the rhino, in its enormous reinforced crate, onto the lowbed.

The four men introduced themselves. The leader said, "*Bwana*, I'm Diop, the group's leader; this is Diallo, Amadou, and Moussa. We're part of a security group that guards gold mines in Senegal. Rhinos are a new experience for us, but the bad guys are the same everywhere, so don't worry about the rhinos' safety. They'll be under guard twenty-four seven."

Ken thanked them. He thought it strange that they spoke Swahili, but all four were relaxed, casual, and smiled easily.

Diop explained that they would need to bring the air tug to the lodge to take the rhino off the lowbed. They would also need a place to store the crates and their equipment.

The trip back to the lodge was without incident, but when they arrived at Rufisi, Marijke thought four thousand people were waiting to see the rhino.

They watched as hydraulic jacks slowly lifted the top-hinged end. Dead silence reigned as the point of a horn, then a snout, moved into view as the rhino smelled its new home. Then it charged out but stopped after fifty metres when it found nothing to fight, confused by the overwhelming sound of four thousand people cheering.

The soldiers dragged their crate away, hauled it onto the lowbed, and drove to the place Ken had allocated for crate storage, five hundred metres from the lodge, hidden in the bush beside the road.

One end of the first crate contained a steel weapons store. The other and both sides held other equipment.

Later that evening, Diop asked Ken, "Please tell me if you want help with anything here at the lodge. Guarding is usually tedious. I also need permission to drive around with your rangers to learn the layout of the reserve and its accesses."

"Please do; you're part of our crew while you're here. Marijke is our doctor, so if you have any medical problems, come to see her."

Diop grinned. "We already know that; when I saw the *jujus*, I asked, and then I thought I might introduce her to the rhinos once they are free of the pen. They ignore people they know. Don't worry if you don't see us around; we'll be out scouting."

After Diop left, Ken asked Marijke, "What do you think of the soldiers?"

"They give me a feeling of security; they display an incredible level of calm confidence and competence. I'm glad they are on our side. And your impression?"

"Four highly trained military men with experience in battle. I've met a few like them in some odd places."

Two days, two more flights and four smaller rhinos later, five rhinos were in the rhino pen, five crates were in the bush, and people were still coming tens of kilometres to lean on the bars and watch them.

The soldiers worked to transform the air tug into a military fighting vehicle and assemble two drones, the parts for which were in the crate.

And Diop picked a spot on the road from the park gates.

35

____

In Dar es Salaam, the leader of the biggest poaching gang was still nursing the wounds caused by Rufisi to his business, but when he learned that Rufisi had five rhinos with horns corralled beside the lodge, he decided the prize was too big to ignore. He contacted his buyer and asked for a man to recruit assistants, kill the rhinos, and take the horns; he didn't tell the buyer he would also destroy the lodge.

The man who came was a mercenary, a ruthless individual who had fought with terrorist groups in Africa and the Middle East. Only four Tanzanians agreed to join the force he formed, so the others were all recruited from the dregs that populated the docksides of Dar, a mixture of nationalities from the hundreds of small boats that plied an illegal trade between Dar and all points north and south. Car thieves stole fifteen pickups at a price, and sixty AK-47s with ammunition came from a dealer who had brought them from the Congo; he also offered two cases of explosives.

The man didn't plan for or choose moonlight; overwhelming firepower would work, and if he lost a few men in a battle, so what? He believed the reports that the lodge had half a dozen armed men and villagers who would vanish at the sound of guns.

A week before the marriage, a man in Oman, watching the satellite view of Rufisi, called Diop and said, "Fifteen vehicles leaving Dar."

Halfway from Dar, the leading vehicle in the column hit a pedestrian on the way to the park. They didn't stop. The trucks drove straight through the park gates. They fired several shots, and one pickup knocked over the pole that carried the telephone wire. It hadn't worked for years, and the man in charge at the gate had a satphone. Once the column had passed through, he came from the toilet where he had hidden and called the police. He reported a terrorist attack, so the police notified the Army. Once labelled a terrorist attack, the label stuck. Then he called Ken at Rufisi and told him.

The last of the fifteen vehicles carried four Tanzanians; two had previously been poachers. Once through the park gates, their truck slowed, the gap to the one ahead increasing until they lost sight of the column at each bend in the road. Unseen, they turned into a poaching track the driver knew. They would go their own way to the rhinos. They had agreed earlier that the bonus promised for a successful hunt, split between sixty, was only a tenth of the value of a horn split four ways.

Ken and Marijke dressed quickly and hurried to the office to look at the satellite view; they could see the column of headlights, the last of them already a kilometre inside the park gates.

"Stay here and keep watching, Marijke. Flick the outside light on and off if there's any change in their route. I'll fetch the crew and pull chains across the road."

Ken dashed out, and Marijke sat to watch, thinking, *This is serious; should I tell the guests to gather somewhere?*

Ken found Amali, gave orders, and then thought of the Senegalese guards and his feeling that they were military professionals. Lucas appeared, so he asked him, "Lucas, where are the rhino guards?"

"They've left already, *Bwana*. They go out every night to guard the rhinos."

"We haven't time to look for them; once the chain is on the road,

I want every armed man along the road at twenty-metre intervals in the bush. Tell them that when the column stops because of the chain, they must shoot as many of the terrorists as they can."

Ken turned and ran back to Marijke.

"*Bwana*, the last vehicle in the column has turned off and is taking a different route; at a guess, it will come along the river's side."

The column of vehicles, ten kilometres from the lodge, drove onto a straight stretch. The driver of the pickup in front could see the road was clear and accelerated, followed by the others, but three hundred metres from the bend, the dark shape of the camouflage-painted guard vehicle came round the corner and stopped in the centre of the road. Diop and Moussa, manning it, had spent three years fighting terrorists; none had ever returned to their base.

The mercenary leader exclaimed, "What the fucking hell is that ..."

He didn't complete the sentence because the heat-seeking missile hit the hot engine block, and the pickup exploded, followed a microsecond later by the explosion of the ten-kilogram box of explosives in the back. In a flaming ball, the pickup rose and fell on the second vehicle, crushing the cab and the men in the rear. Then the second box of explosives triggered, and the firebomb landed on the third pickup, killing all four men.

The column concertinaed. Three of the vehicles hit the one in front, and before the men could understand what had happened, other than being in extreme danger, they heard gunshots from the rear of the column and approaching fast.

The gunshots were explosive. Three hundred metres to each side of the column, drones—each painted a dark camouflaged grey—systematically and with total accuracy fired pulses of laser energy into the tyres, which exploded with the sound the men heard. In complete panic, the men leapt from their vehicles and escaped into the bush; most left their weapons behind.

A minute later, the eleven remaining pickups were on flat tyres. The drones switched back to surveillance.

Ken arrived at the office just in time to see the enormous flare at the head of the line of headlights.

"What's that, Marijke?"

"I don't know; it's dying out, and the vehicles have stopped. I guess it was an explosion."

"I'll stay and watch until they move again."

"There's still the last one, *Bwana*. It stopped, probably to look at the explosion, and now it's moving again."

They didn't move for fifteen minutes, and then Marijke said, "Look where the sixth light was, it's gone dark; I think they switched it off."

Ken replied, "Or the battery is flat. It looks as if they've abandoned the attack. I'll have someone to take a tracker there; they can stop out of sight, and he can sneak up on them. I'll give him a satphone."

"*Bwana*, the last vehicle taking the riverside route has stopped, and the lights have switched off. They are heading for the rhinos. They've decided to walk because the car is too visible. It'll take them an hour."

"Okay, Marijke, I'll ask a ranger to come with me and stand guard before they can reach the rhinos."

"Not without me, you won't. I'm not staying here when I don't know where you are."

"Marijke, it's dangerous; you're much safer here with the guards around the lodge."

"But you aren't. I saved us from death the last time. I'm coming."

Ken tried a last time. "No."

"I am. I'll wear my work pants and shirt that resemble military camouflage. Fetch Mwamba; he can see well at night."

The four poachers taking the route along the riverbank stopped three kilometres before the lodge and marched. They had never hunted rhinos and thought the engine noise would frighten them away. They split into two pairs. Two would walk near the river, the others close to the bush line in case the rhinos sheltered there.

Only three hundred metres later, one of the two near the river found the ground soft and sunk almost to his knees. The other came to his aid, and five minutes later, the glooper had claimed the two victims. One AK lay on the ground a dozen metres from the soft edge. The other two knew nothing about their fate and continued walking.

Diallo and Amadou, the soldiers guarding the rhinos, carried superb equipment. Their night vision binoculars gave them superb vision, and their weapons, designed for the purpose, were a combined semi-automatic sniper rifle with night-vision sights and a short-range machine gun. They could talk to each other via a UHF link with throat mikes and earphones; one had a satphone. The message "1 unit" followed by a GPS position had warned them of the terrorist vehicle. When the GPS readout stopped changing, they knew the car had stopped. They spread out until a hundred metres separated them, Diallo lying beside the bush line, Amadou out on the plain.

From his position on the plain, Amadou watched Ken, Marijke and Mwamba walk along the bush line towards the rhino pen and then hide. He reported it to Diallo, who was annoyed at the extra responsibility, then replied, "We didn't tell *Bwana* where we would be; he's just doing what he thinks best. Keep watching."

Five minutes later, Diallo's earphone whispered, "Got them, two 'terrs', just passed the lodge. Close to the bush line."

Ken said quietly to Mwamba, "We will see them on the plain from here. Go into the bush, find a place and listen for them if they come through it. Don't risk your life, but you can shoot them."

Then he and Marijke hid behind a sparse bush; they could see the plain through the branches.

Below the bush, a savannah hare was quietly munching on fallen berries; when Ken and Marijke sat silently behind the brush, it decided to remain hidden and froze. Several minutes later, Marijke tapped Ken on the shoulder. He had heard the shuffling footsteps and watched through the bush as a man's shadow against the sky came within view. Marijke tapped his shoulder twice, and Ken thought,

There's a second one, so he waited, his AK ready. *I'll fire over their heads when they're both in view and tell them to drop their guns.*

As the man passed before the bush, the hare felt trapped and burst from the brush onto the plain. The man, tensed to breaking point after kilometres of walking in the dark, spun towards the still-shaking bush, the AK lining up to fire a burst into it. Ken flattened Marijke as he pushed her to the ground, expecting to hear the staccato sound of an AK and bullets ripping the bush apart. There was just one sharp explosion.

The second terrorist, twelve metres from the first, saw his partner hurled backwards by an enormous force, heard the report, and saw the massive hole in his chest. The shock of something unknown was enough; he dropped his AK and ran.

Ken heard his fading footsteps. Two minutes later, after listening carefully, Ken whispered, "Darling, don't move. I'll find out what happened."

He crawled out and then found the body with its terrible wound. After collecting Marijke, they returned to the lodge, and after another half hour, Mwamba joined them.

"*Bwana,* what happened?"

Marijke added, "Yes, *Bwana,* I want to know too."

"We were unlucky to have chosen a bush to hide behind where a hare had also hidden, and when it erupted from below the bush, the terrorist reacted to spray the bush with bullets, but his AK exploded and blew him apart. I think packed clay might have blocked the barrel. The other one ran; I'll have the tracker follow him tomorrow."

But Ken knew it wasn't an exploding AK but a sniper rifle.

Forty-four men began walking towards Dar; only eight had guns and were in the lead. A mistake of consequence, because the lions and hyenas, attracted by the smell of burned flesh, killed twelve before they reached the park gates. The Tanzanian Army rounded up the remaining thirty-two. Some tried to escape, but irate villagers led the soldiers to them. The man hit by the leading vehicle on the way to the park had died of his injuries.

The tracker reported the abandoned vehicles, all with flat tyres, so Ken told the rangers to tell the villagers they must take all the wheels and whatever they wanted but leave all guns for the police to collect. The four rhino guards appeared without saying where they had been and left with the rangers. The tracker found the scattered bones of two terrorists and then an AK by the glooper; he drove their pickup to the lodge with three AKs for the gun store. Ken gave the pickup to a village.

Finally, the Army reached the column of terrorist vehicles after midday; none had wheels, seats or windscreens. The police joined the military, and their forensic officers, who discovered a wooden box part with "Explosives" written on it, declared that an accident had detonated the explosives in the first vehicle and that that had triggered the second vehicle's box of explosives.

Later, the judge agreed that explosives marked it as an act of terrorism. As all the men captured were foreigners, it amounted to invasion by an external force, and as they had killed a Tanzanian citizen, he imposed the death penalty. Unusually, after an order from high up, the executions happened three days later. The man organising the raid transferred all the money to a personal account and disappeared. His body floated a month later in Mombasa Harbour.

The park official called Ken and asked if he could clear the road for use.

With no head of the bushmeat trade and no East Africans or foreigners willing to go poaching, Dar had to forgo bushmeat. It would be many years before anyone signed up for a poaching expedition: the equivalent of the bush telegraph exists between sailors and the inhabitants of the world's docksides.

The overseas buyer of rhino horn decided to move his operations elsewhere. Then, after he received a message that said, "Tanzania is off limits for all poaching, ivory or horn", he decided it was better to forget Tanzania existed.

Rufisi was safe, but just in case, a hidden military missile launcher, two laser pulse drones, and some unique hand weapons, all prepared for long-term storage, sat in a sealed steel shed five hundred metres from the lodge.

Ken drove them to Jock's lodge when the four Senegalese rhino guards left. Before they boarded the plane, he shook hands with them and said, "I and all of us at the lodge will remember you guys; I know we have a lot to thank you for."

As they marched away, he called, "Good hunting." The leader turned, grinned at him and saluted smartly.

36

____

The guests began to arrive on the Monday after the terrorist attack. Hendrik and Marie-France came first, flying from France. Leo, Lisa, Louis and Soraya followed with their two guards an hour later.

The flight from Dar to Jock's lodge the following morning had Petrus, his girlfriend, Dr Richter, and his wife.

Jock and Lindiwe came on Wednesday.

On the Monday evening, Hendrik asked Louis and Phillipe to join him for their first-ever shareholders' meeting. Louis replied, "You must include Leo; I'll come, but he will be my proxy in future."

Hendrik opened the proceedings. "I don't think we need to be overly formal. I asked for this meeting because I don't know when we will meet again, and I want to inform you that Phillipe will inherit my shares. I understand from Louis that Leo will inherit his. This lodge is fantastic due to Phillipe and Marijke, and we owe it to them and the future to expand its operations."

Hendrik asked, "Phillipe, we now have rhinos; what is your vision for the future?"

"First, with Marijke's help, the parks board will give us a lease on land ten kilometres from here to build a new lodge. It will take time to construct; I estimate three years. I shall call our current lodge Elephant and the new one, Giraffe. It is in an area that suits giraffes.

We will need young giraffes from Manyara and the Serengeti, and if we can find them, some of the Rothschild's giraffes.

"Then I have another dream. Hunters exterminated the Great Tuskers that roamed this country and Kenya a hundred years ago. Their DNA has disappeared from East Africa, but a DNA pool exists in South Africa. If we can build a herd of Great Tuskers here for the future, Rufisi and our names will go into the history books alongside those who saved the rhino.

"We'll need at least two more lodges to manage the tourist influx. Perhaps we can buy them."

Leo said he would buy the giraffes and guard them. He suggested starting with a tented camp as an annexe to Rufisi, where Rufisi clients could spend two or three days. Louis said he would watch for any opportunity to buy shares in other lodges, and Hendrik said he would investigate the Great Tuskers.

Ken told Marijke, "When I saw you on Table Mountain, I had no idea what would happen, and I'm sure what's happening is due entirely to you."

"*Bwana*, not me, it's Rufisi. There are ancient forces here; all we have done is release them. Now let's get married. The Catholic priest should be here on Friday; he's coming from the Cardinal Rugambwa Hospital for our parents' marriage."

"And who's coming to marry us?"

"The *waganga* found a *mganga* who attended a mission school, became a priest and then became a *mganga*. He's flying to Dar from Arusha, and Lodge Air will bring him with the Catholic priest. When someone asked him if he could come, he said he wouldn't miss the opportunity to meet us."

"So, everything is organised?"

"Yes, all the villagers coming will either arrive on the day or come on Friday; they will camp in the rhino corral now that the rhinos are on the plain. The rangers have set up water tanks and heaps of firewood. Lucas is the director of operations."

"How many?"

"I don't know; I think it may be more than a thousand."

Lisa asked Marijke to show her the wedding dress. "Marijke, you must visit Leo and me in Oman; this dress and your others would inspire our designers. What jewellery are you wearing?"

"Only a tanzanite pendant." Marijke fetched a box and showed her.

"That's magnificent; I've never seen anything like it. Where did you find it?"

"It's an uncut stone; the woodcarver made the ebony frame. I have lots that the people have given me."

Marijke showed Lisa the tanzanite collection and told her that Ken had bought her a tanzanite ring because she couldn't take them to Antwerp for cutting. Lisa replied, "Taking the stones to Belgium for cutting and bringing them back is not criminal. We have diplomatic passports. Leo or I can take them."

"Thanks, Lisa; let me collect a few more. I'll call you when I'm ready."

Marie-France and Hendrik stood together on the lodge veranda before the Catholic priest over an hour before Marijke and Ken were to marry. Wellwishers crowded the plain in front.

Ken thought his father looked happy and proud, and Marijke thought her mother looked radiant. Then Ken looked at Marijke, and she at him, and they both smiled as they felt the same thought—*It's possible to jump at any age.*

After the priest declared them man and wife and Hendrik kissed his bride, a thousand people ululated while all the guests on the veranda wished them well. Marijke disappeared. Ken knew she had gone to don her wedding gown; he had yet to see it. People were streaming onto the plain.

An hour later, Ken stood by the *mganga* priest, watching the lounge door that Marijke would use. He thought the crowd in front was several thousand. When she came out, he felt his heart stop. Mama Keita had produced a fabulous dress and a fantastic headpiece, but Marijke lit up the veranda with her smile of happiness.

Murmurings of amazement filled the porch, and then she strode to the edge in front of the people and raised her arms. The sudden silence made it easy to hear her voice as she spoke in Swahili. "*Nawashukuru nyote kwa kufika siku hii roho ya wote inapofurahi.*—I thank you all for coming on this day when the *mizimu* of all rejoice."

As she turned and joined Ken, cheering broke out. It would have continued for ages if Lucas had not gone to the veranda and signalled for quiet. At Marijke's request, the ceremony was in Swahili; Petrus, his girlfriend and Hendrik stood with Marie-France, who translated for them.

When Ken put the tanzanite ring on her finger and kissed her, the crowd cheered for minutes, and Marijke said, "*Bwana*, the elephants have come to our wedding too. Come with me; we must have their blessing."

No one had noticed the elephants' quiet arrival near the water's edge. But, when Marijke took Ken by the hand and stepped off the veranda to walk toward the water, everyone saw them, and as the crowd separated to allow a lane down which the bridal couple strode hand in hand, silence spread.

Gogo and two other matriarchs came to meet them, and the crowd saw the elephants brush their trunks over them, scenting their hair, bodies, and the *jujus* around their necks.

Lisa whispered to Leo, "The first was the legal marriage; I think this is the one that counts."

When the matriarchs returned to the three united herds, and Marijke returned with Ken through the crowd, people twenty kilometres away heard the ululation of thousands. The elephants trumpeted a chorus.

The guests left in the morning, and Ken and Marijke departed with their parents in the afternoon, leaving a proud Lucas as the Rufisi manager in Ken's absence. Marie-France wanted to show Marijke and Ken where she and Hendrik had spent their childhoods. They flew to France in Hendrik's jet for ten days' holiday at his estate.

Ken visited both estates with his father, who showed him the barrel with 'Rufisi' written on it and promised to bottle it and send the wine in two years.

Finally, they flew directly to Heidelberg. They were expecting to meet Dr Gruber and his wife and were surprised to find Leo and Lisa waiting for them at the airport with the professor.

The professor took them on a tour of Heidelberg and the university. When they finally returned to their hotel and entered the presidential suite, Marijke found an academic gown on the bed. She put it on.

"*Bwana*, I have a medical degree for the first time. It's not the same feeling as when I qualified as a lawyer."

"What's different?"

"It feels like a *juju*, recognition for what I am and what I've done, not what I've learned."

"*Kweli kabisa*, my darling, *kweli kabisa*."

The next day, Marijke dressed in the gown Mama Keita's team had specially designed for the graduation ceremony, wearing her *jujus* and the tanzanite pendant. She wore the academic gown over it. The hotel staff treated them like royalty.

Ken thought, *That's natural; to me, she's the queen of East Africa.*

Hendrik whispered to Marie-France, "When we first met them, Phillipe said she was the province's most famous woman. I think it's now all of East Africa."

The audience gave Marijke an ovation when Professor Gruber handed her the degree after a eulogy recounting her achievements. Hendrik and Marie-France left with tearful promises to visit Rufisi shortly, and Ken and Marijke had a short visit to make on the way back. Lisa had invited them to Oman.

Epilogue

T ime passed, and there came the night that Marijke knew would be *Bwana*'s last. Naked, in bed in the bungalow, she held him in her arms. Their final words to each other are unknown.

When his heart stopped beating, Marijke rose, dressed, and clothed *Bwana* in his marriage costume, then called her daughter Asatira to help.

He lay in state in a glass-covered coffin for three days, fifty metres in front of the lodge, while ten thousand mourners moved by. Some brought flowers, and others brought gifts. A thousand fly whisks, denoting respect, surrounded the coffin.

Halfway to the river, his grave lay open, with the rusting hulk of a pickup beside it. Two rails would allow the rangers to slide it over the grave to protect it from scavengers.

At the end of the third day, the full moon rose, and Marijke walked to the coffin with Asatira; the rangers took away the glass top and sides, and the tractor pulled the massive, spiked chain along the front of the lodge, keeping everyone behind it.

The elephants came to the river, and three matriarchs came to Marijke; they caressed the body in mourning, touched both Marijke and Asatira on the head, and left. Sixteen men from the nearest village carried *Bwana*, laid him in the grave, and then shovelled in the earth while Marijke watched. They pushed the rusting pickup carcass into place, and the men left. The back of the pickup was full of flywhisks and flowers, and over the rear cab window, an etched stainless plate had the picture of an eagle in flight with the words:

Bwana Mkubwa

Phillipe d'Yquem/Ken Phillips

Baba

Elephants visited the grave; they polished the cab roof until it shone in the sunlight.

Marijke withdrew from daily life after Ken died. For three weeks, she sat on the veranda, remembering. At least one person checked on her every ten minutes, and one slept on the porch at night. Marijke lost herself in her memories.

She remembered when Rufisi was one lodge; now it was four, Elephant, the original; Rhino, Cheetah and Giraffe. She remembered when Ken promoted Lucas to manage Giraffe Lodge, now managed by Lucas's son.

She remembered the spa women: those who had married rangers, the one who married a graduate from Dar studying snakes, and others who went to Dar to qualify as therapists.

She remembered the first village to build its farm; now, every settlement had one and sold an excess of vegetables to Dar.

She thought of Dan, the hydrologist, his proposal and how he had left a crew and machine to drill hundreds of pure water wells next to villages.

She felt again the excitement of the time when five rhinos arrived before her wedding. The male proved worthy; the park now had over five hundred.

She couldn't forget when the first tusker arrived from Tembe Elephant Park in South Africa, a two-year-old with the DNA of the Great Tuskers, and how she had introduced him to the herd and the many young elephants that now promised magnificent tusks.

She remembered the battles with poachers, the fight against floods, and the people's health improvements.

She relived the birth of her daughter at the lodge, with two *waganga* in attendance, and how when she held her baby the first time, she had looked into her eyes and known her name.

She felt pride at the memory of when she had asked the *waganga* for every voter to vote at a general election but only for a young candidate who would support a ban on commercial canned hunting. And how a new young parliament had passed the bill in less than a year.

And then how the *waganga* had exercised their newfound political power to push for registration of the *waganga* under the medical act.

She remembered introducing nine-year-old Asatira to the cheetahs and twelve-year-old Asatira to the elephants, and how she had given Asatira her cheetah *juju* when she left at eighteen to study medicine. "Asatira, keep this *juju* around your neck, and before you make any decision that will change your life, hold it and think." And Asatira had returned.

And she remembered her happiness when Shy became the matriarch of the herds.

She paused, remembering, and called to Asatira.

"Yes, Mama," Asatira said, coming to the veranda.

"A few days before the full moon, my *mzimu* will join your father's: it's waiting for me. I promised the woman who gave me these *jujus* and the title of 'The Elephant' that I would pass them on to someone worthy. Please discuss this with your husband; if I give them to you, you can never leave East Africa."

"I don't want to leave, Mama, but I'll confirm with you tomorrow."

"He agrees, Mama. I shall never leave, and last night Shy came to see the babies; she gave me this." She handed her mother a sprig of resurrection.

"Then the elephant *mzimu* approves; place it in my hands when you bury me. I shall give the *jujus* to you when the matriarchs come. When your time comes, you must find a worthy successor. It might not be your daughter; if you have the least doubt visit the *waganga* in

Kenya to find someone. And if you cannot find someone, give them to a museum."

When the matriarchs came three days before the full moon, Marijke and Asatira strode out to meet them, and when they returned, Asatira wore the elephant *jujus*. The news spread—the *mzimu* of the Great Elephant was still with them.

Marijke died two days later; the funeral was identical to that of *Bwana*, except that fifty thousand mourners filed past her coffin. There were no fly whisks, but every village for a hundred kilometres emptied their farms of flowers.

Asatira and her visibly pregnant daughter stood by the uncovered coffin when the elephants came; more than three hundred covered the plain, and all the mothers filed past. They caressed *Bibie*'s body gently.

After burying her and covering the grave with a pickup, the rangers left Asatira and her daughter alone, and the matriarchs returned. The pickup has a similar plate to the other. It has an elephant in place of the eagle and the words:

Bibie Mkubwa

Marijke

Marie-Jeanne d'Yquem

The Great Elephant

Ask, and the people will tell you that a cheetah sleeps on the cab roof above Marijke's grave.

Epitaph

Excerpt from *Legends of Tanzania in the Early Decades of the 21st Century*:

And when Asatira returned to the lodge, the people were happy; the *mzimu* of the Great Elephant was still with them. *Hakuna Matata.*

Above the tombs, the cheetah *mzimu* of *Bibie* and the eagle *mzimu* of *Bwana* watched, and then *Bibie* said, "*Bwana*, shall we jump?"

And the eagle *mzimu* replied, "Let me carry you, my darling."

They rose high into the sky, then circled to look down, and *Bibie* said, "I think we did improve it—if only a little."

"Quite a lot, my love, quite a lot."